Freedom's Promise

Path to Freedom - Book Three

Pegg Thomas

Spinner of Yarns Publishing, LLC

S PINNER OF YARNS PUBLISHING, LLC

Sault Ste. Marie, Michigan

Copyright @2024 by Pegg Thomas
https://peggthomas.com/
Published in the United States of America
ISBN: 979-8-9866966-6-9
Cover Design by Hannah Linder
Cover Art Copyright by Spinner of Yarns Publishing, LLC

Join Pegg's Newsletter
writing updates – sneak peeks – fiber arts updates – personal content
https://www.subscribepage.com/PeggThomas

This book is dedicated to the men and woman who risked everything for freedom.

Those who broke away from slavery risked death or torture if caught. They also risked death in the attempt from cold, heat, starvation, and accidents such as drowning in rivers or encounters with wild animals.

Those who assisted the fugitives risked fines, imprisonment, endangering and impoverishing their families, and the loss of their businesses and/or reputations.

Freedom has never been free.
But it's always been worth it to those who crave it.

Acknowledgments

I want to thank my friends who patiently listen while I prattle away about the people in my stories, and eagerly share the latest tidbit of history I've discovered in my research. In naming anyone, I'm sure to miss someone, and since you know who you are... THANK YOU!

Author's Forenote:

The Quaker use of *thee* is not the same grammatically as the Old English use. The Quakers did not use *thou*, only *thee* and *thy*, a variation they considered more plain.

Chapter 1

F RAGILE BLACK CREPE CRUSHED beneath his fingers as Daniel Whiteford removed the wreath from his front door. What used to be his
front door. He handed the wreath to the butler, Silas, who accepted it
with a solemn nod.

Cook sniffed, and Margaret's maid wiped a tear from the groove in
her cheek.

"I know you shall take good care of this place for the new owner. I
appreciate that he has agreed to keep all of you on staff." Daniel cleared
his throat and pivoted to face the trio. "You have always done your best
for me."

"Good luck, sir," Silas said.

"When you find them, tell Gwen hello from all of us." Cook's chin
wobbled on the last word.

"Indeed." Daniel stepped off the porch and strode to the carriage
without another backward glance.

Arthur held the door until Daniel collapsed onto the plush seat.
He buried his face in his hands. The soft click of the door closing

barely registered past the fog of his grief. The carriage rocked as the bandy-legged old stableman climbed onto the high seat. It jerked into motion with the clatter of iron horseshoes striking cobblestones.

He pulled his hands from his face but refused to look back at the house—the house his children had grown up in. The house his wife had died in. An empty shell awaiting the new owner's arrival.

Not entirely empty. He was glad the new owner had agreed to keep the staff on. He'd considered bringing Silas with him, but the man was getting on in years. His children and grandchildren lived nearby. It hadn't seemed fair to ask it of him.

Daniel would miss Cook's apple fritters and her Sunday fried chicken. There would be cooks in the north, but would they be able to create his favorites? Cook was a wonder in the kitchen, even if she was a gossipy old thing. No, that wasn't fair. She'd not gossiped about the most important thing. Not ever. None of them had. He owed them for that, as well as the care they'd given his family over the years they'd been in his service.

Why had everything gone so wrong?

His wife's death, as much from a broken heart as from the influenza, had been the last straw. Their daughter Constance's horrendous scandal, caught with that low-life captain in the very bedroom she shared with her husband.

Daniel pressed his fingers to his throbbing temples in an attempt to suppress the memories of the past horrid months.

And Jonas, his only son, the one on whom Daniel had leveled such hopes. The one he had groomed to take over the shipping business he'd labored his whole life to build. Jonas would rather make his money running illegal slave ships. North Carolina had outlawed the importation of slaves in 1774, but men like Jonas found ways around the law. They were little better than pirates.

Refusing to have his ships pressed into that sort of service, Daniel had sold the business—every last ship—to keep them out of his son's hands.

Slavery. He abhorred the practice. They'd never had a slave in their home. Daniel hired his employees or bought their indentures. He couldn't abide the thought of one man owning another as if a horse or a cow. He shuddered and drew in a long breath. Over the last few years, he'd lost more than one friend over his stance on the issue. It was a good thing he was relocating north. He needed a new start, far from his disgraceful children, and far from the evils of bondage that seem to grow more prominent every year.

Daniel Whiteford had one more chance to do things right.

Thomas Baldwin, a long-time business acquaintance, had settled in the new Quaker community of Mount Pleasant in the Ohio territory. Surely a new community such as theirs would need a man of business—someone to ship in supplies and keep the flow of commerce open.

Daniel would need to purchase riverboats and establish a freight line, but he was good at what he did. He'd built his shipping business from the ground up, after all. And he'd always had a cordial business relationship with Thomas.

Mount Pleasant was the perfect place for Daniel's new venture.

But that was the lesser reason for traveling to Mount Pleasant.

He was more interested in finding his last family member who remained untainted by the world. The Quakers—who called themselves the Society of Friends—would have seen to that. The boy had been born in April of 1799. He'd be a sturdy four-year-old next month, the perfect age to begin molding him to be a man of character, a man of worth, a man as unlike Jonas as Daniel could imagine.

In Mount Pleasant, Daniel would find Gwen Morgan⁄and reclaim his grandson.

"Pull it!" The shout came from the other side of the addition to Mark Allen Teed's house.

Zachary Brown clicked to Annabelle, and the mule leaned into her harness. The rope tightened and creaked under its load as the steady mule plodded forward, front hooves digging into the soft earth, releasing the scent of crushed grass.

"Stop her there." Micah Pike's hand splayed above the peak of the roof.

"Whoa, girl." Zachary cupped his hand over the bridge of the mule's long face, and she stopped.

"Hold on." The hand disappeared as Micah no doubt secured the beam on the other side of the house.

Zachary removed his hat and mopped the sweat from his brow. He plopped his hat back on his head, letting the brim shade his face. It was early April, but the sun beat down as if it couldn't wait for full summer. He wouldn't complain.

His pastures were already growing lush, his cows filling out, and their milk richer for the fresh fodder. All six of his cows had birthed their calves, four of them giving him heifers. He could sell them for a good price on the frontier and build onto his barn this summer.

Mark Allen and Micah, his closest neighbors, would come to help. He was thankful for all God's blessings, and especially for those two steadfast friends. The three of them made a good team. Zachary's dairy was thriving, Mark Allen's orchard was growing, and Micah's farm was expanding as he cleared more land.

So why wasn't Zachary happier?

The rope slackened before the shout of "Unloaded!" reached him. He unhooked it and walked toward the house, tying Annabelle and the rope to the hitching post before walking around the new addition.

"Is it not time for lunch?" he called to the two men on the partially constructed roof.

Micah squinted into the sun. "'Twould appear so."

"Good." Mark Allen hooked his mallet's head on top of the last beam he'd pegged in place. "My belly fears my throat's been cut."

The door on the finished side of the house opened, and Faye Teed filled the doorway. Curly black hair escaped the linen cap to frame her face. Her sleeves pushed up, her apron wrinkled as if she'd just dried her hands on it. She folded her arms across her extended middle, the very reason the men hurried to complete the addition.

She cocked her head at Zachary. "Was that my husband claiming starvation?"

Zachary grinned. "It sounded like him." What a change—a metamorphosis—the past two years had been for the young woman before him. Gone was the selfish creature who had stepped off the riverboat with her haughty air of superiority. In its place had grown a confident woman, a capable wife, and a loving partner to Mark Allen.

He squelched the stir of jealousy that often plagued him of late. Not that he wished to have caught Faye's eye, far from it. But surrounded by his friends and their wives and growing families, Zachary struggled with loneliness.

"Tell that wife of mine I am coming to the table with the hunger of a hibernating bear."

"And thee can tell him for me—"

"Nay." Zachary held both hands palms out toward her. "Thee will not put me in the middle of this."

"'Tis always the way with these two." Micah climbed down the ladder and leaned close to Zachary. "Which makes me all the more thankful for my docile wife."

"Micah, the things thee will say." Gwen Pike pushed past her sister and into the sunlight, carrying a tray laden with food toward the trestle table under a nearby shade tree. A tow-headed boy followed her, holding the hand of a dark-haired toddler. "Stop thy nonsense and come eat."

Mark Allen climbed down, and they took their seats on the benches, bowing for the Quaker's silent prayer. When Mark Allen cleared his throat, the women passed around platters of bread, meat, and cheese and a bowl filled with steamed asparagus, Zachary's favorite. He took a large spoonful.

"I hope thee enjoys it," Gwen said. "'Tis up early this year with the fine weather."

Zachary sank his teeth into the soft greens and swallowed. "Perfect."

She flushed at the praise but didn't linger over it, tending to Owen and Sally Faye, her children.

The men spoke little, filling the holes in their middles that working since daybreak had left. The women ate around helping the little ones until Faye rose and fetched a dried-apple pie from the house. She refilled the men's cups with cider from the pitcher before sitting again.

It was such a homey moment. So unlike the starkness of Zachary's one-room house. The silence. The hours filled with work and more work and resting by himself in the evening.

"Papa says we can get a dog," Owen said around a mouthful of cheese.

"Do not speak with thy mouth full," Micah chided his son.

The boy took a slurp from his cup. "But thee did say."

"Indeed, I did." He quirked an eyebrow at Gwen. "But dogs do not grow up from the ground like our corn. It may take some time to find one."

Owen slumped on the bench, his chin resting on the table.

"'Tis springtime," Zachary said. "Dogs will be having their puppies soon, I should expect."

That, and the slice of pie Gwen slid in front of the boy, perked him up.

"Aye." Micah glanced around his fields, bordered by hardwood forests dotted with pines. "'Twill be good to have a dog about the place to warn of strangers and keep the vermin away from the corn," he said.

Mark Allen waved a half-eaten slice of bread his way. "Have thee had strangers coming by?"

"None that we have seen, but there have been footprints near the creek."

"And eggs have gone missing some days." Gwen pulled Sally Faye, who was mashing her asparagus rather than eating it, into her lap. "So we know there have been people about." She glanced at Zachary. "Barefoot people."

Zachary swallowed his bite of pie and set down his fork. "Then a dog is a good idea." Barefoot likely meant escaped slaves, since Indians from the area had moved farther west. He'd seen some fugitives before, always at a distance, most memorable a boy with a floppy hat who had been around the past two summers. He didn't look more than ten years old, but it was hard to say without getting closer. Several Friends had reported seeing him, but the boy didn't let anyone get close.

Here Zachary was, feeling sorry for himself in his lonesome state, while escaped slaves ran for their lives across this very countryside, risking everything for a shot at the very freedom he enjoyed. Guilt squashed what was left of his appetite.

Who was he to complain about his circumstances? He had his freedom, his own land, his own cows, plenty to eat, and good clothes to wear. He was a respected member of the Friends community—called Quakers by those outside—and blessed with good neighbors. Even if he never had a family of his own, he had so much more than others.

"On a much happier topic." Micah raised his cup as if toasting his wife. "There will be another addition to the Pike household come the fall."

Exclamations of surprise and congratulations ringed the table, except for Faye. Naturally, the sisters would have already shared this exciting news.

"So we will be building an addition to thy cabin soon, I take it?" Mark Allen said.

"If the Lord wills." Micah beamed with pride.

"Are thee hoping for a boy or a girl?" Faye asked, smoothing her hands over her belly.

"Since we already have one of each," Gwen said, "I do not think it matters."

"Then we shall pray for a healthy babe and mother." Zachary also raised his cup and took a sip, swallowing the envy that rose inside him and despising himself for the feeling. He truly was happy for his friends. He had no right to be envious.

God had given him a good life. Why could he not be grateful for it and satisfied with his circumstances?

Chapter 2

N EW BERN HAD CHANGED since Daniel's last visit four years prior. It was bigger, noisier, and more crowded. While his ships had come and gone from the ports here, he'd stayed in Greenesville, content never to set foot on the oceanside docks again. His agent had been more than capable of managing things. And there had been plenty of work in Greenesville to keep him busy with the riverboat traffic. At least, that was what he'd told himself. But as the carriage wove through the busy streets, he couldn't lie to himself anymore.

He'd avoided the town after sending his grandson away.

Knowing he'd done his best for the boy, giving him a life with the Quakers and making sure there was a trustworthy young woman to raise him, had soothed his conscience at first. But as rumors of Jonas's activities reached him, his thoughts had turned more often to the lad.

Was he happy with the Quakers? They were good people, and Daniel had no fear that they would mistreat his grandson, but they were odd in their ways. Strict and somber. Did they bring any joy into his grandson's life? Did they have the means—the finances—to properly care for him?

When the scandal around Constance broke, Margaret had taken to her bed, horrified at their daughter's behavior.

Daniel, on the other hand, had buried himself in his ledgers, making more money than ever before. His shipping and supply business, already lucrative, had thrived. As it grew, and as word confirming Jonas's exploits reached him, it became clear that he couldn't hand the business to his son to make an abomination of it.

He'd approached Margaret with the idea of retrieving their grandson.

Would his wife still be alive if he hadn't? Already in her bed, Margaret had stopped talking to him. Then stopped eating. He'd had every doctor in the city to see her, but to no avail. She'd simply given up. Died of a broken heart, unable to face the scandal, too weak to fend off the influenza. And he hadn't been able to do anything about it.

He'd failed as a father and as a husband. His last chance to save his family lay with his grandson, and it was time to become a proper grandparent to the boy. That journey started today.

He knocked the head of his cane against the top of the carriage. "Drive around to the docks. The ticket office."

"Aye, sir."

A few moments later, the carriage halted, and Arthur climbed down and opened the door.

"Thank you, Arthur." Daniel climbed out, straightened his coat, and marched to the office. The familiar odors of brine, fish, and chimney smoke flavored the cool air. Placards on both sides of the office door advertised the names of ships and approximate arrival and departure dates written in heavy chalk. He walked past them and into the stuffy room beyond.

"Can I help you, sir?" The thin man behind the counter peered over a pair of round spectacles.

"I need a ticket on the first ship to Alexandria."

The clerk opened a book and ran his finger down the page. "One will sail on Thursday next."

"A week?" Daniel barked out the words, not bothering to modify his tone. "I am in a hurry, man. Can you not get me a berth sooner than that?"

"I am sorry, sir, but one left just hours ago. I am afraid you missed it."

"And so I must wait a week?"

"If the *Ruby Ann* be on time, aye." The clerk flipped his hands over in a futile gesture. "But that one be as likely to run late as any."

Daniel ground his teeth to keep the frustrated words inside. He'd made his decision, and he wished to follow through with it, not waste precious time awaiting a tardy ship. But the clerk couldn't produce a vessel on demand. It wasn't like the uncertainty of voyages was unknown to Daniel. He'd dealt with such things throughout his career.

He just hadn't expected it to delay the search for his grandson. Short-sighted on his part.

"I shall take the berth on... what did you call it?"

"The *Ruby Ann*, sir."

"That one." Daniel pulled out his wallet and withdrew a check. That was another thing. He still needed to have his money—at least a good portion of it—moved to a bank closer to Mount Pleasant. His banker would know of one in that area. Daniel could see to that while he waited.

"Here you be, sir." The clerk slid a ticket across the counter and named the price.

Daniel wrote the check and gave it to the clerk. "Do you have a recommendation for a nearby hotel?"

"One of the popular ones is back a block and around the corner to the left. Boston fellow bought it a few years ago and spruced it up a mite. The sign is purple with a ship on it."

"Thank you." Daniel pocketed the ticket and returned to the carriage, giving Arthur the directions to the hotel.

The lobby of The Royal Ship was less than Daniel had expected for a booming city like New Bern. The furnishings were clean but worn, the draperies a deep purple that darkened the room as much as the walnut paneling, but it was close to the docks and the business district.

Margaret would have insisted they stay elsewhere.

He missed his wife.

They had drifted apart the past dozen years, she with society functions and he with the business. He should have spent more time with her. Should have spent more time with the children when they were young. Should have done a lot of things differently. But regret didn't produce results. He'd do better as a grandfather.

The room rented for a week, he followed the clerk upstairs to the third floor and went to the window. His view was the business district with people milling along the street.

"Where do you want your bags, sir?" Arthur asked.

"Anywhere." Daniel turned from the window to the stableman he'd employed for going on twenty-five years. He reached into his coat and pulled out a bill of sale. He tapped it against his palm, and then handed it to Arthur. "The others were kept on with the new owner, but you were not. Therefore, I feel it only right to leave you with this."

Arthur accepted the paper as if it might turn into a snake and bite him.

"'Tis a bill of sale for the carriage and horses."

Arthur pushed it back toward him. "Nay, sir. I could not—"

"Of course you can. Consider it your pension. You can sell them or hire yourself out, whatever pleases you. They are yours. I have paid the stable fee for two full weeks, including a room for you above. I only request that you continue to drive me around the city as I have a need until I board the ship on Thursday."

The old man's hand trembled. "I know not what to say, sir."

"Say nothing. The deed is done and legal. They are yours in appreciation for the care you have always taken with my horses, and my family, for the past quarter of a century. You have earned it, man."

Arthur pulled the paper close to his chest. "Thank you, sir."

"I will not require your services for the rest of today." He gestured to the window. "My bank is within walking distance and the exercise will do me good."

"Very good, sir." Arthur backed out of the room, still clutching the paper to his chest.

Filled with restless energy, Daniel headed out the door. He might as well get his business done before the wait settled in. Then maybe he could visit with some old friends before he left, those few who hadn't shunned him for his anti-slavery stance.

Zachary pulled the three-legged stool close to the cow in the last stanchion and settled on it, moving the empty bucket under her.

"There now, Bossy." He stroked her brown hide. She was his favorite, one of two cows he'd brought from North Carolina. He planned to keep the heifer she'd dropped a few weeks ago to build his herd, as he had two of her other heifers which were already milked and waiting to be released from the stanchions behind him.

He settled into the rhythmic motion of stripping her milk while leaving enough for the heifer to grow well. Bossy had eaten her grain ration, but instead of contentedly chewing her cud while he milked, she kept pushing her nose through the wooden slats that separated her from the box stall on the other side. Very odd. He used that stall when needed to keep a sick animal away from the herd, and it'd been empty for months.

Testing the weight of her udder, he asked, "That is all thee has for me?" The bucket was less than half full, and Bossy was still his best milker. The bucket should have been closer to two-thirds full, even with her feeding the heifer.

"What has thee off thy milk production today?" He rose and moved the bucket and stool out of the way, then examined Bossy thoroughly, running his hands over her, even slipping a finger into her mouth to make sure her palate didn't have a thorn in it. But she was the picture of health.

He backed her out of the narrow space and released the rest of the cows, shooing them out of the barn. When he returned for the bucket, a rustling came from the box stall.

Zachary grabbed a pitchfork. He didn't mind raccoons and opossums in the woods, but they were not welcome in his barn. The creatures stole his grain and messed in the hay, making it inedible for the cows. He raised the pitchfork as he eased the door to the box stall open.

A scrawny boy was curled in the corner, his arms wrapped protectively over his head, the white of his eyes showing. "Doan kill me." A floppy hat rested in the straw next to him.

Zachary set the pitchfork aside. "Who are thee, boy?"

"It doan matter.'" A hacking cough shook him. "I be leavin' now. Please doan tell nobody you seen me." He tried to rise but fell back against the side of the stall.

"Thee are too sick to go anywhere." Zachary approached, and the boy shrunk as if fearing a blow. "I will not hurt thee."

Another coughing spasm had the boy curling into a ball.

In his gentlest voice, Zachary said, "Thee are sick and need care." He hoisted to lad to his feet. The boy weighed nothing, so he scooped him into his arms. "Rest easy, I am a Friend. Thee are safe with me."

Glassy eyes rolled back as the boy's head slumped against Zachary's shoulder.

His dark skin seared Zachary's. He was burning up.

The first thing Zachary needed to do was bring the fever down. He headed for the creek and when they arrived, he walked into the shallow water and sat down, immersing them both up to the shoulders. The boy roused for a moment and looked around, but said nothing before he went limp again in Zachary's arms.

"So thee are the lad we have seen." The floppy hat had been mentioned by others. And that he was thin as a scarecrow and dark as night, darker even than Zachary. What was the boy's story? An escaped slave, to be sure, but where did he live? He'd been seen over the past two summers, yet only rarely, and nobody had spoken to him that Zachary knew of. How had he survived?

Zachary ran his hand over the lad's stomach, which was round and full. Bossy's milk, of course. He'd be lucky to keep it down, what with his fever as high as it was. A restorative broth was what he needed, and Zachary had been meaning to cull the young rooster who'd taken to challenging the older one. But not yet. He held still in the cold spring creek water until his teeth chattered, keeping the boy's head above water.

Rising, he walked as fast as his cold-stiffened muscles would allow, getting the boy to the house, out of his wet clothes, and into the bed. The lad never stirred, but he wasn't burning up anymore. Zachary shucked out of his wet clothing and piled all the garments in a wash basin. He'd deal with them later.

Once dressed in dry clothing, he took the ax from its peg near the back door before going in search of the rooster.

Many Quakers had helped slaves gain their freedom, as Eli Bass had helped Zachary. Eli had been passing through North Carolina on his way back to Tennessee when he'd come across the estate sale of Zachary's deceased master. Eli had been moved to compassion and purchased Zachary, then just fifteen years old, spending everything he had. Every last penny.

Zachary looked back on that day with equal amounts of gratitude and sorrow. Gratitude that Eli had bought him to set him free, and sorrow that he hadn't been able to purchase Momma. How Zachary had suffered, still suffered on occasion, all these years later, from the nightmares of Momma's face as he was hauled away. She'd been left shackled in the line yet to be auctioned off.

What nightmares did the boy in his bed suffer from?

Zachary returned to the house with the chicken. He stoked the fire in the hearth, cleaned the bird, put it in the pot with water, and swung it over the fire. He pushed a handful of dried willow bark into a smaller pot, covered it with water, and set it to steep on the other side of the hearth.

He crossed the single room of his house and touched the boy's face, which was still too hot but not as bad as before. The tea would help bring it down, but sleep was also important. It would wait until the boy awoke.

The laws regarding escaped slaves had stiffened in recent years. Even Friends were hesitant to reach out, at least overtly, to help the men and women fleeing to freedom. Stiff fines and jail time were often levied against those who were caught assisting the fugitives. And the slave catchers who roamed the country, on both sides of the Ohio River, were not above terrorizing the residents in their searches. They'd beaten one Friend half to death after finding a woman hiding in his smokehouse. It was unclear if the man had even known she was there.

How much worse it would be for Zachary, a free black man, if they found an escaped slave on his property?

Settled into the rocking chair by the bed, Zachary leaned back and looked to the rafters. "What do Thee have in mind, Lord, bringing me this boy?"

Chapter 3

W AITING HAD NEVER BEEN something Daniel did well, and waiting for the ship was no exception. He paced down the street, glancing in a window here or there, but not shopping, just walking. Burning the hours until the *Ruby Ann* was due to sail at dawn. She'd arrived on time, which was a blessing. Even now, the sailors were hard at work unloading her cargo before loading the next. Daniel had been down to check on her, to reassure himself he'd be on the water and on his way soon.

But that still left him with hours to fill, and he was sick of his hotel room.

He paused, withdrew his pocket watch from his waistcoat, and flipped it open with his thumbnail. A miniature of Margaret looked up at him. She'd been so young when he'd had it painted. Not much older than Constance was now. If only his daughter had been half the woman his wife had been, there would have been no scandal. Margaret would still be alive. She hadn't been the perfect wife, but he hadn't been the perfect husband either.

He snapped the watch cover shut, closing off the memories and regrets. It was almost four o'clock. Another hour of walking should ensure that he would sleep that night despite his anxiousness to get on with his journey.

He turned onto a street he hadn't ventured down before. It was narrower, hemmed in by buildings less ornate than those along the main district. There was a large gathering of men outside an imposing square structure. Looking for something to divert his attention, he headed that way to see what had attracted them.

The call of the auctioneer didn't register until he'd stepped into the crowd. He wouldn't mind learning what horses were currently selling for here, even though they'd likely be scarce on the frontier and twice the cost. He'd need a good riding mount when he arrived. Not a tall man, he had difficulty seeing over the shoulders in front of him.

"That one looks choice, I say." A man in front of him elbowed the fellow next to him. "I shall bid on her."

"She is a trifle on the young side," his companion answered.

"Easier to break them in that way."

There was something sinister in the man's voice, as if he'd mistreat the horse in the process of...

The crowd shifted and revealed a girl on a low platform in front of the auctioneer.

A slave.

He'd stumbled into a slave auction.

The girl's eyes met his. Dark and deep and hollow. How could anyone so young look so... hopeless?

"You always did like them young. I prefer women with a little more meat on their bones."

Revulsion rolled over Daniel. And remorse. He took a step back. Silas had warned him years ago about Jonas's pursuit of their servant girl, Gwen, but he'd dismissed it as just a young man perfecting his flirting skills. Although indentured and not a slave, Gwen had been under his roof and had deserved his protection, even from his son, a man not unlike those surrounding him now.

The girl on the platform was prodded by the man next to her and told to turn around. She did, and he lifted the back of her shapeless shirt. "No marks, gentleman," the auctioneer called out. "She is a biddable wench, not defiant. You will have no problems with this one."

He named a starting bid.

The man in front of Daniel raised his hand, as did several others in the crowd.

Daniel took another step back, wanting out of this awful scene.

When the girl was forced to face the crowd, she once again looked at Daniel.

A shudder went through him. *God in heaven, how could these men treat her this way?* Before he could think about it, he raised his hand. There was another flurry of calls from the auctioneer, more waving of hands—including Daniel's. After the auctioneer banged his gavel, he pointed it right at Daniel.

"Lucky bugger," the man in front of him muttered. "Wish my pockets were that deep today."

"The wench is not worth it," his companion said. "Next week's lot will have more."

The crowd dispersed around Daniel, so the girl must have been the final one to auction for the day. He approached the auctioneer, not sure what he should do next.

A man to the side behind a table waved him over. "Eight hundred and fifty dollars."

Daniel fished a check from his pocket and stared at it for a moment, trying to fathom what he was about to do.

Had he actually purchased another human being?

It went against everything he believed, but if he hadn't done it, she'd be the legal property of that lecherous man he'd overheard, or someone of his ilk. The thought turned Daniel's stomach. He leaned over the table and scribbled the amount and his signature.

"Very good, sir." The clerk, or whatever the slave pusher was called, handed a bill of sale across the table for Daniel.

A bill of sale, not unlike the one he'd given Arthur for the horses and carriage. He pocketed it.

"Go with him, girl." The man pointed at Daniel. "He be your master now."

Those hollow eyes met his again, and he offered a smile. It probably looked as sickly as he felt, but the girl approached him.

"What is your name?"

"It be anything you like, sir," the clerk said.

"I was asking her," he snapped, then faced the girl. "Come with me."

He wasn't going to talk to her in front of that clod. He retraced his steps to the broader street, the street he shouldn't have left in the first place. When he reached it, he stopped and turned because she'd walked three paces behind him, just as he'd seen slaves walk behind their masters for as long as he could remember.

"What is your name, child?"

"Dinah," she said in little more than a whisper. The voice of a young girl who shouldn't be away from her mother came from a somber face far too old for her years.

If she'd been purchased by those men back there, she'd have been a Dinah for sure, used as poorly as her biblical namesake. Daniel had bought her, but he'd bought her to save her from that. Now, what was he going to do with her?

"How old are you?"

She looked back down the street they'd left. "They say I be fifteen."

Not likely. "How old do you say you are?"

"Eleven." She flinched as if expecting a slap.

A child, but old enough to be helpful, and he'd need help with his grandson, a girl to tend to the boy's needs.

He wouldn't keep a slave, but once they crossed into Ohio Territory, he could write her an indenture. She could work off her freedom. After all, he couldn't just set her free, turn the child out on her own. She'd be snapped up by the first slave catcher who came by. She'd be defenseless.

But what was he to do with her until then?

Despite another dunking in the creek and the little broth Zachary had managed to spoon into him, the boy's fever was dangerously high again by noon the next day. There was no help for it. Zachary needed to fetch Paul. The boy needed a doctor.

It was risky, leaving him unattended. But who would come by except his fellow Friends?

Slave catchers, that was who. Zachary hadn't seen them himself, but word had filtered in from the river to be on the lookout for gangs of three or four men hunting fugitives.

Micah's idea to get a dog wasn't a bad one. Any extra warning would be welcome. And yet, would the boy be here if Zachary'd had a dog? He studied the figure in his bed. The only discernable movement was the slight rise and fall of his chest. If he hadn't made it into the barn, would he be dead in the woods somewhere? Unknown and unmourned by anyone?

Zachary would need to weigh the pros and cons before he decided on a dog.

For now, the boy's health was his most pressing concern.

He scooped his hat off the table and plopped it on his head as he closed the door behind him. In the barn, he hitched the team of horses, Justice and Jubal, and climbed onto the wagon's high seat. It wasn't far to town, but the wind carried a hint of rain. Zachary chirped to the horses, and they quickened their pace, large hooves thudding on the soft earth. Someday they'd have real gravel roads in this area. The elders were already talking about improving the town streets next summer. Mount Pleasant was growing and they needed to start planning for more amenities.

A gust of wind threatened to snatch Zachary's hat away. He clamped a hand on it and tilted the brim against the blast. When he straightened, a man was riding toward him, sitting erect in the saddle.

"Whoa, Justice. Whoa, Jubal." He tugged back on the reins, and the matched blacks stopped.

Paul pulled his horse to a halt beside the wagon. "Hello, Zachary."

"Thee are all smiles this afternoon." He couldn't remember seeing the man's grin so wide.

"How can I not be when today I as well as made my mother a grandmother."

"What?" Zachary blurted out his first thought. "Thee have no wife."

Paul laughed. "'Tis true, but Faye's babe arrived this morning. Mother will be thrilled. A fine girl, doing well, as is Faye."

"I should have realized." And would have had he not been preoccupied with the boy. "Happy news, indeed." There was always the rush of joy and relief when another soul joined the world without incident. "And Mark Allen?"

"Ah, that one is the worse for wear. Poor man aged five years overnight." Paul's horse snorted and pranced sideways, but he got it under control. "Are thee on the way to visit them?"

"Nay, in fact, 'twas thee I was going to see."

Paul's brows drew together. "Thee are in need of a doctor?"

"Not I, but someone at my house."

"Someone?"

Although there was nobody in sight, there were concealing trees nearby, so Zachary lowered his voice. "The less said the better. He is on my bed. Go in haste. I will catch up with thee."

Paul touched his heels to his horse and charged off.

Zachary clicked to the team and turned the wagon, following at a rapid trot. He drove straight to the barn and unhitched the horses, turning them out to pasture. Then, leaning against the wind, he untied Paul's horse from the hitching rail and took it to the barn, tying it in an empty stall. Fat raindrops slapped his hat and shoulders as he raced for the porch. He eased the door open and slipped inside, keeping quiet.

Paul leaned over the bed, tapping on the boy's chest. He straightened when he saw Zachary, then joined him by the door.

"Where did thee find him?" His tone was serious and hushed.

"In my barn."

"What do thee know about him?"

"Almost nothing. He did not give me his name when I—"

"He was speaking?" Paul whipped a look at the bed and then pinned his attention back to Zachary. "How long ago did thee find him?"

"Yesterday."

"And thee are just now—?"

"Aye." Zachary raised his hands, palms toward the doctor. "I cooled him twice in the creek, and I have spooned a restorative broth into him, as much as I could. Thee know how"—he spread his hands—"sensitive the situation is."

"Indeed." Paul pursed his lips and pressed the knuckle of his thumb against them. "I find no infection in him, but his unresponsiveness is disconcerting. He needs more liquids, as much as thee can manage." He shook his head. "I should take him to my house."

"Nay, do not."

"But I could tend him there."

"Thee have heard the news, have thee not?"

"The slave catchers? They would not bother a simple country doctor."

"If they thought to make a coin on it, they would." Zachary lowered his voice. "And what of thy mother and thy women servants? Those types would not hesitate to push their way in."

Paul frowned, but didn't argue. There were too many instances reported to back up what Zachary had said. The slave catchers would use intimidation, force, or whatever means they wished. They were a law unto themselves on the frontier.

A feeble cough from the bed broke the tension.

Zachary followed Paul to the boy's side, where dark eyes stared at them.

Paul sat on the bed's edge. "What is thy name?"

"You a Quaker?" The boy's voice was thin and reedy, but the words clear.

"I am." Paul nodded toward Zachary. "As is Zachary. Thee are in a safe place."

"He ain't no Quaker." The boy pointed at Zachary. "No slave be Quaker."

"I am not a slave." Zachary knelt beside the bed to be on the boy's level. "Not anymore. Will thee not tell us thy name?"

"Titus."

"Ah." Paul smiled. "A good, strong name. A lad with a name like that should recover quickly, should he not, Zachary?"

"Is it thy true name, the one given by thy mother?" He ignored Paul's puzzled glance.

"Aye. But"—the boy seemed to withdraw even farther beneath the blankets—"Massah called me—"

Zachary pressed his fingers to the boy's lips. "That name means nothing. Thee are Titus. Paul is right, it is a good, strong name." A smile flickered under his fingertips, and then the boy's eyes shut.

Paul backed away from the bed. "I wish he had stayed awake long enough to drink, but have the broth ready for the next time. He may drift in and out for the next couple of days. I find nothing wrong with him that rest, drink, and food will not repair."

"I will tend to him."

"I know thee will. And thank thee for reminding me to have a care for the women in my house."

"Thee has not had experience with men like these."

"Not yet, but I fear we shall all be exposed to them before long." The doctor rubbed his chin. "What was that about the boy's name? Did I say something amiss?"

"Nay, thee did not. But names are given to slaves at the whim of the master, yet each also has a name given by his or her mother. That is their true name, one they are often not allowed to use if it does not please the master."

"Why would it not?"

Paul struggled to understand something too foreign for him to comprehend, and Zachary envied him his innocence.

"Taking away a person's name," Zachary explained, "giving him another, is a way of stripping off the last vestiges of himself. It forces one to acknowledge that he is not a person. He is a possession."

"That is... barbaric."

Zachary nodded toward Titus. "They will do far worse than that to the boy if they catch him."

"Part of me does not want to know, but the doctor in me has to ask." Paul left his words hanging.

Raised in the north and educated in Scotland, Paul had lived a sheltered life. Not that Zachary looked down on him for it. Rather, he envied him. And while he was reluctant to share the information, the doctor should know what he might encounter in the future as more and more slaves made their way to the free territory. Zachary stiffened his heart against the painful memories he'd suppressed for so long.

"Each master has his own way of handling things, of course," he said. "After he is whipped, the boy could be branded with a hot iron, marking him as a runaway." He ignored Paul's quiet gasp and pushed on, reliving what he'd seen, what he'd heard told around evening fires from his youth. "Or they might cut a tendon in his leg so he could not run again, or hack off a few of his toes."

Paul raised a hand, his face tight. "I am not sorry I asked, but I think I understand without more detail."

Zachary stopped. There was no sense upsetting the good doctor with things he couldn't change. But understand? No. The man couldn't understand. How could anyone understand such a barbaric system unless they'd lived it?

Unless he'd held a brother in his arms, blood soaking into his clothes.

Chapter 4

T HE SUN WAS ALREADY climbing the sky the next day when Zachary emerged from the barn and blinked grainy eyes. He set the milk can down and smothered a yawn before stretching his back. He'd sat by the boy all night and fed him broth whenever he awoke, which had been every couple of hours. He'd managed to doze in the ladder-back chair between feedings, but it hadn't been enough. And while his body said a nap was in order, the cornfield needed to be planted. It was well into May, and he'd spent the entire day before with the boy—Titus, best to think of him that way—so Zachary didn't have the luxury of another day off.

He hefted the milk can and headed for the springhouse. Inside, he settled it into the cold water next to three other cans. He'd need to take the milk around to his customers soon, or he'd run out of cans. After drinking several handfuls of the spring water, he headed to the house.

Letting the door bang on his way in, because the boy was due to eat again anyway, he approached the bed as Titus struggled to sit up. "Let me help thee."

"I can sit." But Titus swayed like a willow twig in the breeze.

"Sure thee can." Zachary clamped a hand on his shoulder and squeezed as if in greeting and not that he was holding the boy upright. "Are thee hungry?"

"I's always hungry."

That was likely the truth. Thin past the point of lean, there was also a hollowness under his eyes. His unevenly cut hair lacked any sheen. When was the last time he'd eaten his fill? Had he ever?

Memories of life in the slave quarters threatened to escape, but Zachary squashed them down. "Thee have finished the broth. How about eggs and cheese this morning?"

That brought a lively gleam to the dark eyes studying him.

"I will cook if thee promises to remain in bed." Zachary cocked his head.

Titus nodded and slid back between the covers.

Zachary cut a bit of salt pork into the flat bottom of the iron spider and then pushed its three legs into the ashes of the fire he'd started in the hearth before milking. While it heated, he broke six eggs into a bowl, added a generous splash of cream, and whisked it with a fork. He added a pinch of salt, another of pepper, and then grated a little nutmeg on top.

"Why you be safe here?" Titus broke the silence. "Why doan the slave catchers take you back?"

"I am not a runaway." Zachary glanced at him. "I have my freedom papers."

The boy's mouth opened, but no sound came out.

"A Friend bought me, those others call Quakers, and—"

"Quakers doan buy slaves." There was a challenging set to his young jaw. "Everyone knows that."

"Thee are very young." Zachary stirred the snapping pieces of salt pork, releasing their savory aroma into the room. "Before the laws changed, many Quakers who could afford to would purchase slaves and give them their freedom papers." He poured the egg mixture over the salt pork, letting Titus digest the history lesson. Then he put the lid on the spider and moved it to the edge of the hearth to finish baking the eggs.

"But there were too many men who wanted our people to remain in bondage, and so those who wished to protect slavery changed the laws to make freeing slaves illegal. Still, some Quakers bought slaves and took them north to free them. When they returned home, many were fined, some even arrested and imprisoned."

"That what happen to the man who freed you?" Skepticism filled the boy's voice.

"Eli bought me in North Carolina, but he lived in Tennessee. He took me home and drew up my freedom papers there, where it was not illegal. Not then, anyway."

"And then you come north?" The boy was sitting again, and his stomach let out a long rumble.

Zachary chuckled. "I will tell thee the rest another time." He took a loaf of bread from his pantry shelf. It was three days old, but it was all he had. "Are thee steady enough to sit at the table now?"

Titus shot to his feet and swayed, clutching the bedpost.

"Slowly, lest thee fall." He set out two plates, two forks, and two cups, then took the pitcher of milk from the shelf and a half round of cheese. The boy needed nourishment and so did Zachary if he was going to plant corn all day. He yawned as he lifted the lid from the spider and dished out the baked eggs.

Titus made his way to the table, sat and grabbed his fork. Zachary stopped him with a hand over his. "In this house, we give thanks to the Lord before we eat."

"Oh." The boy dropped the fork as if it'd been heated in the fire.

"Quakers say a silent prayer." Zachary bowed his head. *Lord, I know not what You have in mind for Titus and me, but help me to meet his needs while honoring Thee and keeping both of us safe.* "Amen."

Titus stared at him until Zachary nodded, then he attacked the food like a ravenous wolf.

"Slow down or 'twill come back up. The food is for thee. Nobody will take it away."

Cheeks bulging like a chipmunk's, the boy only nodded, but his frantic chewing slowed, and he set his fork beside his plate.

"I must work in the field today. I will leave the leftover food on the table should thee awaken hungry again."

"Who you work for?" Titus asked around a mouthful of bread.

It wasn't the time to address table manners. "I work for myself." He gestured around with his empty fork. "The house, the land, the cows, the chickens, the horses and mule, they are mine."

"And doan nobody try and take them from you?"

Zachary shook his head and took another bite of eggs. Nobody tried to take anything from him, but he had nobody to share anything with either. Oh, his friends, of course, but nobody special. No family.

If only the boy could stay. He certainly needed someone to care for him, but it wasn't safe for him to be here. There would be men after him. Slave catchers who would force him back across the river where his life would be made worse than miserable—if he were allowed to live at all.

And Zachary? He could lose his freedom papers if he was caught helping an escaped slave. And losing them would mean...

He could be forced across the river and sold back into slavery.

On the deck of the *Ruby Ann*, Daniel lifted a hand to Arthur. The stableman, waving his cap from beside the carriage, grew smaller as the ship slipped away from the dock. Odd, but it felt good to know that someone would miss him here, even if only a hired man.

Unlike Jonas and Constance. Not that it mattered. He hadn't told either of them his plans. Hadn't told them he'd sold the house or the business. Maybe—someday—he'd write them each a letter. After all, disappointments or not, they were his children. Not his responsibility anymore, but still his children.

An ocean breeze filled the huge sails above him. Canvas rippled to life, sailors shouted, and people milled away from the railing as New Bern receded into the distance. It should take only a few days to reach Alexandria, where they'd exchange the ship for a riverboat to take them to the Ohio River and into Ohio Territory.

Daniel took a step back and bumped into someone. "I beg your pardon—" He turned to Dinah, staring up at him with alarm in her eyes.

"I's sorry, Massah. I closed my eyes for a minute and—"

"No matter." He wasn't used to having someone shadow his every move. He'd quite forgotten about her. The poor thing had slept on the floor of his room last night on a blanket—if she'd slept at all. He couldn't fault her for being exhausted this morning.

Two well-dressed men walked past. Daniel nodded, but they ignored him and eyed Dinah while the girl stared at the deck's planking.

He studied the girl himself. He'd been in such a state of shock over purchasing her that he hadn't really seen past her eyes, the eyes that had tugged at his soul. She was tall for her age, and willowy, her shapeless shirt and skirt of unbleached cotton. Her hair was covered with an intricately folded piece of calico.

She looked up at him then, dark eyes in a smooth face with wide, high cheekbones that tapered to a delicate chin. Her light skin said she had white blood. Was her father her former owner? Daniel wanted to deny the possibility, but his eyes wouldn't allow it.

"Your girl is a young beauty," a gray-bearded man said around the pipe in his mouth. "You should have a care with her onboard." He removed his pipe and pointed with it to another man down the deck, and then to two sailors on the rear deck above, all watching them. Watching Dinah. "She is already drawing too much attention."

"Indeed."

"Are you selling her in Alexandria?"

Daniel bristled. "I am not. We are bound for Ohio Territory."

"Now why would a man with a slave want to go there?"

"I have my reasons."

Gray brows drew into a straight line. "Ohio entered the country as free territory, but there are plenty of those from the other side of the Ohio who moved in for the land. They believe in the right to own slaves." He scratched under his beard. "If you think to free the girl there, heed my words. Not everyone will be your friend."

"I hear you."

The old man grunted and slipped his pipe between his lips. "Keep her below deck, and keep your cabin locked." He ambled away, the strange old coot.

Was he telling the truth?

Whether he knew Ohio Territory or not, he had the right of it as far as the ship was concerned. "Come." Daniel dug the key from his waistcoat pocket and led Dinah to the stairs that would take them to the guest cabins below. They didn't have far to go, his cabin being near the stairs. He unlocked it and pushed the door open.

The room was narrow with a round porthole at the end. Two bunks with thin mattresses were fixed to one wall, one above the other, and covered with wool blankets. At least the girl would have a better place to sleep than the hotel room's floor. Two uncomfortable-looking chairs and a small chipped table filled the rest of the space other than a curtained-off corner that probably concealed a chamber pot. Nothing luxurious, but the room provided the necessities. And Daniel planned to spend most of his time above deck, if the weather held anyway.

He pointed to one of the chairs. "Sit down."

Dinah edged around him, careful not to touch him, and perched on the very edge of the chair, in danger of falling off.

"Sit back, girl. Be at ease."

She scooted backward an inch at best.

Daniel sighed. What had the poor girl been through that she was so terrified? Never had he wished for Silas's steady hand in charge more than now. The old butler would know how to handle things. But Daniel was on his own.

For the first time in his life.

He cleared his throat. "Dinah, you have no need to be afraid of me. I will not hurt you, this I promise. Do you understand?"

She nodded, but nothing in her eyes indicated that she believed.

Maybe she'd settle better if he told her his plans. "We are going to the Ohio Territory to make a new life there, you and I. I have a grandson there, just four years old, and I will require help with him once I claim him again. Have you worked with young children?"

Another nod, but no softening of her posture.

"We shall be on this ship for a few days, and I think it best if you remain in this cabin because the men"—he pointed up—"are not to be trusted."

Her eyes grew larger.

"Do you understand?"

Her nod was vigorous, terror in her expression. Perhaps the child knew more than she should about such things. The thought sickened him. Something must have shown on his face because she shrank back into the chair.

"Nay, child." He gentled his voice as if he were speaking with a nervous colt. "You have nothing to fear." He pressed his hand to his chest. "Not from me."

He stood, the key between his fingers. "I am going up on deck, but I will lock you inside. 'Tis not to contain you, understand, but to keep you safe."

At last, the girl relaxed a little, and the tightness in her face eased. "Thank you, Massah."

He wanted to correct her, tell her to refer to him as Master White-ford as his other employees had, but he didn't want her to retreat into fear again. They'd have time later to work out the details of how they were to live going forward. For now, he wanted to get above and watch the wind blow them closer to Alexandria.

Closer to his grandson.

Chapter 5

Z ACHARY ROLLED OUT OF his blankets on the floor. He sat up and
worked the kinks from his neck, the pops and cracks loud in the
predawn hour. Two days of planting corn was bad enough, but two
nights of sleeping on the floor was more than he could handle. Today,
he would rig a smaller bed for Titus so he could reclaim his.

A few minutes later, he was walking to the barn, swinging the milk
pail, and breathing in the damp coolness of the dew-drenched landscape.

The morning rhythm of feeding and milking eased the last of the
soreness from Zachary's muscles. He was finishing milking Bossy when
the barn door eased open and shut behind him.

"Zachary?" came the half-whisper.

"Bran?" What was Paul's hired man—more boy than man—doing
at Zachary's farm at this hour? He stood and pulled the bucket from
under the cow. "Is something wrong?"

"You could say that." The young man moved into the light of a
window, pulling someone behind him. "We need your help."

That someone was a woman wearing a dress so thin and tattered it was nearly transparent. Her black hair was streaked with gray and spiked in wild disarray. She was tall, her features dark, though not as dark as his, and her eyes a striking light brown, the whites showing.

"Who is this?"

"Her name be Tess."

"Hello, Tess."

The woman bowed her head, eyes to the floor.

"Thee can look at me, Tess."

That snapped her head up. "Thee? You be a Quaker?"

Why was everyone so shocked that a black man could be a Quaker? He should be used to it by now, but somehow, it always stung when it was one of his own people who asked.

"I am. And thee are safe here."

"Maybe so, but not for long." Bran pulled a disgusted face. "Slave catchers is on this side o' the river. I seen 'em myself."

Titus.

Fear bit into Zachary's middle. How was he going to protect the boy *and* this woman?

"Yours be the closest place I could bring her, and you got that nice root cellar..." Bran let his words drift off.

The root cellar was six feet square and half filled with provisions. Zachary could make space for Tess to lie down and sleep through the day, but what about Titus? Would the dank space cause a setback in his recovery? And was it a good idea to let Bran know about the boy?

"I can fetch her up to the house while you tend the milk." Bran headed for the door.

"Nay. Wait." Zachary pressed the heel of his hand to his forehead. "Perhaps it would be better to keep her here, in the barn."

"They be searching barns from the river to here. But they ain't bold enough to force their way into houses. Yet." He spit on the dirt floor. "They even stuck hay forks into last year's haystacks at one place, I heard tell."

That meant the root cellar was the only safe spot. "Untie the cows and turn them out on pasture. I shall put the milk in the springhouse, then meet me at the house." Maybe he should've warned them about Titus, but there wasn't time.

He'd settled his last can of milk into the spring's cold water, poured a bucket of chilled milk to take inside, and then started across the yard.

Bran had Tess by the hand and was pulling her across the yard. Sunlight poured across the farm, and anyone approaching would be able to see them. They needed to get Tess and Titus into the root cellar—fast.

They reached the porch at the same time. Zachary held the door open and waited while they entered, scanning the countryside for any sign of movement before he entered and pulled the door shut behind him.

"Titus?" Bran's voice rose in astonishment.

So they knew each other. Somehow, Zachary wasn't surprised. Bran seemed to know things that other people didn't.

"I been worried fit to gray my hair." Bran dropped Tess's hand and hurried to the bed, sitting on the edge. "You sickly?"

The two boys were similar in age and height, both reed-thin, one dark and the other as white as the trillium that blossomed in the forest. Bran's straw-colored hair was straight but just as unruly as Titus's black curls. Their grins, however, said it all. They were friends, and had been for some time. So this was why Titus had been spotted in the area so many times.

Zachary crossed his arms. "I take it thee know each other."

A flush of pink graced Bran's cheeks, and he didn't meet Zachary's look. "We do."

There wasn't time for more. "Bran says there are slave catchers on this side of the river. We need to settle thee and Tess into the root cellar." He moved the table and exposed the subtle cracks of the trapdoor, then used a pry bar to open it, exposing the ladder nailed to one wall. Earthy mustiness rose from the cool depths.

"I need to stack a few crates to make more room." Zachary climbed down and shuffled things around. Above him, the boys' voices chattered on.

"I hear hoofbeats," Tess said from near the cellar opening.

"Zachary, hurry!" Bran's frantic voice was accompanied by shuffling and thumping above.

Zachary set the crate in his arms on top of a stack and sprinted up the ladder.

"Uh-oh." Bran stepped back from the window and faced Zachary. "'Tis Paul."

Relief weakened Zachary's legs, and he steadied himself against the table. "Thank God."

"But he will see Titus and..." Bran glanced at the boy and back to Zachary. "He will figure out what I been doin'."

"If all thee have done is help people, I doubt he will object."

The boy's throat bobbed, but he nodded.

Surely Paul wouldn't fault the boy for that, would he?

"Who is this man?" Tess's voice trembled.

"He is our town doctor," Zachary explained, "And another Friend—Quaker. Thee are safe."

Her light eyes held more suspicion than trust, but she nodded.

Boots thumped on the porch before the knock.

Zachary opened the door. "Welcome, Paul." He stepped aside and gave him room. "We have grown in number since thy last visit."

"Grown in number?" Paul entered and scanned the room. "Bran?"

The boy nodded.

"And who is this?" Paul gestured toward Tess, who all but huddled in the far corner.

Bran stepped over to her. "This here be Tess. She was in a bad way when I found her, so I brung her here, it bein' the closest house."

"Thee found her?"

Bran nodded.

Paul's eyebrow rose. "What were thee doing when thee found her?"

Bran opened his mouth, then snapped it shut, shoulders inching toward his ears.

"The point is," Zachary said, "Bran has seen slave catchers on this side of the river." He pointed to the open trapdoor. "I was preparing the root cellar for Tess and Titus to hide in."

Paul strode to the open cellar, leaned over, and sniffed, his nose wrinkling. "I do not like the idea of Titus spending too much time there in his condition."

"His condition?" Bran asked.

Paul shot him a hard look. "He has been ill. 'Twould be better if he not breathe the stagnant air down there."

"'Twould be better if he be not caught," Bran shot back.

"Indeed." Paul went to the window. "Thee has a good view of the road from here, but of course, slave catchers might not travel by road."

"I thought, if we left the trapdoor open, we would have enough warning to get them below and the door shut before anyone could approach the house." Zachary shrugged. "But I would need to be here to lower the door and move the table over it."

"And thee has work to do, I presume."

"In fact, I must deliver milk today. I filled my last can this morning. If I cannot deliver it, I shall have to pour some of it out."

Paul tapped his bottom lip, shooting a glance at Bran. "Bran could make thy deliveries for thee. He would need help loading the wagon, but he can drive and pour from the cans, I should think."

The boy puffed out his chest. "I can do it."

"I have several calls to make this morning, but let me have a look at Titus first." He strode to the bed and examined the boy. "How are thee today, Titus?"

"Fine as frog's hair and ready to run." The boy's voice was stronger, but not as hearty as his words.

"No running yet, I say." Paul rose from the bedside. "But thee are doing well. Much better, in fact. Zachary's fresh milk is no doubt the best medicine."

Paul left the bedside and crossed the room to Tess. "And how about thee? Is there anything thee needs a doctor to see to?"

Tess shook her head but held her ground, not stepping away. "I be just fine, suh."

"No need for the 'sir' here, Tess. Paul is my name. We Quakers recognize no titles. None of us is above any other."

"I hear that said 'bout you all."

"'Tis true. And while I know more about the body than I do women's clothing, even I can see thee has a need." He snapped a finger at Bran. "See if Bridget has a dress she can spare, or even an apron. Give her no details, of course. Say that the request comes from me." He turned back to Tess. "Our cook is of a similar height and generous of heart. We shall see what she comes up with for thee."

"Thank you, suh." She ducked her head and whispered, "Paul."

"Very well. I must be on my way. I shall return in two or three days, when I expect young Titus will be fit as a fiddle."

"Thank thee, for everything." Zachary opened the door and followed Paul out to his horse. When they were away from the house, he said, "Bran and Titus are well acquainted. I have heard rumors of a boy matching Titus's description for the past two summers, even caught a glimpse of him once. I suspect Bran has been assisting him."

"But if he indeed escaped, why is he still here?"

"A very good question. I will see what I can learn. Perhaps with Tess here, he will open up a little more."

"Hmm. Perhaps." Paul mounted his horse. "But do not be surprised if he remains elusive." With that, he turned the horse and cantered away.

Perhaps Paul had more knowledge of runaways than Zachary did.

Bran came out and joined him. "Want me to hitch the team?"

"I shall help thee, and introduce thee to them. They are a good team, but young. Thee will need to have a care not to let them run and churn my milk into butter before the goodwives of Mount Pleasant fill their buckets."

"I can handle them." Bran strutted for the barn. "I handled Paul's team from Roberts Landing, after all."

"Indeed, I remember." Zachary hid his smile at the boy's bravado. "I have a list of the places to stop. Thee can read, can thee not?"

Bran stuck his thumbs under his braces. "'Twas me who taught Mark Allen."

"Perhaps we should keep thee in mind when we open the school-house next year."

"Oh, no." Bran raised both hands as if to ward off something evil. "Like to spend my time in the fresh air."

"Bran." Zachary stopped him with a touch on his shoulder. "How have thee been helping Titus?"

The boy shrugged. "Nothin' much. I give him a bit of food some-times, a shirt once." He glanced toward where Paul had disappeared over a hill. "I ain't never stolen from Paul, not even to help Titus, but sometimes Bridget gives me extra, you know, me bein' a growin' boy and all."

It was well known that Paul's cook doted on the boy like a younger brother, but to his bones, Zachary felt there was something more.

"And?"

Bran jabbed his hands into the pockets of his breeches. "He needed a place to stay a few times, and I let him sleep in Mark Allen's old bed in the stable."

Zachary drew in a sharp breath. "Thee must not do so again without Paul's consent."

"He always left before first light and—"

"It matters not. If Titus had been discovered, 'twould be Paul in trouble, not thee. And who would take care of the women of the house should that happen?"

Bran hung his head. "I should of thought of that."

"Indeed, thee should have. 'Tis the man's role to care for the women around him."

"I will not do it again."

"Good." Zachary started for the barn again. "And Bran?"

"Aye?"

"Thee can always bring him here. Or anyone like him whom thee 'find' in the wee hours of the morning."

Bran flashed him a grin, the gap between his front teeth showing. "'Tis good to know."

"Why is it I have the feeling that thee knows many things?"

Bran shrugged.

They hitched the team and loaded the milk cans. Bran maneuvered slowly and carefully down the road, the milk not getting jostled, just as Zachary had instructed.

He could teach him about handling the team and delivering milk, but would Bran ever teach Zachary what he knew about escaped slaves? Where did they go from here? Canada? How could they make it that far? Were there people—Friends, maybe—helping them along the way? He had so many questions.

Maybe the best person to start asking his questions to was the one lying in his bed.

Chapter 6

T HE RIVERBOAT WAS MUCH more crowded than the ship had been. Its clamorous din rose from numerous crates of chickens, two of piglets, and several lowing calves tied on the back deck of the boat, the annoyance only matched by the odors surrounding them.

Daniel paced the length of the boat to the stern, which wasn't far, and headed back to the front. The sailors ignored him, going about their business with methodical movements.

Poor Dinah huddled on a barrel near what passed for a cabin, hunched over one of his shirts, mending a seam. He could keep an eye on her there while he took some exercise. At least she was out in the sunlight and not stuck in the dark interior of the cabin, which had only rifle slots to let light through. Their quarters were more fortress than cabin, a thought that didn't bring any comfort. If they needed a fortress, then there was inherent danger to this place.

Daniel reached the front of the boat and turned toward the back again. Each footfall rang hollow on the aged and weathered wood beneath his feet.

Why had Thomas Baldwin taken his grandson to a place fraught with danger?

A little voice in the back of his head asked, *Why did Thomas Baldwin take your grandson at all?*

What else could Daniel have done? His daughter's life would have been ruined had they kept the child. In hindsight, she'd managed to do that anyway. But there'd been Margaret to think of, and his business. It chafed to admit it—even to himself—but he'd put his standing in the community above the well-being of the child.

He had chosen the Baldwins to take him in, and the girl, of course. He'd made sure the boy had a mother. He hadn't delivered him to some orphanage and walked away. And he could have. It would have been within his rights.

Even so, he'd been wrong. Wrong about so many things. It was time to correct things. With the money from the sale of the business, the house, and all their belongings, he was prepared to start anew. And this time, he had to do it right.

The captain of the riverboat met him halfway down the side. "Should reach Roberts Landing by evening."

Daniel rubbed his hands together. "Splendid. I look forward to it."

"Do not get your hopes up. 'Tis not much of a town, although it has grown these past few years."

"It matters not. I shall not be staying there, but pushing on to Mount Pleasant as soon as I can hire a driver."

"That new Quaker community?" The captain eyed him up and down, no doubt taking in the cut of his clothing, the lace at his neck, the silver buckles on his shoes, and the gold watch chain dangling from his embroidered waistcoat pocket.

"Indeed, I hope to establish a business there."

"I hear tell them Quakers like to keep to their own."

Daniel waved the comment away. "I have many years of experience working with them. In fact, the group in Mount Pleasant moved from New Bern, where my business was headquartered. I know them well."

"Then you know they will not take kindly to your slave girl."

"That is an issue I am prepared to deal with." Not that it was any of this man's business.

"Would you be selling her then?"

"Selling? I should say not."

"Hmm, too bad. Pretty little creature. She would fetch a good price on the south side of the river." The captain touched the brim of his cap and moved on. "Good luck to you, sir."

Creature, as if Dinah were one of the piglets or calves the captain was hauling west.

Daniel turned back to the front of the boat and stopped next to Dinah. "The captain says we shall leave the boat by this evening. Please have my belongings packed and ready."

The girl set the sewing aside. "Yes, Massah." She stood and moved toward the cabin.

"Dinah." He waited for her to face him again. "Please refer to me as..." He balked at the word master. Even Master Whiteford seemed too... too southern. They were moving north for a reason, and he needed to start the changes. "As Mr. Whiteford."

Her dark eyes rounded.

"I realize 'tis different than you are accustomed to, but we shall be living in a different area with a different type of people. I think it appropriate."

"Yes, Mass—Mr. Whiteford." She barely breathed his name, but it was a start.

"I told you, best you doan know." Titus crossed his arms and glared at Zachary.

The boy refused to give him any information about his activities in the area regarding fugitives escaping to freedom, and now he wanted Zachary's help with Tess—but only on the condition that Zachary remain ignorant of what was happening.

It rubbed like a hair shirt.

"So I am just supposed to go fishing, enjoy myself as if nothing is out of the ordinary, and then return home with an empty cart?"

Titus nodded, and Tess followed suit. The two had been whispering, heads together, ever since a rider had passed the house earlier that day, sending them both into the root cellar.

"Please, suh." Tess couldn't seem to manage using his name. "I doan want to cause you no trouble."

Yet they were asking him to blindly stick out his neck for them. And he'd do it.

"Tell me the plan again."

Titus scooted to the edge of his chair. "You know where Short Creek bends into a horseshoe, maybe a mile northwest of here?"

Zachary nodded.

"Drive there in the cart. Me and Tess will rig it for her to hide in. There be a row of trees, tall trees, for you to tie the mule. Then you go fishin', and Tess be on her way."

"I could drive her farther—"

"Why?" Titus interrupted.

"To help her get farther away from the river and—"

"You ever go farther than that?"

"Nay, but I thought—"

"You do somethin' unusual, people notice. A man goin' fishin' is just a man goin' fishin'. A man drivin' where he doan usually drive, people notice."

And it was all about not being noticed. Zachary understood. He didn't like it, but he understood.

Tess, wearing the dress Bridget had sent, twisted her hands together but lifted her light-colored eyes to his.

"I can nevah thank you enough for what you already done." She plucked at the sleeve of the dress. It wasn't new, and its faded gray wouldn't stand out. It would go unnoticed. "I just ask you for this one last thing."

"Thee will need food. Bake biscuits this afternoon. Thee will find everything thee need on the pantry shelf, and thee can take as much cheese as thee can carry unnoticed."

She started to protest, but he cut her off.

"I insist." Zachary stood. "And since I shall be fishing tomorrow, I must get my farm work done today."

"You fetch me a channel cat or two, and I fry you a fish dinner to remember." Titus's grin was infectious, and maybe the idea of a catfish dinner didn't hurt either, but Zachary left the house a little less discontent than when they'd sprung the idea on him after the noon meal.

After all, he'd be doing something to help. And maybe this would establish trust with Titus. The boy was intent on keeping Zachary at arm's length, but for whatever reason, that only made Zachary want to bridge the gap more.

"Come along." Daniel stomped down the dock leading to the town, leaving his remaining worldly possessions in his trunks on the dock, where the sailors had stacked them. Roberts Landing wasn't a proper port at all. There were no dock workers to hire. In fact, there was nobody in sight. At least he shouldn't have to worry about his belongings being stolen.

Dinah hurried after him, her bare feet slapping on the wood.

He stopped abruptly and turned. The girl stepped to the side to avoid colliding with him. He grabbed her arm to keep her from spilling into the river, and she squeaked in surprise or fear, he wasn't sure which. He glanced at his trunks and back to her. She had only the dress he'd bought her in. No shoes. No apron. Not even one of those pockets to carry anything in. But then, if she owned nothing, what would she have to carry?

He needed to outfit her properly before they arrived in Mount Pleasant. She couldn't arrive looking so much like a... a slave. Why hadn't he thought of that before? Because Margaret had always seen to the needs of the family and the household. He knew nothing.

"Hmm." He pivoted and continued his march toward the buildings in the distance. Why had someone built them so far from the riverbank? His shoes sank into the boggy ground as they stepped off the dock. And it was May. How wet must it be in the early spring when the river ran high? The distance made sense, but he would have preferred having a cart or wagon he could hire, rather than walking.

The sun was heading for the horizon, and the shops they passed were closed for the day. Noise and light spilled from the open windows of a tavern in the middle of the block, so Daniel headed there. He paused at the doorway. Should he tell Dinah to wait outside, or would someone try to snatch her? Maybe it was best she stay in his shadow.

"Stay close to me," he said over his shoulder as he strode into the tavern.

It was much like any other small-town tavern. Men gathered in knots around tables, discussing the world's problems and complaining about the price of beef or flour or cotton. Maybe not cotton up here, but men gathered together would complain about the price of anything. Pipe smoke hung in a haze across the room, and the scents of yeasty ale and unwashed bodies vied for his attention.

Daniel approached a man wearing a stained apron at the bar. "I need a room for the night and someone to fetch my trunks from the dock."

"There be a room upstairs." The man leaned over and eyed Dinah before quoting the price for two people. "Bob over there"—he nodded toward the table by the entry door—"in the red cap, he be the man to hire for a bit of work."

"Thank you." Daniel pulled coins from his waistcoat pocket to cover the cost of the room, then approached the table indicated by the bartender. "Are you Bob?"

"I am." The man rose, towering over Daniel by at least two handspans, muscles filling out the sleeves of his homespun shirt. "What can I do for you?"

"Have you a wagon?"

"I do."

"I have seven trunks at the dock to be brought up, and I would like to hire you to deliver me and the trunks to Mount Pleasant tomorrow, if that suits you."

Bob rubbed his chin, then named a price Daniel found exorbitant, but he wasn't there to haggle, and he needed the ride. "That will be fine. I should like to leave as soon as I purchase some things from the mercantile when it opens."

"I will fetch your belongings now and keep them on the wagon until then." He stuck out a hand that nearly swallowed Daniel's.

"Very good." Daniel returned to the bar and requested whatever could be had for supper to be sent to their room. He moved through the crowd, ignoring the stares that were aimed not at him so much as at Dinah, and climbed the stairs, his shadow so close he could feel the fear wafting off her.

Their room was at the end of the hall and much quieter than below. He pushed the door open and stepped inside.

The room smelled stale. "Open the window." He made a shooing gesture to Dinah, who hurried past him to the window overlooking the stable behind the tavern. Its odors came in on the breeze, but even that was an improvement. It was a tiny room with one bed, a washstand with a pitcher and basin, a single chair, and a rickety table with a stub of a candle on it. There was no fireplace, but two copper warming pans hanging on the wall said they should at least have hot coals for warmth in the evening.

What would he find in Mount Pleasant?

A knock sounded.

At his nod, Dinah hurried to open the door to a girl not much older than herself who held out a tray containing two bowls of something steaming, a loaf of bread, and two mugs. Dinah took it and set it on the rickety table by the window.

"We shall require another blanket," Daniel said.

The girl nodded and left without a word.

Daniel grabbed a mug and drained the contents, a very pleasant cider with a bit of a tang to it. He glanced around the small room before settling on the bed and pointing to the chair. "Sit, eat. You must be as hungry as I."

Dinah perched on the seat but made no move toward the food.

"Tear the loaf in half and help yourself to one of the bowls and the other mug. 'Tis for us to share."

She gingerly tore a small piece from the bread and picked up a bowl, but her discomfort was palpable.

Daniel sighed and took the other bowl. "We must learn to get along. 'Tis just you and I for now. No reason to stand on ceremony. Eat, girl." If he was this awkward with Dinah, a girl would do anything he bid her to, how was he going to manage with his four-year-old grandson? Daniel pushed that thought aside.

What would Margaret have said, him sitting on a bed in a cramped and smelly room, eating with a servant? She'd be scandalized.

But where had all the fine manners and trappings of wealth gotten him? He and Dinah were starting on a new path. For both of them, it meant leaving all they knew behind. He because he wanted something better. She because she had no choice.

He finished the stew, its savory goodness a welcome surprise, and mopped up the last bits with a swab of bread.

The tavern girl brought the blanket and left with the tray. Dinah had kept back the bread they hadn't finished. Daniel wouldn't have thought to do that, but doubtless, the girl had gone without before, whereas he always assumed he could purchase more.

"Dinah." She startled but looked at him from her chair. "'Twill not always be like this. We will settle in Mount Pleasant and make a home there. You are too young to be given your freedom papers, but I will do right by you. And when you reach majority age, I will give you your freedom papers. You have my word on it."

"You gonna set me free?" For the first time, her voice was loud and clear in her shocked response.

"When I can, but you understand, I cannot do it until you turn one and twenty."

"Oh, Mass—Mr. Whiteford. I doan know what to say."

"Say that you will help me raise my grandson. 'Tis all I ask." He needed her help, or someone's help, because he lacked any knowledge of the everyday things it took to run a household. Or a family.

"Yes, suh. I will. You can be sure I will." Her dark eyes shone in the growing darkness of the room. "And thank you, suh."

"Go to sleep. We must be up early and on our way."

To find his grandson.

Chapter 7

"WHOA, ANNABELLE." ZACHARY PULLED the mule to a halt near the trees where Titus had instructed him. He wasn't supposed to speak to Tess because there was always the risk of someone wandering by. But he could talk to the mule. "This looks like a good place for thee while I fish. The trees will shade thee, and there are plenty of leaves to munch on."

He dismounted from the cart and tied Annabelle before taking his fishing pole and basket from the seat. Nothing moved, and he was tempted to whisper something. Instead, he thumped the mule on her rump as he passed. "Enjoy thy rest, old girl."

He baited his hook and cast the line, then settled on the creek's bank and waited. And listened. Birds chirped from the trees behind him. Insects buzzed and hummed and skimmed across the crystal water of the creek. A bullfrog croaked its complaints to the world. Above, a hawk made lazy circles, riding the breeze and surveying its kingdom.

If he hadn't been straining to hear something different—anything to indicate Tess had made her escape—he'd have enjoyed the morning.

Even more so an hour later when a channel cat struck his line and bent his pole almost double. It took him a long time to work the big fish around and tire it out enough to get it near shore. Even then, he waded in to get a hand on it to flip it onto the bank. The thing was longer than Zachary's arm and nearly as thick. He'd never landed a fish of that size before, and the thrill of seeing it flop on the shore shot through him.

"What you got there, boy?"

Zachary froze.

Three men walked toward him. They wore breeches and linen shirts with the common waistcoat of working men. Two were lean and average height with nondescript hair and eyes. They were like bookends, the kind of men one wouldn't notice in a crowd. Although one carried a coil of rope over his shoulder.

They weren't in a crowd.

The other man was shorter and pudgier, with hair so light-blond it was almost white. He'd been the one to call out, and he spoke again. "Answer me, boy."

Zachary stepped out of the creek. They reached him and had to crane their necks due to his height. That shouldn't have mattered, but he allowed himself a small measure of smugness over it. He'd repent of that later.

"As thee can see, I am fishing." He needed to keep them talking and focused on him, in case Tess was still nearby.

"Thee?" The man with the rope glanced at his counterpart, then back at Zachary. "You a Quaker?"

"No such thing as a Quaker slave." The blond man appeared to be the one in charge.

"I am a free man." Zachary kept his voice even. "The Lord recognizes no distinctions among men. Jesus Christ came to seek and save sinners of every kind."

"He sure sounds Quaker," the bookend without the rope said.

"Quaker or not, who do you belong to?" the blond man demanded.

"I belong to no man. I have my freedom papers." But a sweat broke out on the back of his neck. His papers were in his house. And so was Titus.

"He don't match any description we got," the rope man said.

"Which proves nothing." The leader crossed his arms and squinted up at Zachary. "Where are you from?"

"My farm is outside of Mount Pleasant, just about a mile from here."

"What farmer has time to spend fishing on a fine day like this?"

"One who worked extra hard yesterday to make time."

The man without the rope pointed to the channel cat, no longer flopping on the grass. "He was fishing, for sure."

"And now I shall return to my farm." Zachary picked up the fish, careful of its spines, and gathered the basket and pole in his other hand.

"With just one fish?" The blond man asked.

"I have only myself to feed." He lifted the fish to his shoulder height so the men had to look up at it. "This one will feed me for a few days. I wish thee a good day, gentlemen." Heart pounding, half expecting one of them to try to stop him, Zachary headed for his cart.

Please, Lord, let Tess be far away from here by now. And lead these men in the wrong direction to find her, if it be Thy will.

"It be that woman we want," one of the men said behind him. "We got no reason to hold on to him, even if we could."

"And if he is a Quaker, we could stir up a hornet's nest by touching him."

"You scared of Quakers? They are pacifists. You can smack one, and he will not even smack you back." It was the nasal twang and disdainful tone of the blond man.

"I ain't never seen a Quaker as big as him."

Their voices faded as Zachary reached the trees.

Squashing the urge to throw the fish in the cart, jump on the seat, and whip Annabelle into a run, he moved with slow purpose. Like a man out for a day of fishing. Not a man hiding fugitive slaves or helping them escape.

He was a man doing his best to go unnoticed.

He laid the fish on the floor of the cart, casting a glance under the seat as he did so. The tarp was folded and flat. No sign of Tess.

Thank Thee, Lord.

"Come on, girl." He untied the mule and backed her out of the trees. Taking his time, he climbed into the seat and gathered the reins. He glanced back at the three men, who remained by the creek, watching him. Zachary touched the brim of his hat and clicked to Annabelle. The mule set off at her usual plodding pace, and he didn't hurry her.

So many things could have gone wrong back there.

But none had.

Tess was on her way. Zachary had a fish for dinner. And those three slave catchers were none the wiser. His emotions swung from elation to relief to fear to anger and back again, and he couldn't have said which was the stronger. But he was rock-solid sure of one thing.

No matter what Titus said or thought, Zachary was going to help more fugitives escape.

Daniel gritted his teeth as the sturdy wagon bounced over yet another crater in what Bob had called a road.

Dinah gave a little squeal, clinging to the straps of the trunk she sat upon.

"'Tisn't much of a road, but 'tis the only way to Mount Pleasant." Bob's tone was entirely too cheerful under the circumstances.

The sun beat down as if it were August and not late May. Or maybe it was just hotter away from the breeze off the river. Daniel removed his hat and wiped the sweat from his forehead with a kerchief before replacing it. "How much farther?"

Bob pointed to where the land rose in a gentle hillside. "Once we top that rise, the town be just beyond."

At last.

How long would it take him to locate the boy? Mount Pleasant couldn't be very large. Its distance from the Ohio River would see to its slow growth. The Quakers would have been better served had they stayed nearer the water, especially as the roads were so poorly developed.

But Quakers were odd. Good people. As trustworthy as any—more trustworthy than most. But odd. They did things their own way for their own reasons, all of which they attributed to God. It didn't make much sense to Daniel, but then, neither did the minister's sermons in his own church. Daniel had been too busy making a living and raising a family to worry on spiritual matters when he was younger.

Perhaps that was where he'd gone wrong. He'd have to think on that when he was settled and had the time. But first, he needed to find the boy.

What had Gwen named him? He couldn't keep thinking of him as *the boy*. He must have a name. But what if it wasn't appropriate to his new station in life as Daniel's grandson and heir? Daniel couldn't remember being four years old, so surely it wasn't too late to change a name. Simple enough, really.

What name would he choose? Something strong, commanding, a name men would remember. He drummed his fingers on the cracked wood of the wagon's seat. George was a strong name, but probably too English. As were Charles and Edward. What about Andrew? Yes, that would do nicely. A strong name with a connection to the Bible. The Quakers would approve of that, would they not?

The wagon lurched again, Dinah squealed again, and Daniel reined in his impatience.

Once they crested the hill, before them spread a tiny town flanked by more rolling hills, woodlands, and swaths of farmland with dark soil that testified to its richness.

"That Mount Pleasant?" Dinah asked.

"Aye. As pretty a town as you will find out here," Bob said. "All planned out proper with streets and all, not cobbled together like Roberts Landing."

"Glory be," Dinah whispered.

Daniel had to agree with the driver. It was a pretty town. There were houses made of milled boards and cabins constructed of whole logs, and rising from the edge of town was a brick building. The church? No, Quakers didn't call it a church, what did they call it?

"That there's the new meeting house." Bob supplied the correct term. "Be the only brick building in the area. I heard the Quakers brought in some men who know how to make bricks. I expect there will be brick houses to follow."

That would do for Daniel's new house. Brick and square and elegant without the frills Margaret would have insisted on. A fine place to start his new life.

They rode down the hill and entered the town, passing houses with women and children tending kitchen gardens. Some houses issued tantalizing smells from the open windows. Two barefooted boys with a red hound on a length of rope ran alongside the wagon and called a greeting to Bob. Daniel could picture his grandson growing up in such a lovely setting. Of course, his grandson would wear proper shoes.

They reached the center of town where the businesses were clustered. There was a mercantile with a swinging sign, followed by a blacksmith and wheelwright shop that was shuttered closed. A barbershop came next that, by the sign in the window, also sold tobacco. Across the street was a cooper, a cobbler, and a tavern.

"Take us to the tavern." Daniel pointed to the green sign depicting a mug and chair on the front of a wooden building that stood taller than those around it.

Bob stopped the wagon in front of it.

"Stay on the wagon," Daniel told Dinah. "I shall return shortly." It might be easier to obtain a room before anyone inside saw her. They'd caused enough heads to swivel as they'd passed the houses.

He pushed the door open and entered a long room with round tables and poor lighting. It was similar to the one in Roberts Landing, but newer and cleaner. It was empty at that middle hour of the afternoon.

A man came from a doorway in the back, wiping his hands on a towel. "What can I do for thee?"

Thee. Of course he'd be a Quaker. "I am in need of a room to rent on a long-term basis."

"Long-term, thee say?" He eyed Daniel up and down, no doubt coming to the conclusion that he was not a Quaker from the lace on his shirtfront and the silver buckles on his shoes.

"Indeed. I wish to make my home here and start a business."

The tall man set the towel on the table beside him. "Welcome to Mount Pleasant." He offered his hand, which Daniel took. "My name is John Greene."

"Daniel Whiteford."

The man froze, then removed his hand from Daniel's. "Daniel Whiteford, father of Jonas Whiteford?"

Not the reception Daniel had hoped for. He cleared his throat. "Indeed, I am he." Had Jonas's exploits reached this far into the frontier? Was Daniel to be denied the chance to start over because of the son he'd already disowned?

"I have no room for thee." The words came with a brisk note of finality.

"Then perhaps you can recommend a boarding house?"

"There is none in Mount Pleasant." The man crossed his arms. "'Tis a quiet community where we strive to live in peace with all men."

"Indeed, that is just what I am searching for." Daniel gestured toward the door. "I have a young girl with me, and we need shelter."

"A girl?"

"Do you know Thomas Baldwin?" At the man's nod, he continued, "He knows me well. We did business together for years. I think he would vouch for my character."

"I would not be so sure."

Anger simmered in the pit of Daniel's stomach. He hadn't come this far to be dismissed by some tavern keeper. "At least rent me a room for a fortnight. Is that too much to ask?"

"I am not sure—"

"I will pay you double the going rate."

That gave the man pause, as well it should. There wasn't a line of people forming outside the door, clamoring to get in. And this far from the river, who else was he going to rent a room to?

"Very well, for a fortnight. After that, 'twill be up to the elders if thee are to stay on or not." The tavern keeper plucked a key from a peg and handed it to him, the other hand outstretched as he named the price.

Daniel took the key and opened his money purse, a little surprised the man hadn't charged him more. "I will have the hired man carry in my trunks."

"First room at the top of the stairs. The missus and I live in the back rooms."

Relieved he'd overcome this first obstacle, Daniel strode to the door. "Come, Dinah. Bob, bring the trunks."

The burley driver touched his hat brim, then dismounted and hefted the first trunk to his shoulder.

Dinah scurried down, grabbing her bag of belongings, which he'd purchased that morning at Roberts Landing. She clutched it to her chest as if it held the crown jewels. The childish gesture tugged a grin from him.

But then, to her, that bag probably represented something as valuable as jewels. His grin faded away. As light as her skin was, and wearing a new dress and shoes, which he'd learned she'd never worn before, she could almost pass for a white child, as long as she kept her hair covered. There was no mistaking those tight, dark curls.

He should have thought of a hat or a cap or something other than the fold of calico that marked her a slave.

Daniel held the door for Bob to pass, then ushered Dinah into the tavern.

"What is this?" The tavern keeper's voice rose.

"This is Dinah, the girl I told you about."

"Thee did not mention her being a slave." The man moved to the base of the stairs to block Bob's progress. "We Quakers do not hold with owning slaves."

"Indeed." Daniel's patience, already worn thin, snapped. "Neither do I. Now I have paid the required fee. Allow Bob to deposit my trunks. We shall endeavor to see as little of you as possible during our stay."

The tavern owner stepped aside. Daniel followed Bob up the stairs and unlocked the door. He moved out of the way to let the hired man and the girl enter first.

"'Tis nicer than the last one," Dinah said.

It was, but it didn't quell his anger. It needed an outlet, but he wasn't going to snap at the girl, who was just coming out of her shell. "Indeed."

Pacing the length of the room while Bob finished carrying the trunks, he then tipped the man above the agreed-upon fee and shut the door behind him before pointing at a pitcher and basin on a dry sink in the corner. "Wash the trail dirt from your face and hands. I shall do the same, and then we shall find Thomas Baldwin."

Then he'd find out what had happened regarding Jonas, and Daniel would see his grandson.

Chapter 8

ZACHARY WAS HOEING IN the kitchen garden when Titus came from the house. The boy's strength was returning—after he'd almost eaten Zachary out of house and home. But milk and cheese were easily replaced since his cows had lush spring pasture to eat from. And there was still half a catfish keeping cold in the springhouse.

The boy hadn't bragged when he'd said he knew how to cook it. Zachary's mouth watered at the memory of last night's dinner.

But Titus shouldn't be outside where someone could see him. "What are thee doing out here?"

Thin shoulders lifted and dropped. "'Bout time for me to earn my keep."

"'Tis too dangerous. Did I not tell thee of the three men at the creek yesterday?"

"You were lucky." Titus grimaced. "Had they been bad ones, you would have been taken or beaten half to death."

He was probably right. The thought had dogged Zachary all the way home. He'd gotten away from them too easily. They'd been looking for a frightened woman, not a man of his stature. But others—those like Jonas Whiteford—would have tried to capture him. And without his papers, they might have succeeded in getting him across the river.

Back into slavery.

Zachary crossed his arms and peered down at Titus. "All the more reason for thee to remain hidden."

"I need to work off what I owe you."

"Thee owe me nothing."

Titus sputtered a rude noise. "I know how much I ate." He stooped and plucked a weed from between the sprouting pea plants.

"Truly, Titus." Zachary grasped him above the elbow and pulled him to his feet. "Thee should remain in the house."

"If someone comes along, tell them you own me."

"Nobody would believe such a thing."

"Why not?"

"A black man? Owning a slave?"

Titus crossed his arms. "Plenty of free black men own slaves."

Zachary was as shocked as if someone had poured ice water over his head. "What do thee mean?"

Another rude noise. "My massah hired me out to whoever paid him, some of them black men. One, he was the meanest man I ever worked for. Liked to tear my hide off me, he did."

If there'd been a chair nearby, Zachary would have sat. Free black men owning slaves, or hiring slaves, and mistreating them? How—?

"You doan know nothin' 'bout how things are, do you?"

"I thought I did."

"Was any of them slave catchers black?"

"Thee cannot mean..." Zachary walked to the edge of the garden and sank to the ground.

"Plenty of blacks is used to catch slaves. I seen some of them myself." Titus sat beside him. "Who better to know how a slave thinks?"

"But for free men to—"

"Who said they free?" Titus shook his head. "They slaves too, just doin' what they told so they doan get beat."

Zachary looked toward the heavens, letting the sun's warmth chase the chill from his soul.

How had man gotten so evil?

"Even if a black man might own and hire slaves, I am a Quaker.

Nobody would believe a Quaker would own another human."

"You might be right there." Titus pushed at a clod of dirt with his toe. "But you doan have to say all them thees and thys, do you?"

"I suppose not, if I could remember not to."

Titus cocked his head. "How come you doan talk like a slave if you was one?"

Zachary gathered his thoughts. How best to explain it? The truth, of course. Always the truth. "I worked at it for a long time, learning to pronounce words like Eli did, the man who bought me and set me free. I wanted to be like him."

"Because he set you free."

"Partly that, of course, but also because he was kind and educated and generous and..." Zachary met the boy's eyes. "He was everything I wanted to be."

Titus seemed to look right through him. "Everything a slave could never be."

How simply he'd summed up the root of it all.

"When I get my sisters free, we goin' to Canada." The boy's voice carried a fierce edge to it. "And there, we goin' to learn to not be slaves too."

A pit formed in Zachary's middle. "So thee are going back south across the river?"

Titus nodded. "I got Tabitha free last fall, the baby of the family. She in... she in a safe place."

"How many sisters do thee have?"

"Three. Miriam, the oldest, and Dinah, two years younger than me. They is still slaves."

"And thee know where they are?"

"Not Miriam. Dinah and Tabitha sold to the same place, but Dinah was in the big house, watched too close. I could only get Tabitha free."

So much rested on the young man's shoulders. What would it be like to be reunited with his own brothers? Or maybe—if she still lived—his mother? It would be... indescribable.

It would be worth any risk. If only he knew how to find them.

"How can I help thee?"

Titus stared at him, long and hard, before shaking his head. "Best I go alone. You too big, too easy to spot. But I thank you for askin'."

He'd do a whole lot more if he could.

"Thee are always welcome here. Thee and whoever thee brings along."

Titus stuck out his hand, and Zachary shook it. It wasn't much, but if that was all Titus would allow, then Zachary's dairy farm would be a safe place.

"I shall return as soon as I learn the whereabouts of my grandson." Daniel checked his reflection in the room's tiny looking glass, straightening his neckcloth. It was good he'd decided to wait until the morning to find Thomas and his grandson. He'd needed the night before to calm down and adjust to the fact that these people knew Jonas—and not in a good way.

"What you want me to do?" Dinah asked.

What indeed? He'd decided against taking her with him. Her presence would raise questions he didn't want to answer until after he found his grandson.

The girl should be safe among the Quakers. None of them would snatch her and take her back to slavery. But she couldn't just sit in a room all day with nothing to occupy her time. A young thing like her needed to be active.

"Come with me." He headed down the stairs, but instead of going out of the front door, he walked to the door leading to—he assumed—the tavern's kitchen and knocked.

A woman of middle years opened the door, her eyes darting to Dinah. "Can I help thee?"

"Perhaps." Daniel stepped aside to allow her a better look at the girl. "I have some personal business to attend to. Could Dinah assist here in the kitchen while I am gone? 'Twould give her something to do."

"My John, he would not hold with a slave working in our tavern."

"If she were not working, if she were learning from you, would that be acceptable?" He glanced at Dinah, who lifted bright eyes to him. Already she was so different from when he'd first seen her. "She will be lonely stuck up in our room all day. 'Tis much more pleasant in your kitchen."

"Well..." The woman was wavering.

"I be happy to help, missus," Dinah said.

"'Tis Eliza." The woman motioned the girl forward. "And thee are welcome to keep me company, at least until John says differently."

"Thank you, ma'am," Daniel said. "She will be far happier with you today than following me around or sitting alone in the room." He eased back into the common room and let the door swing shut.

He rubbed his hands together. Now to find Thomas Baldwin.

The man was a wheelwright, so the blacksmith and wheelwright shop was the logical place to start. He set off for the shop they'd passed on the way into town, but it was still shuttered. Was there not enough work to keep the business open?

Next door was the barber, and if anyone knew all the goings-on in a town, it was the barber. Daniel stepped into the shop, which smelled of tobacco, soap, and bay rum.

"What can I do for thee?" asked the man sitting in the barber's chair.

"Can you tell me when the shop next door opens?"

"If thee needs the blacksmith, he is out of town for a couple more days. Gone visiting his wife's family, her mother having taken ill, poor thing."

"And the wheelwright? Is it Thomas Baldwin?"

The man's eyebrows rose. "Thee knows Thomas?"

"Indeed. We did business together for many years in New Bern."

"Ah, well. He works when needed, but that not being often with our town still so small, thee can find him at home." He rose and walked to the front window, pointing. "If thee turn down that street past the cobbler's shop, and walk two blocks, 'tis the second house on the right. A fine board house with three rosebushes out front. Betsy loves those rosebushes."

"Thank you, you have been most helpful."

"Come back when thee need a haircut or a shave." The man returned to his chair, presumably to wait for a customer.

Daniel stepped outside and followed the man's directions to the simple square house of whitewashed milled boards that matched many of those around it, the plain lines without frills, attesting to the Quakers within. But the neatly pruned rosebushes, although not yet blooming so early in the season, set it apart. He climbed the three steps to the porch and knocked on the door.

Thomas answered it and stared at him, mouth agape within his bushy gray beard.

"Hello, Thomas."

"Daniel?" The man shook his head as if to clear it. "What are thee doing here?"

Not exactly the welcome he'd expected. "I have come to settle here and start a new business."

"Impossible."

"What do you mean?" Anger stirred inside Daniel again. He wasn't used to being treated so rudely.

Why had he not been invited in? Why was he being told he wasn't welcome? It was intolerable.

"Who is it, dear?" Betsy appeared behind Thomas and gasped, covering her mouth with one hand.

"What is the matter?" Daniel demanded.

"How can thee not know?" Betsy glared at him, gray hair tucked neatly beneath her cap, hands planted on her hips. "After what thee did?"

"If this has something to do with Jonas—"

Thomas raised his hand. "That is a different issue."

"Then what? I did not expect such a cold greeting at the home of someone I have known for years. Someone I entrusted..." He let that thought slide away. After all, he'd never admitted to being the boy's grandfather.

"Thy grandson to." Thomas's voice was hard, his eyes like flint.

"You know."

"Indeed." Thomas glanced up and down the street, where several people were watching from doorways. "'Tis best thee step inside." He backed up and Daniel followed him.

"Where is the boy?"

"Not here, thank the Lord." Betsy's voice was even harsher than her husband's, the lines in her face deep with disapproval.

"Is that why thee have come?" Thomas asked. "To see him?"

To see the boy? Nay. To *claim* him. But it was plain that such an admission would not be welcome. "He is my grandson, after all."

"Thee gave that title away"—Thomas crossed his arms—"when thee gave him over to me."

"When thee forced Gwen to sign that unholy oath." Disgust thickened Betsy's voice.

Was that how they saw it? He'd given the girl her freedom. Did they not remember that part?

Thomas gestured to the table. "Come. Sit. 'Twould appear we have much to discuss."

Daniel slid onto a bench and planted his elbows on the table, hands clasped. "Where is my grandson?"

"With his mother and father," Thomas stressed the family titles.

"Father? The girl married?" He'd never considered that.

"She did." Betsy didn't sit, but stood like a guard behind her husband's shoulder. "And he has a sister and another sibling on the way."

Daniel's grandson had a *family*.

He removed his hat and pushed his fingers through his thinning hair. "I had not thought—"

"'Twas apparent from the start," Thomas said.

"Thomas." He worked to keep his tone even despite the emotions tumbling through him.

His grandson had a family.

He'd thought to find the boy living here, with Thomas and Betsy sheltering Gwen as a single mother. He'd expected them to be relieved at his appearance. That he would take the boy off their hands. He'd expected to be welcomed.

He'd been wrong. So very wrong.

"You know me," he fumbled for the words. "Have I ever dealt ill with you or your people?"

"I did not think so until thy son found us."

"Jonas?" Daniel cringed. Could the situation get any worse? He didn't want to ask the next question, but he needed the answer. "What has he done?"

"Thee mean to tell me, man to man, that his appearing among our people was not brought about by thy orders?"

"I never sent him to find you."

Thomas and Betsy shared a look he couldn't read, but Thomas gave his wife the smallest nod.

She, on the other hand, rolled her eyes.

But when Thomas turned back to Daniel, there was a slight relaxing of his posture.

"Jonas found us when we wintered in Pennsylvania the year we left New Bern. He and another man caused grief among us, and almost succeeded in capturing one of our people to return him to slavery."

Daniel pressed the heel of his hand to his forehead, elbow on the table, and stifled a groan. Or at least mostly stifled it. Then he raised his head and looked from Thomas to Betsy and back again. "I have never held with slavery. Never. I have purchased indentures, but I have fulfilled my part at the end of each. What Jonas has done, what he had become..." He shook his head. "I have sold my business to prevent him from inheriting it. To prevent him from using it to ship in more slaves."

Thomas straightened on his bench. "'Tis illegal now to ship in slaves, is it not?"

"Indeed, which only makes it worse." He let his hand fall to the table. "My son is little more than a pirate. Nay. He *is* a pirate."

"'Tis why thee have come in search of the boy." There was a wealth of understanding in the other man's voice.

Daniel nodded.

"Thee cannot have hoped to uproot the lad." Betsy's tone made it clear that she hadn't warmed to him. "To take him from his mother and father?"

"I have come to make a new life here." That much Daniel could admit to. The rest... he needed time to reevaluate the situation.

"Here?" Thomas tugged on his beard, a habit Daniel remembered that said the man was pondering.

"Indeed, here in Mount Pleasant. To start a new business." He cleared his throat. "Near my grandson." They would obviously stand against him if he made a move to legally claim the boy and remove him from his... his family. That thought cut deep, hurting more than Daniel could deal with at the moment. But he would see the boy, and maybe, in time, when they all saw the advantages he could offer...

"'Tis something the elders will need to discuss."

"I am not Quaker. Why would the elders care?"

"The elders own the land in town. If thee wishes to start a new business, thee must deal with them to purchase land."

"I cannot see why they would object—"

"Because they know of the unholy oath thee pressed Gwen to sign," Betsy said.

Why did she keep calling it unholy? Had Daniel and Gwen not both gotten what they wanted at the time? 'Twas a simple business transaction. But if the Quakers didn't think so, Daniel would jump whatever fences they placed in front of him so he could stay.

Because he wasn't leaving without his grandson.

A knock sounded at the door, and Betsy rose to answer it.

"Hello, Betsy. Is Thomas in? I have a wheel in need of his special touch."

That voice...

Daniel turned on the bench and faced his old stable boy, now a man fully grown. What was his name?

The man stared at Daniel with something akin to horror in his expression.

"Master Whiteford?"

Chapter 9

F RANTIC HOOFBEATS BROUGHT ZACHARY to the barn door, where he shielded his eyes against the sun's glare.

The flea-bitten gray racing toward his house belonged to Mark Allen, but he'd never seen the man push the old horse so hard.

Something terrible must have happened.

Zachary raced for the house, arriving at the porch as Mark Allen swung to the ground, although Jughead hadn't come to a complete stop.

"What is it?"

"Daniel Whiteford is in Mount Pleasant." Mark Allen gulped a deep breath.

"What?" Zachary took a step back. "Is his son with him?"

Still heaving, Mark Allen shook his head.

That was a relief.

Zachary's skin crawled at the memory of Jonas and his plan to abduct him, which might have succeeded if not for Gwen.

"Jughead has gone as far as he can. Would thee allow me to borrow

Annabelle?"

"Indeed. I will fetch her saddle—"

Mark Allen stalled him with a raised hand. "No time. I can ride her bareback. I must get the news to Faye—and Gwen."

"Of course. Thee will find Annabelle in the paddock behind the barn. There is a rope over the gate to use for reins. I will care for Jughead."

"Thank thee," Mark Allen shouted over his shoulder as he sprinted away.

Zachary gathered the reins of the horse. Its head was down, its sides heaving. The poor old beast had run his heart out.

Annabelle came around the corner of the barn already in a full gallop and disappeared down the road. She wasn't as fast as Jughead, but she'd get Mark Allen home to Faye and then to his sister-in-law's place to spread the news.

What could Daniel Whiteford want in Mount Pleasant? The answer was too obvious and too horrible to consider.

Owen.

"Must be bad news to travel so fast." Titus came onto the porch.

"Indeed." Would Daniel have any legal standing to remove Owen from Gwen and Micah? Was he heartless enough to wrest the boy from the only family he knew?

Would the Quaker elders allow it?

Could they legally stop him?

Zachary owed Gwen so much—his very freedom, if not his life. Anything he could do to keep the boy with her, he would. Anything.

But—

Titus cocked his head at him. "What happened?"

What if coming forward as Gwen's defender endangered Zachary's plans to assist more fugitive slaves and keep a safe house for Titus? Could he remain unnoticed—as Titus had insisted he must—if he stirred the waters with Daniel Whiteford?

Would Zachary be forced to choose?

Daniel fussed with the hem of his sleeve, refusing to make eye contact with Betsy Baldwin. The woman had been staring daggers at him since they'd entered the carriage. A very nice carriage, borrowed from the town doctor, or so he'd been told. What sort of frontier doctor could afford such a conveyance?

It didn't matter.

All that mattered was his grandson, and the Baldwins were taking him to see the boy.

The carriage rocked to a stop, and the half-grown boy who'd driven them hopped down and opened the door. Daniel waited for him to assist Betsy to the ground, then waited for Thomas to join his wife before finally pushing his way out of the carriage. The scene before him was wholly inappropriate for his grandson.

A log cabin, nothing more. It had two glass windows in the front, the only refined thing about it. Oh, it appeared well-built, but it was not a proper house. And the barns beyond were almost identical log structures, squat and sturdy and no doubt useful, but a far cry from the brick structure Daniel envisioned behind his future brick house in Mount Pleasant. Backing the fields of rich brown soil were trees, mostly hardwoods with some pine. A thin column of smoke in the distance was the only evidence of neighbors behind the trees.

All that flashed through his mind and out when the door opened and Gwen emerged, a lanky man behind her. She'd changed, of course. She must be all of twenty now and had filled out in womanly curves. Ah, yes, Betsy had said she was in the family way.

Mark Allen—his name had been supplied the night before—stepped out of the cabin behind her.

But where was his grandson?

"Gwen, Micah," Thomas said. "I see Mark Allen has apprised thee of the situation."

The lanky man stepped in front of Gwen who must be Micah Pike. Thomas had related the story of their meeting on the wagon train west, where they fell in love and then married upon reaching Mount Pleasant. "What is the meaning of this, Thomas? Why would thee bring him here? To our home?" Anger punctuated his tone despite the Quaker words.

Thomas raised his hands in a calming gesture. "He would have found thy place sooner or later. 'Tis better that he comes with us."

The man didn't bother to glance at Daniel. "He is not welcome here."

Gwen stepped beside her husband, and placed her hand on his arm. "'Tis all right, Micah. Daniel Whiteford never mistreated me."

"Never—" Micah's mouth dropped open as he gaped at his wife. "He forced thee to sign that oath. That is mistreatment in my book."

"Nay, he did not force me. He..." She looked at Daniel then, sadness in her blue eyes. "He made me an offer I willingly accepted. 'Twas my sin as well as his."

"Sin?" Daniel couldn't stop the question. "What sin?"

"The sin of false witness." Thomas's words were even, though tinged with a lingering... anger? Resentment? "Thee fostered Gwen to us under a lie. And furthermore, thee threatened her should she ever speak of the lie to which thee had bound her."

Oh, that.

"Only for us to learn months later,"—Betsy skewered Daniel with another of her sharp looks—"that thee gave up thy own grandchild. Turned thy back on thy own flesh and blood. What sort of man are thee, Daniel Whiteford?" The question hung in the air for a long moment.

The sort who didn't stand for a dressing down by some Quaker goodwife. But also the sort who felt the pinch of guilt at her words.

"Betsy." Thomas's single word had the woman turning her back on Daniel and marching to stand beside Gwen, wrapping her arm around the young woman's shoulders.

"As thee can see,"—Thomas gestured to those gathered—"we care deeply for Gwen and Micah and their family, which includes young Owen."

"Owen?" Was that what she'd named his grandson? It sounded so... foreign.

"What do thee want of us?" Micah demanded.

"I want to see my grandson."

"Thee no longer have a grandson." Micah pointed to Thomas. "Thomas is the only grandfather Owen has ever known. He is the grandfather Owen loves."

If the man had wished to inflict pain, he'd succeeded.

And like a wounded bear, Daniel rose to the bait. "The boy is *my* flesh and blood, as you have admitted. I have legal rights. Legal standing. I will see the boy, or I will pursue those legal standings, in all haste."

Gwen stepped forward, shaking off Betsy's restraining arm. "I can see that thee have regrets, and to be sure, I do as well." She stopped halfway to him. "But I must think of what is best for Owen. He is not old enough to understand how things came to be. 'Twould only confuse him and perhaps unsettle him. Thee can understand this, I trust?"

"You have joined the Quakers?"

She nodded. "Thee were wise to send me to them. For that, I owe thee a debt of gratitude."

"Then let me see my grandson."

"He is not here. We felt it best to have this first meeting without him."

"Where is he?"

"Safe with another Friend." Micah came forward. "As is our daughter."

Gwen settled a restraining hand on her husband's forearm. "Such a confrontation as this would have upset the children." There was no anger in her voice, no condemnation in her expression, unlike those who flanked her. Even Mark Allen who, if Daniel remembered Silas's words correctly, had been in love with Gwen when they'd both served him.

Yet there he was, in open support of her and her husband. Indeed, he had brought them word of Daniel's arrival.

So much loyalty to one young woman.

It brought an odd sort of peace to Daniel, knowing that the woman he'd chosen to raise his grandson engendered such feelings in others. It spoke well of her character.

Drawing on that peace, he summoned a patient tone. "When will I be able to see him?"

"May I suggest that meeting take place at our house?" Thomas asked.

Betsy's lips thinned to a flat line, but she nodded. "Monday would be suitable."

Monday? Wait another four days? Preposterous.

Before he could protest, Thomas turned to him. "During that time, thee and I can approach the elders regarding thy desire to purchase land in Mount Pleasant."

"Purchase land?" Micah's voice rose in fury despite supposedly being a pacifist. "To what purpose?"

"To build a house and start a business." Daniel straightened to his full height, which lacked several inches of the younger man. "'Tis my intention to start over, right here in Mount Pleasant."

"And Jonas?" Gwen's voice trembled on the name, no doubt with good reason.

"My son and I are no longer in contact with each other." He lowered his head, swallowing the shame that overwhelmed him, and then raised his eyes to her. "For anything he did while you lived under my roof, I apologize to you now. I had a... blind spot where my son was concerned. But no longer."

She nodded, a simple gesture that offered him grace and forgiveness. "And Missus Whiteford?"

"Passed away back in March."

Gwen came near and touched his arm. "I am sorry for thy loss."

No wonder so many had come to this woman's defense. Her sympathy was beyond expectation, under the circumstances. Daniel cleared his throat of the emotions clogging it. "'Tis kind of you."

"If there is one thing I have learned among the Quakers, 'tis the power of kindness to heal any hurt."

"Then perhaps it can heal the breach between my grandson and me."

She gave him an unsteady smile. "With God, all things are possible."

With God.

Was that where Daniel needed to start? If he could find a way to relate to these Quakers more on their level and understand what made them different, it could only help his business relationship with them and help make his case for regaining guardianship of his grandson. It might work.

Butting heads with them wasn't going to.

Daniel stuffed his disappointment deep down inside. He wanted to scoop up his grandson and leave, but that wasn't going to happen. For one thing, the boy wasn't there. For another, Daniel owned no home to take him to. And last, the boy had a family. A real family. Not just the young woman who had taken him in. She'd found a husband who had accepted her and the boy.

That possibility had never crossed Daniel's mind.

Zachary was in the middle of the evening milking when hoofbeats approached the barn.

"Get in the loft," he called to Titus.

The young man scurried up the ladder and disappeared.

Zachary set the milk pail out of harm's way, then strode to the door, breathing a sigh of relief when Mark Allen slid from Annabelle's back.

"I have returned her in good condition, if a little leg-weary."

"Tell me what happened." As Mark Allen filled him in, Zachary took the mule's lead rope and led her to her stall, adding a generous scoop of grain to her trough.

Owen's grandfather had come to disrupt the boy's life. Slave catchers roamed the countryside in search of their prey. An escaped slave was even now in the loft above Zachary's head. Mount Pleasant had seemed set apart, a safe place, but these events proved there was no such place.

"So what happens now?" he asked.

"They will meet at Thomas and Betsy's on Monday. Thomas will introduce Daniel to the rest of the elders before then. They must decide if they wish to sell him land to start a business or not."

The last thing Zachary wanted was the father of a slave catcher living in Mount Pleasant. Especially the slave catcher who had almost enslaved him again. But the elders wouldn't sell Daniel land if they saw him as a threat to the community. Would they? "We must trust in their leadership."

"Aye." Mark Allen let the word draw out.

"What are thee thinking?"

"'Tis just that"—Mark Allen shrugged—"he does seem changed. Not the same man I worked for. I cannot put my finger on it exactly, but he is... milder."

"Or simply out of his element." Zachary wouldn't give him any credit, not the man who'd raised Jonas, even if Daniel claimed they were no longer speaking.

"Could be. But when he said he was no longer in contact with Jonas, the pain on his face was too real to be a deception."

"Unless he is a better actor than thee know."

"I worked for him for five years. I do not think he is an actor at all." Mark Allen untied the gray and backed him out of the stall. "Thank thee for caring for Jughead. Now I best get home and return the children to Micah and Gwen."

"Give them my regards. And if they need anything at all—"

"I will tell them to contact thee."

The horse's hoofbeats hadn't died away when Titus appeared at his elbow. "You doan like this man who come to town." It wasn't a question.

"He once owned Mark Allen and Gwen by indenture. And his son tried to capture me and return me to slavery." He turned to Titus. "So thee are correct, I do not like him. Or more to the point, I do not trust him."

"He a slave owner?"

"Nay, Daniel did not own slaves. Jonas, his son, however, was happy to make his money off the backs of others."

Titus braced his feet and crossed his arms. "Then I doan like him either."

"Thee would be wise to stay far away from Daniel Whiteford."

"I must be goin' soon." Titus returned to the cows waiting to be milked. "The moon turns full in another week. I need to leave before then."

A few days, no more, and Zachary would be alone on the farm again.

"Will thee return? Here?"

The boy stopped and faced him across the barn. "I hope so."

"As do I."

With a curt nod, Titus settled beside a cow and got to work. He was a fine farm hand. If things were different...

But they weren't. And as long as men rode on this side of the river looking for fugitives, Titus would never be safe here. It was best Zachary remembered that and didn't get too attached.

If it wasn't already too late.

Chapter 10

T HE ONLY THING THAT connected the men before Daniel was their plain manner of dress, their age, and their expressions. Seated in a half-circle in the large room of the brick meeting house, all were gray-haired and most bearded. Some were tall, some short, one skinny as a rope, others lean, and some threatening to burst buttons on their waistcoats. But none of the eight was smiling as they faced him, not even Thomas.

It was as if Daniel were on trial. And maybe he was, a disconcerting thought. He'd always been the man in charge, even when dealing with municipalities. After all, he was a man with a vision for the future... and money. Money had always gotten him what he wanted in the end.

The introductions were made, but he didn't bother to remember their names. They wouldn't matter unless he got what he wanted. And the grim faces before him engendered little hope.

"In New Bern, some of thee know that we often did business with Daniel," Thomas said after the introductions. "I found him to be honest and trustworthy, never shorting an order, and always able to supply the materials needed for our community in a timely manner."

"I remember." The skinny one crossed one leg over the other. "But I also remember the oath he forced Gwen to sign."

Thomas raised his hand. "Gwen admits to signing the oath willingly, though she was but a youth and did not understand the ramifications of her actions at the time."

One of the portly men leaned forward, further threatening a row of buttons. "What about his son, the one who tried to steal away with Zachary?"

Daniel tried not to squirm. Thomas had filled him in on Jonas's disgraceful actions on the carriage ride back to town after meeting with Gwen and Micah. The real shame was that it hadn't surprised him.

"We cannot hold the father to account for the sins of the son," said the tallest man.

"Nay, but we cannot have the son inherit property here if he is still in the slave trade, now can we?" The portly man pushed his case, which set all the men to muttering among themselves.

"If I may," Daniel said, "Jonas is no longer my legal heir. He will inherit nothing from me when I pass. In fact..." He cleared his throat. "'Tis my intention to name my grandson, whom you know as Owen Pike, as my heir."

That set off another round of murmurings and some nodding.

All but Thomas seemed pleased by his announcement—all but Thomas, who crossed his arms. "Why would thee do that?"

"Because he is my grandson."

"How can thee think to bequeath such a thing on a boy thee have never met?"

"He is my only grandchild, the last of my line." Daniel tried to keep the frustration from his voice. "To whom else would I leave it?"

"Back to the business," the tall man said. "Do thee plan to continue in the same manner, with importing goods to the area?"

"I do."

"Thee will need to move such goods a long distance, Roberts Landing being the closest port to us here in Mount Pleasant." The skinny man tapped his cheek, squinting into the distance. "A warehouse must be built. 'Twill require the purchase of horses and wagons and hiring teamsters to drive, load, and unload. Perhaps even thy own river barges and crew. Such a business will require a good deal of capital."

"Capital is not an issue. I have money from the sale of my other business, as well as the sale of my house in Greenesville." At this assurance, several of the men relaxed in their chairs. As always—even with Quakers—money smoothed things over.

Except with Thomas, who didn't seem mollified. "But will our people do business with thee?"

"Why would they not?"

"Because thee are not a Quaker, and because all know of the unholy oath thee signed with Gwen."

Why must Thomas keep calling it unholy? Daniel tamped down his irritation. "Much has happened since that day. I regret my decision, but I do not regret entrusting the boy to your care, Thomas. Even in my anguish over what happened, and my wife's emotional frailty at that time, I knew you would be the one to take care of the boy, that you would do what was best for him. You see, even then, I had the boy's best interest in mind."

Thomas stared at him, gray beard hiding much of his expression, but clearly not impressed by Daniel's admission.

One of the lean men cleared his throat. "There is also the issue of the slave you currently own, Daniel Whiteford."

A gasp rippled through the gathering.

Thomas shot to his feet. "What slave?"

Daniel had hoped he'd done a good job of hiding Dinah, but of course, she was bound to be discovered sooner or later. "While I do—at this moment—own a slave girl, the circumstances of my acquiring her necessitated what I did."

"There is nothing that necessitates owning another human being." Thomas moved toward the door. "I think we are done here."

"Please." Daniel stood and raised his voice over the sudden din of murmurs and, if he had to guess, prayers for his soul. "I purchased Dinah at a slave auction in New Bern while awaiting my ship to sail north. I did not know of the auction until I stumbled upon it. And when I did..." He plowed his fingers through his hair. "She looked at me from the platform, her eyes so sad, and the men in front of me were plotting to purchase her for..." He shook a finger at Thomas. "I saved that girl from a much worse fate, I can assure you."

"What do thee intend to do with her?" Thomas remained by the door, stiff as a fence post.

"I intend to issue her freedom papers when she is of age, but the girl is only eleven years old." He spread his hands. "Were I to give her those papers now, they would have no merit. Any slave catcher who found her would whisk her back across the river, and none of us could stop him." He let his arms fall to his sides. "I cannot legally free her—even on this side of the river—until she is an adult because she has no family, no guardian. You all know the laws as well as I do."

Daniel dropped back into his chair. "I could not let those men take the child and do what they had planned. God as my witness, I could not."

Silence gripped the gathering.

Darkness crept across Zachary's farm. Bats swooped and dove, catching moths and other nocturnal insects. The day's heat had waned, and a blessed cool dampness settled over the land. A cow in the pasture lowed to its calf. It was the first of June, the start of summer, and the moon would be full in a few more days.

Zachary had come up with a plan while hoeing the corn that afternoon. He needed to add onto the barn. He'd kept back three young heifers to grow his herd because he had plenty of customers for his milk, butter, and cheese, but he needed more barn space.

Titus came from the springhouse and joined him. "What you starin' at?"

"I am going to build an addition to the barn." He turned to face the boy. "And I am going to build a secret room above it. 'Twill be a wide space, but not tall, so 'twill not be visible from outside. 'Twill look like the usual sloped roof to anyone passing by."

"A secret room." Titus's voice was low and steady, but it hummed with excitement. "You gotta build out the back, near the treeline, so folks can get close without bein' seen." He cocked his head. "And make the entrance from the outside, not inside."

"Why?"

"Slave catchers come lookin', they gonna enter the barn. Door on the outside gives slaves a chance to escape."

Zachary would never have thought of that.

"Hinge the door on top, so the wind can't catch it and blow it open."

"Anything else?"

The boy shot him a glare as if he suspected Zachary was mocking him.

"Thee knows more about this than I do." Zachary spread his hands. "Whatever thee can tell me will only make it better. 'Twill make it safer."

Titus walked closer to the barn, and Zachary followed. "Folks need a ladder of some sort, but it can't look like a ladder. It gotta look like somethin' the barn needs to be there."

"If I use logs to build it, notched and joined at the ends, instead of milled boards and do not cut the ends flush..."

Titus grinned. "Natural ladder."

"But how will fugitives know of the place?"

"Doan you worry none 'bout that. You build it, word will get around."

"Should I make two entrances, one on the inside as well as the one on the outside? 'Twould be easier to get food and supplies to people."

"Too risky. Slave catchers is used to lookin' up for trap doors to attics."

"I see."

"They is used to lookin' for trap doors to cellars too, so this idea of yours," Titus nodded, "I like it."

"Then I shall build it."

"How soon?"

"I can start as soon as the corn is hoed."

"I mean"—Titus leaned closer and peered up at him—"how soon you get it done?"

"Oh." Zachary rubbed the back of his head. He needed a haircut, but that was a random thought, and he needed to concentrate. It was time to start cheese-making while the milk was rich from the lush pastures. He'd been skimming and saving the cream in the springhouse for weeks.

Titus tapped his bare toes on the ground. The impatient boy in front of Zachary barely resembled the weak, ill creature he'd found in his barn. This boy—almost a young man—was quick-witted and re-sourceful. No wonder he'd escaped the slave catchers thus far. *Please, Lord, let him continue to do so.*

"Three weeks at least, probably four." At Titus's frown, he added, "I will need help to raise the logs, and every man is busy this time of year. But I promise thee, I will work as fast as I can."

"Good." Titus pulled in a long breath and stretched his arms wide, flexing his back. "'Cause I leave tonight, and I plan to come back through in three weeks."

He'd known the time was short, but Zachary still felt a kick in the ribs. "I have something for thee in the house." He headed that way, Titus falling into step beside him.

In the house, Zachary lit the lantern. He pulled a paper-wrapped parcel from the trunk in the corner and handed it to Titus.

"What is it?"

"Open it and see."

The boy eyed the parcel as if it might contain a rattlesnake or a copperhead.

"Go ahead." He stifled a grin. "'Twill not bite thee."

That earned him a frown, but Titus untied the string and folded back the brown paper. Inside was a set of clothing. Not new, because new would be noticed, but there was more life left in them than the rags the boy wore.

"Where did you get these?"

"Cora Johnson was cleaning out some of her closets, and I told her I can always use rags for cheese-making. She said I could have the whole lot if I gave her a discount on her cheese this winter."

"You got more than this?"

"Indeed, several bags full, but those are the best size for thee."

"What you plan to do with the rest?"

"I figure to put them in that room when I get it built, for others in need."

Titus's eyes glistened in the lantern's light.

"Thee should change, and I shall scrub thy old clothes for wrapping cheese."

While the boy did as he said, Zachary packed a sack with bread, hard biscuits, cooked bacon, and cheese, wishing he had more to send. But more would attract notice.

Titus, dressed in his new outfit, accepted the sack.

"Thee will be careful."

"I always is."

"And thee will return?"

"If I be able to."

It wasn't the answer Zachary wanted, but it was all he was going to get.

"Now I need to git while the dark can hide me."

"Where will thee go?"

Titus shook his head. "Best you doan know."

"If I am to help—"

"There be lots of helpers around the country. Doan nobody know more than they got to. Safer that way. Safer for you, and safer for those on the run." He grasped Zachary's forearm. "Trust me." Then the boy left, the door easing shut behind him. And Zachary was alone again.

Never had his little house felt so empty.

Daniel waited in his chair while the other men filed out of the meeting house, and only Thomas remained.

Thomas took a seat beside Daniel. "Thee have been through much these past few years."

"Indeed. The burdens have been great."

"I am very sorry for the loss of thy wife. I cannot imagine going on without my Betsy and pray God will never ask me to."

Daniel rubbed his nose and glanced out the window. "I am glad you do not have to."

"And thy son." Thomas sighed. "I have lost three children, buried them back in New Bern. 'Tis a burden I will always carry. But 'twas disease that stole them away from me."

"While I disowned my children."

"I do not mean to judge, but thy daughter as well?"

"Indeed." Daniel saw no point in beating about the bush. "She disgraced herself and our family."

"Because of Owen?"

"Nay, not that. I was successful in covering up for her that time." He paused and let the hurt wash over him. "But she was found in a compromising situation with someone not her husband. The news spread through Greenesville as only gossip can." He faced Thomas.

"The shock led to Margaret's decline. My wife died of a broken heart."

Thomas clamped a hand on his shoulder and held firm, silence surrounding them. After a few moments, Thomas released his shoulder and leaned back.

"What thee did for the girl—Dinah, you said?"

Daniel nodded.

"'Twas no small thing."

"'Twas not. I had no idea what I was getting into. Not only the cost—she fetched a much higher price than I imagined—but also keeping her safe. Getting her this far has not been easy. 'Twould seem that men see her only as... Several offered to buy her on my journey here. And now, I know not what to do with her."

"Where is she?"

"Helping the tavern owner's wife in the kitchen. The girl was agreeable to it, and I thought 'twould keep her out of mischief."

"Eliza is a kind soul."

"So the girl has told me."

"But 'tisn't a long-term solution."

"Once I have a house built—if I am allowed land on which to build one—she could become my housekeeper, but until then..."

"There is a family in need of a mother's helper, a young mother expecting her third child." The look he leveled at Daniel was telling.

"You speak of Gwen."

"Indeed."

Perhaps, if he loaned the girl out to them, Gwen and Micah would be more agreeable to him having a presence in his grandson's life—which could lead to more as the boy grew and matured and became Daniel's heir.

"Why do thee not bring the girl on Monday? They could meet her, and thee could offer her services."

"Do you think they would accept?"

"I suspect 'twill depend upon how thee presents the issue. If thee presents the girl as a gift, then not likely. But if thee presents her as a favor to thee, having a safe place for the girl..." Thomas shrugged. "Perhaps."

"I shall do as you say."

Thomas stood. "Come. I will walk with thee to the tavern."

Daniel followed him outside into the cool of the evening. "How do you think the other elders will rule?"

"'Tis hard to say, but thee gave them much to think over."

"How soon will I hear back from them—from you?"

"The final decision will be made after meeting on Sunday."

"So I will have the answer before I meet my grandson."

Thomas's measured stride stiffened at Daniel's last two words. As well they might, since the man considered Owen to be *his* grandson—and not Daniel's.

Monday could not come soon enough.

Chapter 11

I T HAD BEEN DIFFICULT for Zachary to refrain from working on the barn addition on a Sunday, but it being the Lord's Day. He'd adhered to the Friend's belief in a strict day of rest—other than milking and feeding the cows, of course. He couldn't neglect them, no matter the day of the week. But now it was Monday, his farm work was finished, and he should start on the addition. Except...

He untied the last cow from her stanchion and shooed her out to pasture with the rest. He could start squaring the trees he'd felled, but he felt a gentle nudge in his spirit, and he'd learned to listen to those. After all, Gwen had saved him from slavery. He owed her his support in whatever way he could provide it.

And she was taking her son to meet Daniel Whiteford at the Baldwins' this evening.

The team hadn't been hitched in a while, so he grabbed lead ropes and brought Justice and Jubal in from the pasture. He gave their black hinds a quick brushing before buckling on the harnesses. They were fresh, so once they got underway, he let them lengthen their trot until the wagon was skimming over the road. He had to mash his hat down tightly to avoid losing it. In no time, he pulled up in front of the Baldwins' house.

Micah's wagon wasn't there yet.

Zachary set the brake and tied the team, then stepped onto the porch.

Thomas opened the door. "Welcome, Zachary. What brings thee this evening?"

"I thought, what with Gwen bringing Owen..." Why was he reluctant to admit to feeling the nudge of the Spirit to one of the elders?

"That she would appreciate a friendly face. No doubt thee are correct. Come in." Thomas stepped back. "Betsy, pour another mug of cider."

"I did not mean to intrude—"

"Thee are always welcome here."

"Of course thee are." Betsy beckoned him farther into the house that smelled of fresh bread, cinnamon, and something savory.

Thomas combed his beard with his fingers. "And perhaps thy calming influence will be what Micah needs when he arrives."

Micah had no legal claim on Owen, but that didn't make him any less the boy's father. Zachary was still feeling the loss of Titus, who had only lived with him a fortnight. How much worse would it be for Micah to lose his son?

How much worse for Gwen?

The rattle of a wagon reached them as Betsy pressed a mug into Zachary's hands.

"There they are." Thomas opened the door with an unsteady hand.

So it wasn't just Micah who might need a calming influence.

Owen tumbled from the wagon and raced to the porch, golden hair shining in the sun's slanted rays. "Grandfather!" He launched himself into Thomas's arms, and the old man lifted him and clutched him for a long moment.

Betsy pressed against his side, fussing over the boy as if she hadn't seen him in months instead of at meeting the day before.

Micah tied his team and escorted Gwen, who held Sally Faye in her arms, to the house. "Zachary, 'tis good to see thee."

"And thee as well."

Gwen raised her eyes to Zachary, worry dimming their usual blue brightness. "Thank thee for being here."

"Whatever thee need, thee only need ask."

She gave him a wan smile.

At the sound of footsteps, all heads turned.

Daniel Whiteford approached the house on foot with... Zachary blinked and stared. With a slave girl?

Anger heated his blood until the thump of it filled his ears.

"Welcome, Daniel." Thomas set Owen down but gripped his hand as he walked to the edge of the porch. "And this must be Dinah."

The other faces around Zachary mirrored his surprise—horror—and yet, Thomas knew of it.

Dinah?

Where had Zachary heard that name recently? It wasn't common. None of the Friends were called by that name.

"Thank you for having us," Daniel said, never taking his eyes from the boy who clung to Thomas's hand. His grandson.

"Come into the house, everyone." Betsy ushered them all back inside to take seats set up around the tidy parlor. Sally Faye on Gwen's lap, Owen sitting on the rag rug at Micah's feet. Zachary remained standing, back against the wall near the corner by the door.

"Well." Thomas slapped his palms against his knees. "We have introductions to make. Daniel, thee should go first."

"Me?" The man looked startled, then glanced at Dinah, who had settled on a colorful rag rug near him. "Oh, of course. This is Dinah. She had been with me since New Bern, on my journey here."

The girl smiled at him, a true smile, not the fake fool-the-master smile he'd seen—and given—plenty of times when he'd been her age. She hugged her knees to her chest and rocked on her haunches. Was she of simple mind? Or was she truly content to be with this man?

"Thee own a slave?" Micah's question was forceful.

"In a manner of speaking." Daniel shifted forward and rested his clasped hands on his knees. "'Twas never my intention, but the girl was... not in a good place."

Zachary's anger broke out in a sweat across his shoulders.

Did the man think them all fools? He'd *bought* the girl. He owned a slave. What made him think the Friends would ever allow it?

And yet, Thomas had known. Which meant the rest of the elders also knew. And not a one had spoken of it at meeting the day prior. It made no sense.

"The elders have met with Daniel," Thomas said, "who has assured us that he intends to give the girl her freedom papers when she reaches the age of majority."

"Why? Why not free her now?" The words exploded from Zachary.

"Dinah is but eleven years old and has no family—no guardian." Thomas didn't match his anger. "To free her now would be to let anyone capture and return her across the river. She would have no protection."

Daniel raised his hands, then let them drop into his lap. "So you see my dilemma. I did not wish to own Dinah, but neither could I let her fall into the hands of the men who would have purchased her."

"You purchased her!" Zachary took a step toward Daniel.

"He been nothin' but kind to me." Dinah's words stopped him. "He let me help Eliza in the kitchen. I learnin' to cook." She dug her hand into the small pocket tied around her waist. "He even give me this." She uncurled her fingers, exposed a silver coin, then tucked it back in the pocket, dipping her head shyly as she did so.

"We will discuss the issue of Dinah more later." Thomas cleared his throat. "'Tis time to finish the introductions."

Zachary gritted his teeth. Give the girl or coin or not, he wasn't satisfied with the man's answers. Not even a little. But he would wait for his turn to ask questions—after he supported Gwen in whatever way she needed.

At last.

Daniel had hardly taken his eyes off the boy. He was Constance's son, but he looked so much like Jonas at that age. Memories of their childhood innocence bombarded him.

Where had he gone so wrong as a father?

Gwen called to Owen, "Come stand by me, son." Once he was at her side, she met Daniel's eyes. "Owen, this man is Daniel Whiteford, thy grandfather."

The boy's fair brows drew together. "He cannot be." He pointed at Thomas. "He is my grandfather."

Gwen slid her arm around the boy's slight waist. "Of course he is, but thee can have more than one."

Owen stiffened and looked at Micah. "Can I?"

"When I was thy age, I had four grandfathers." Micah shot a glare at Daniel, but continued. "There was Grandfather Pike, Grandfather Warren, Great-grandfather Pike, and Great-grandfather Simmons. My great-grandfathers were very old."

The little boy pointed a finger at Daniel. "Who is he?"

Daniel held his breath. Part of him wanted to tell the boy that he was his only blood relative, but another part told him to hold his tongue. After all, he didn't wish to scare the boy away—or annoy Micah.

Gwen turned Owen until he faced her again and smiled. "Thee may call him Grandfather Whiteford."

"Is he thy father?"

"Nay." Gwen brushed the fair hair from the boy's forehead. "But worry not about that now. 'Tis time for thee to say hello."

Owen pressed closer to her side but faced Daniel. "Hello."

Daniel drew in an unsteady breath. "I am very pleased to meet you, Owen."

The boy's forehead crinkled again. "Why do thee talk that way?"

"He is not one of the Friends," Gwen told him.

A mutinous look Daniel remembered too well from Jonas crossed the boy's face. "Then how can he be my grandfather?"

"'Tis a long story for another time." Gwen's voice was gentle and reassuring, and Daniel's respect for her grew. Truly, he'd chosen wisely when he'd left the boy in her care.

Who was he kidding? He'd chosen her because she'd been available. Because he'd needed to get her away from Jonas. And because he could blackmail her into keeping her mouth shut.

The shame of it crashed down on him as he studied the beautiful blond-haired child.

How could he remove Owen from this woman who loved him like a mother? Or her hawk-eyed husband, who looked as if he'd like to rip Daniel out of his chair and toss him to the street—pacifist Quaker or not?

Because Micah loved the boy too—as a father loved his son.

Daniel understood that. He respected it.

But accepting it meant giving up his plans, or at least some of his plans. He couldn't remove the boy from their home, separate him from the only family he'd ever known.

But he could still relocate here to Mount Pleasant and start a business to hand over to young Owen one day.

"'As your mother said, 'tis a long story." Daniel leaned toward the child, desperate to touch him. But he kept his distance, not willing to risk scaring him away. Or angering Micah. Or maybe most of all, hurting Gwen, the woman who had truly become his grandson's mother. "And as I am planning to build a house and start a business here, we shall get to know each other in time."

"Thee are staying?" said the black man, the one still looking daggers at him from the corner.

He wasn't accustomed to being questioned by servants, much less one not in his employ. But he kept this tone respectful, not wishing to create a scene. "The elders have given their blessing for me to purchase the land."

The black man turned to Thomas but pointed at Dinah. "What about Dinah?"

"Indeed." Thomas motioned toward Daniel. "Thee had a request to make to Micah and Gwen, did thee not?"

"I did." He'd thought long and hard about how best to word it. "You see, I have no place for Dinah until my house is built, and that could be many weeks. 'Tisn't right for her to live above the tavern. A girl her age needs to be busy, to be around people. I wondered if you would be willing to house her—I would cover all her expenses, of course—until my house is ready. You have the children, and she would be much happier with a family than stuck in a stuffy room with me."

Dinah rose to her knees and faced him. "Have I displeased you, Mass—Mr. Whiteford?" Her dark eyes took on the haunted look he'd seen at the auction.

"Of course not." He smiled at the girl. "But as I said, I have no place suitable for you."

"I be just fine sleepin' on the floor. I doan mind."

"Dinah, would you not be happier on the farm with these good people?"

"But I wants to serve you, suh. You done so much for me."

"You would be serving me." He looked over her head at Gwen. "You would be helping to watch over my grandson. Nothing could please me more."

Dinah glanced over her shoulder at Gwen. "That true?" Her voice was barely a whisper.

Gwen gripped her husband's hand, which rested on her shoulder.

"Would thee like that?" Micah asked Dinah.

"If it be what Mr. Whiteford wishes."

"But what do *thee* wish, Dinah?" asked the black man. Who was he, and why was he even there?

"I wish to please Mr. Whiteford because he been so good to me."

By his dark expression, that answer didn't satisfy him.

"Do thee like being with children?" Gwen offered the girl a lovely smile, the kind a mother would bestow on her own offspring. What an amazing young woman she'd matured into.

Dinah brightened. "I do. Granny Anna had me helpin' with the younguns on the plantation."

"Then we would love to have thee come and live with us until Daniel's house is built." She paused and made eye contact with Daniel, speaking directly to him. "And thee can see him whenever he comes to visit Owen."

Acceptance. That's what she was offering Daniel. He blinked and nodded, not sure his voice would work.

Zachary gulped the cider he'd almost forgotten was in his hands. He needed to get out of the house. Needed to get away from Daniel Whiteford—the slave owner. How had Daniel managed to turn the heads of Thomas and the elders?

And why was Gwen so accommodating toward him? Why wasn't she demanding that he leave Mount Pleasant and never return? Why wasn't Micah?

Most of all, why had Zachary felt the nudge to be here to witness this... this farce?

None of it made sense.

And Zachary certainly wasn't the calming influence Thomas had thought he'd be.

He set the mug on the small table by the door and slipped outside without a word to anyone.

Thomas joined him before he got the team untied.

"Zachary." He stopped him with a hand on Jubal's bridle. "We should speak."

"About the slave owner in thy house?" The words came out like knives, but he couldn't stop them. "How could thee, Thomas? How could the elders—knowing he owns Dinah—have agreed to sell him land? Agreed to letting him live among us?"

"I have known Daniel for many years. He has been through more than thee know, and it has changed him."

"He bought that girl."

"To save her from a worse fate."

Zachary whirled, nose a handspan away from Thomas's. "And thee believe him? This man who forced Gwen to sign that unholy oath?"

The old man's eyes held their usual calm assurance. "I do."

"Well, I do not." Zachary stepped back and slashed the air with his hand. "His son tried to capture me, and now he owns Dinah. Nothing about that says he is trustworthy."

"Do thee not believe people can change?"

"Of course I do."

Thomas gripped his shoulder. "Why did thee come here tonight?"

"Because of Gwen."

Thomas kept his grip firm and waited.

"Because..." Zachary had to tell him the whole of it. "I felt led to be here."

"Why, do thee suppose? Did the Lord want thee to see and hear what just happened?"

Zachary stepped away from the older man's touch and climbed onto the wagon. "I know not."

"Then perhaps"—Thomas moved away from the horses—"that is the question thee really need answered."

Zachary backed the horses from the hitching rail and turned the wagon onto the street. Without a backward glance, he smacked the reins across the broad rumps in front of him and allowed the team to lunge into their collars, jerking the wagon into motion. He held them to a fast trot until they cleared the town street, then let them run.

It was stupid. It was dangerous in the growing darkness. But it matched Zachary's dark mood. As they neared the farm, he pulled them back to a trot, then down to a walk so they could catch their breaths and calm down.

If only he could do the same.

He unhitched Justice and Jubal and turned them out on pasture, then built a fire behind the barn, a roaring blaze to give off light. He fetched the adz and rolled one of the felled and trimmed trees near the fire. With a mighty swing, the tool bit deep into the wood.

Why, Lord?

Why did Thee allow me to become involved in helping my people escape to freedom, only to bring a slave owner into our midst? 'Tisn't right, Lord.

Another swing, another deep bite.

'Tisn't right.

Chapter 12

HOOFBEATS CAUGHT ZACHARY'S ATTENTION the next morning, and he set the adz aside. He grabbed the rag he'd hung on a nearby bush and mopped sweat from his face and neck as Mark Allen rode into view around the barn.

"Thee are busy this morning." Mark Allen dismounted from his old gray horse.

Zachary didn't feel the need to explain that he'd been working all night and had resumed after the milking. But now that he'd stopped, fatigue pulled at him.

"I need more space in my barn for the heifers."

"If thy farm gets much larger, thee will need to take on a farm hand."

"I suppose I might." If only he could hire Titus, but the boy wouldn't be safe without his freedom papers.

"I came to tell thee that Edward Johnson died last night. Paul brought us the news. The funeral will be tomorrow morning at ten."

Zachary had always enjoyed the old man's company, his stories from his younger life, the wisdom he'd freely shared. "I shall miss him. How is Cora holding up?"

"I have not seen her yet, but she is a strong woman, and much younger than Edward."

She'd been Edward's third wife, his first dying in childbirth before their first anniversary, and the second from smallpox a few years later. He'd been alone for many years before courting Cora. Many thought her too young for him, but they'd been happy together. Zachary envied them the years they'd had.

Envy seemed to be his companion too often these days. Envy and loneliness.

"He will have left her well provided for, I am certain." Zachary mopped his face again and tossed the rag back on the bush to dry. "But on a happier note, how are Faye and Cordelia doing?"

Pride lit the other man's features. "I cannot believe how much Cordelia has grown in only a month. Paul says she is healthy and perfect. He has become her doting uncle. And Faye took to motherhood like a duck to water."

"Thee are a lucky man."

"And well I know it." Mark Allen pointed to the logs still needing to be squared. "I must deliver the news about Edward to the others on this side of town. After the funeral, I can give thee a hand with these."

"If thee have the time to spare."

"I can make time." Mark Allen swung into the saddle and gathered his reins. "Oh, I almost forgot to mention, there has been a black man in ragged clothing sighted this side of town. Likely a fugitive."

"A big man?"

"Average size, they said."

"I shall keep my eyes open."

Mark Allen studied him for a moment, then nodded and reined his horse around. "Until tomorrow."

Zachary walked to the house and opened the bags filled with the old clothing Cora had given him. He pulled out a pair of breeches and a shirt. They'd fit an average-sized man. He took them behind the barn where he'd been working and laid them over a bush near the tree line. "Lord, I know not who might be in need of these clothes," he said out loud, "but if thee do, Lord, bring him here that he may help himself. Amen."

He returned to the house and collapsed on his bed, too tired to think.

"I can write you a draft from my bank in Pittsburgh." Daniel scanned the faces of the Quaker elders. "That was the closest bank I could transfer my funds to." They were back in the meeting house, seated in the same half-circle as before. Same somber faces, but without the hostility he'd encountered during that first meeting. He'd won them over.

"We have need of a bank in this area." Thomas removed his pipe and pointed the stem at Daniel. "Thee would not consider opening a bank instead of a shipping business, would thee?"

"I'm afraid I know very little about banking. Certainly not enough to run one."

"Pity." Thomas replaced his pipe.

"For thy house lot, there is a large parcel near the meeting house on the west side, square and on the corner—or what will be a corner once the next street is made on that side of town." The elder in charge of the property allotments ran his finger over a map. "And for thy business, there is a parcel on the south side across from the livery stable." He looked up at Daniel. "'Twould be handy for keeping thy horses for the wagons, I should think."

Eventually, he'd have his own stable, but in the beginning, it would be advantageous. "I believe that would suit me."

"Fine." The gentleman pushed back in his chair and laced his fingers together before naming a price.

Daniel almost asked him to repeat it, so low was the figure. Surely, even on this frontier, they could get more than that for two parcels of land. But he pulled his purse from his coat pocket. "I will write you the note today."

"Splendid." Thomas stood. "I would be happy to walk with thee to see the land. Of course, should it not suit, we can transfer the note to a more acceptable parcel, can we not?"

Gray heads nodded around the room as Daniel handed over the banknote. "Thank you, gentlemen. I look forward to starting imme-diately."

He and Thomas left the meeting house.

"'Tis this corner up ahead." Thomas pointed the way. "Thee would be close to the meeting house, should thee come to join our congregation."

"Become a Quaker?"

"We call ourselves Friends, not Quakers, but that is how the world knows us."

"I would not know how to follow so many rules."

Thomas chuckled. "We do not have so many rules. We only hope to please the Lord with how we live."

Daniel mulled that over as they walked across the property. It was a large lot with plenty of room for a modestly grand house, a large stable, and a kitchen garden. An ancient oak tree towered over one corner, and a row of untrimmed bushes bordered the east side, separating the empty lot from the neighboring one, where a house was being built. The tang of freshly sawn wood lingered in the air.

It would be a good place to call home. Margaret would have approved.

"What do thee think?"

"I can build a nice house here."

"Hmm." Thomas tapped the ashes from his pipe and stowed it in a pocket. "Let us walk to the other property."

"How difficult will it be to hire workers from among the Quake—Friends?"

Striding toward the street, Thomas tugged at his beard. "There are four structures currently under construction, so it may require more time than thee would like. But there is always the option of hiring off the river."

"Off the river?"

"Indeed. 'Tis risky. Some of the men down there are not of good moral character, but others are just men willing to work for pay."

"If they can do the job, 'twould suit me fine."

"I expect 'twill be thy best chance of having thy buildings up by fall."

Not until fall? "I had hoped to get started sooner."

"Thee would need to hire more men and—"

"Then I shall."

"And thee would risk hiring more of the, shall I say, unsavory characters."

"If they can lay a brick or pound a peg, that is all I require."

"Hmm." Thomas pointed down a street on the backside of the business district with only a few buildings on it, and those appeared to have been hastily constructed. They turned onto it.

It wasn't hard to find the livery stable, it was a lopsided shack with corrals behind it.

"Not the most appealing of places." Daniel wasn't sure he wanted to look out his window at that every day.

"Built from the wood of the barge that brought Lawrence here. He has plans to improve it when he can afford to." Thomas pointed to the land across the street. "And here is thy parcel. It runs the length of the street and half as deep. As yet, there is no street behind thee, but in time."

The view behind his new property was rolling hills and forest groves, creating a pleasing landscape. Daniel could build something here. Something long-lasting. A business that would benefit the town for many years to come. A business for Owen to inherit.

Owen. The name was growing on him. It would have to, as he had no option to change it. Perhaps in eight years or so, Gwen would allow him to apprentice the boy, teach him everything he knew. Set him up to be a prosperous man of business.

And in the process, keep him from ever becoming like Jonas.

Zachary awoke with a pounding headache, the slanting afternoon sun coming through the window not helping it at all. When had he last eaten? As best he could remember, noon the day before. He fumbled his hand across the bedside table and grasped his pocket watch. It was four o'clock. He'd need to start the milking in another hour. His stomach grumbled.

But first—food.

He sat and held his head in his hands, letting the dizziness pass. He needed water. He rose and stumbled to the bucket beside the hearth. The water was warm and stale, but he drank four dippers full before stopping. The remains of a wheel of cheese and half a loaf of Gwen's bread hid under a linen cloth on the table. He filled a mug with cider from the jug, then sat and ate everything. He could have eaten another full loaf of bread, but it was his last.

It was past time for another milk delivery, but he'd worked the night through and slept most of the day away.

Stupid man. What had that gained him?

The anger of the evening before still lingered in his veins.

He went to the barn and called in the cows. Bossy, the herd leader, raised her head and stared at him as if to say he was early. But if he got the cows milked, he could take a delivery to Micah and Gwen. She might have bread to trade, and he could see how Dinah was doing.

"Come in, Bossy. I have things to do yet today. Hurry up." He opened the barn door to the pasture when the memory hit him.

The clothing.

Zachary hurried around to the back of the barn.

The bush was empty. Shirt and breeches gone. He scanned the nearby woodlot but nothing seemed out of the ordinary. The man was likely long gone, but Zachary said, "Go with God." He'd done it. He'd helped another fugitive. That put a spring in his step on his way back into the barn.

Bossy ambled in, and the rest of the cows followed, Zachary leading each to her place and securing their heads in the stanchions. Thoughts raced as he fell into the rhythmic motion of milking. Had the fugitive been watching the house, the barn? Had Titus given the man directions to find him? What else could Zachary do since he hadn't even started raising the addition yet? He stood and poured the full bucket into a milk can.

If he left the springhouse unlocked, the man could help himself to the milk there. But that would leave the springhouse vulnerable to bears. Zachary had learned the hard way that a simple drop bar locking device was no deterrent to a hungry or determined bear. The iron hasp and keyed lock had corrected the problem.

But it also kept the fugitives out.

What if he left the key in the lock? A man would know to turn the key and unlock the device. A bear wouldn't be able to.

Zachary had enough milk to supply his weekly customers and himself with some left over. And if he ran a little short, he could do without.

By the time the cows were back out on pasture and the milk cans in the springhouse, Zachary's headache was long gone. He loaded one can on the cart and hitched Annabelle.

"Thee know what, Annabelle?" He let his voice carry while scratching the underside of the mule's neck. "We have extra milk in the springhouse. I would appreciate if anyone who needs some would leave the cream pans undisturbed. I need that for my next batch of cheese."

With one last scratch and not looking toward the tree line, he got in the cart and clicked to the mule.

The trip to Micah and Gwen's was slow as he let the mule plod along, careful not to slosh the milk in the can, but when their cabin came into view, his stomach knotted with anger again. It wasn't right that Dinah was stuck in slavery for another ten years. Ten years with that man.

Even if she was with Micah and Gwen now, she still belonged to Daniel Whiteford.

He stopped Annabelle near the cabin door, and Gwen stepped out with one hand raised to shield her eyes from the sun's slanting rays, Sally Faye balanced on her hip.

"Thy timing is perfect. Could thee smell my baking from thy place?"

"Nay, but I devoured the last of thy loaves earlier today, so I was hoping." He tied Annabelle and lifted the can from the cart. "I will take this to thy springhouse. Is Micah in the barn?"

"He is."

Then a dark face appeared at Gwen's elbow. Dinah smiled at Zachary as she drew Owen outside by the hand.

"Zacree!" Owen let go and dashed toward him. He could pronounce Zachary's name now, but he clung to the childish nickname that he'd first used. "Come on, Dinah." He motioned for the girl to follow before stopping just short of barreling into Zachary's legs. "Can I open the springhouse for thee?"

"I hoped thee would."

Owen whooped and ran back to his mother, who was already holding out the key. "Do not drop it."

"Come on, Dinah." He raced around the cabin, the dark girl following.

"He is quite taken with her." Gwen joined Zachary on the walk to the springhouse. "They were fast friends before we snuffed the candles last evening."

"Me too," said Sally Faye, then popped her thumb in her mouth.

"And thee?" He looked at Gwen. "Are thee taken with her as well?"

"How can I not be? She is a delightful child, so willing to please."

"Do thee remember being willing to please so thee did not upset the master?" Bitterness tinged his voice, but he couldn't stop it.

Gwen stopped and looked up at him. "That is not what I see in Dinah."

"Watch for it. 'Tis an art learned from an early age. Thee were not always a servant, but she has never known anything else."

"I had not thought of it that way."

They continued, and Zachary exchanged the full milk can for their empty one.

"Dinah," Gwen said, "would thee take Owen and Sally Faye to the house and help them wash for supper? I will be along shortly."

"Yes, ma'am." The girl settled the two-year-old on her hip in a perfect imitation of Gwen, then grabbed Owen's hand. "Come on now, you heard your momma. Time to wash up."

Zachary started for the barn, but Gwen's touch on his arm stopped him.

"Thee are angry."

He shot a look after the departing Dinah. "How can I not be?"

"Are thee angry with me?"

"Nay!" The word burst from him. "Thee have done nothing wrong. Thy generosity, taking in the girl, speaks only of thy loving nature."

"Thee have always been my champion."

"And always will be."

She tilted her head, lines forming at the corners of her eyes. "I wish thee would find another to champion. Someone special to thee. I worry about thy aloneness."

Her words hit like the adz biting into wood—only they carved a notch in his heart. "I would like that, if it be the Lord's will and in His time."

She planted her hands on her hips, exposing the gentle swell of the next young Pike under her apron. "I wish He would hasten sometimes."

Zachary laughed. They had been friends for four years, and she never failed to cheer him when he needed it.

"Who is this laughing with my wife?" Micah approached, grin belying his challenging words.

"No one to cause thee any worry, husband." Gwen started for the cabin. "I expect thee to stay to supper, Zachary. Do not disappoint me."

"That woman." Micah shook his head. "She bosses us all around."

"I would give much to find a woman like her, but one more my age." He winked at Micah to cover the seriousness of his words.

"Thee are hardly an old man."

Zachary chuckled. "Thee may not think so now, but I shall remind thee of those words in twelve years when thee reach this age."

Micah clapped him on the back. "Come. If we are late to supper, my wife will get testy."

"A moment first." Zachary looked at the house and back again. "Thee are agreeable to Dinah being here?"

Micah sighed. "Agreeable because she is a child in need of a proper home, I am. Agreeable because we are helping the man who once owned my wife? Not as much."

"Thomas thought I might be a calming influence last evening, and instead, 'twas I who acted the hothead." Zachary crossed his arms. "'Tis just that... she is a slave." That last word came out half-strangled.

"I know. I hate that as well. But Thomas is correct. To free her now would be to put her in greater danger."

"It does not mean I have to like it." Zachary bit out the words.

"Indeed. I feel the same way. But rest assured, as long as she is under my roof, she will be treated like one of my family. Thee has my word on that."

Zachary nodded. "I never thought otherwise. 'Tis Daniel White-ford's presence that goads me."

"Ah, my friend. On that, we can also agree." Micah pointed to the cabin. "Oddly enough, Gwen is at peace with it."

Perhaps so, but Zachary didn't want to be at peace with it—and that was the problem.

Chapter 13

A FULL WEEK HAD passed and Daniel was no closer to starting on his buildings. Frustration gnawed at him like a rabid animal. He paced the rickety dock at Roberts Landing. Today might bring a barge with men willing to work for him. He'd come up empty the past three days, since he'd caught a ride to this town, and if nothing happened today, he'd have to go back to Mount Pleasant and wait until the Quakers finished their current building projects.

Which would put him far behind his desired schedule.

Always a man of business, he hated being behind schedule. He hated idleness. He hated feeling... helpless. In his younger years, he would have started on a building himself, but years behind a desk had left his muscles lacking as well as his stamina. Not that he was old, still four years from sixty, but neither was he fit enough to erect a building on his own.

He was turning for another lap down the dock when a barge emerged from the morning's mist. It was a typical river barge, squat and flat and piled with crates. But this one was heading straight for the dock. If Daniel had been a praying man, this would have been a good time to ask for a favorable outcome. Somehow over the years, he'd stopped praying.

Yet he was about to sink his life into a community of praying people, so what could it hurt?

"Lord, if there are men on that barge willing to work for me, I would appreciate it." His words startled a family of wood ducks. The momma duck quacked and ushered her little ones away from the dock. At least someone had heard him.

Soon, the sailors had the barge snugged to the dock, but they didn't start unloading the barge's cargo. Daniel approached the one he assumed to be in charge. "Captain? Are you not unloading?"

The man swung around to face him. "I am not. I was paid to get this tub to Roberts Landing, and here it is. My work is done." With that, the man stomped down the dock toward town.

Daniel approached one of the crewmembers as they were filing off the barge. "Where are you men going?"

"Back to Pittsburgh, I reckon," said the burly man closest to Daniel.

"I am looking to hire a crew to build a house. Do any of you men have experience in building?"

The burly one nodded as the others gathered closer. There were six of them, one a stripling youth, but most looked to be in their thirties and one closer to Daniel's age.

"The house will be built of bricks. Is anyone experienced with brickwork?"

The older man stepped forward. "Aye. I was apprenticed to a mason for many a year. I can build a brick house." He flicked a hand at the others. "I can show them what to do."

"How about the rest of you," Daniel asked. "Any building experience?"

"I helped my pa build our house." The youth grinned at his crewmates. "And it still be standin'."

Chuckles rose from the men, and one of them cuffed the youth good-naturedly on the shoulder.

One, his face hidden behind a thick black beard, stepped forward. "I spent some time buildin' things. I can handle most any tool for woodwork."

Daniel rubbed his hands together. "How many are interested in staying to work for me?" He named a fair price per day worked and stressed the need to work six full days a week with only Sundays off. There was no way the Quakers would sanction his working men on Sunday, and he needed to stay in their good graces to encourage their business.

A man who'd stayed near the back stepped away. "I am needed back in Pittsburgh. The wife is expecting our firstborn in a month." The other men laughed and a couple mocked him, but he slung a satchel over his shoulder and walked toward town.

Good man. Too bad he wouldn't stay and work, but Daniel admired him for putting his family first. If only Daniel had learned that lesson when he'd been younger. Things might have turned out differently.

The other five agreed to go with Daniel. They shouldered their belongings and followed him into Roberts Landing. He'd already arranged for Bob to drive him back to Mount Pleasant with whomever he could hire, so it didn't take long before they were on the road.

The ride provided some insights into the men. They were a rough crew, especially in language. Daniel had spent enough time near docks to not be shocked by the level of profanity, but the Quakers wouldn't approve. However, his properties were both on the edges of town, so with any luck, nobody would hear them for most of the day.

He'd planned to put them up in the tavern. However, it might be prudent to rent space at the stable instead. It was obvious the owner needed the income, and these men were used to sleeping on a boat.

Daniel turned to the older man who knew masonry. "What is your name?"

"Isaac Wilson."

"Well, Isaac, I had planned on my house being brick and the business being wood, but with your knowledge and skill, perhaps I should have both structures made of brick."

"Where will the bricks come from? We been on the wagon half an hour already."

"Not to worry. There is a brickmaker in Mount Pleasant. He is already working on my order."

Isaac nodded. "Bricks last longer than boards, that be a fact."

Exactly what Daniel wanted. A structure that would last. A legacy to hand down to Owen.

They did a round of proper introductions. The youth was Jimmy, and the three men in their thirties were Henry, Will, and Tad. All short names and easy to remember. Tad said he had experience with driving teams, so Daniel would employ him with carting supplies from the river as needed. On his first day back in Roberts Landing, he'd sent a letter to the new agent he'd acquired during the stopover in Pittsburgh that included an exhaustive list of things he'd need.

So many plans, so much to be done, but it would be worth it. He would have a steady, prosperous business running within the year.

"Zachary!" The urgent call was an odd combination of a whisper and a shout.

Zachary rolled over on his bed. It was still dark. Had he been dreaming?

"Zachary!"

He knew that voice. He was off the bed and across the room in one fluid motion. He threw the door open wide in one fluid motion.

"Titus?"

The youth stood before him, one arm wrapped around a young woman who appeared on the edge of collapse.

"Come in." Zachary took the woman's other arm, ignoring how she flinched away from him. "Let us settle her on the bed."

She pulled against him with what little was left of her strength then.

"'Tis all right." Titus kept her moving toward the bed. "He ain't gonna hurt you."

As soon as they got her to the mattress, her eyes rolled back and she flopped forward.

"I shall fetch Paul." Zachary grabbed his breeches and pulled them on, tucking in the long shirt he slept in.

"She be exhausted," Titus said, "not sickly."

"How can thee be sure?"

"I found her in a bad way, with dogs on her trail." Titus sank onto a chair, weariness leaching the youth from his features. "Took us three days to escape them." He poked a thumb toward the sleeping woman. "She been a house slave."

"And therefore not in a condition to survive such a grueling run as a field worker or farm hand would be."

Titus's head lifted and fell in what might have been a nod, if he weren't so exhausted. "And she been on her own two days before I found her." There was respect in his voice. "She be a brave one to try runnin' on her own."

"Is she one of thy sisters?"

Titus shook his head. "I be goin' back for them, but I had to help this one first." He pointed out the dark window. "You got the new addition on."

"I did, with help from Mark Allen and Micah."

"And the secret room? They know 'bout that?"

Zachary waved a hand in dismissal. "Nay. They helped me raise the log sides, but I am finishing the rest. 'Tis almost done."

"I could not have gotten Lizzy up the ladder by myself."

"Thee did right to bring her here. We can move her at milking time. Until then, she and thee need to sleep."

"I could shut my eyes for a bit." Titus yawned until his jaw cracked.

Zachary pulled a blanket from a chest and tossed it to his young friend. "Sleep. I will stay awake to listen and watch."

Titus curled into a ball along the wall opposite the fireplace.

The night was warm, so they didn't need a fire, but his guests would need food, and probably a lot of it when they awoke. Zachary kindled a fire without lighting a lamp. He grabbed his pocket watch from the bedside table and held it close to the fire. Three o'clock. Plenty of time to get a stew simmering before morning chores. He peeled and cut potatoes, carrots, and turnips into the stewpot by the firelight. They were last year's harvest, and somewhat shriveled, but they would cook up good enough, and he'd add smoked catfish to it once they were done for more flavor.

He couldn't cook a catfish as tasty as Titus had prepared, but he'd caught a trio on Sunday afternoon and smoked them. He couldn't work on the barn on Sunday, but the Friends considered fishing relaxation—not work. And Zachary would need to keep food on hand that he could smoke or cook in a hurry—or give over without cooking to any fugitive who needed to eat. And most of them would.

Gwen had raised her eyebrows at his request for more bread when he'd delivered her milk last time, but she was happy enough to trade for extra milk, now that she had one more mouth to feed.

Was Daniel keeping up his end of the bargain and paying for Dinah's expenses?

Zachary shot a glance at the bed and frowned. How could the Friends allow that man, a man who owned another person, to stay in their community? Daniel's business might bring in needed provisions they were currently doing without, but was it worth the moral compromise?

Not as far as he was concerned.

Not that anyone had asked him.

He pushed the pot over the fire, which he'd kept small, and then slipped outside. The moon was past full but still cast light over the landscape. Stars lit the rest of the heavens. The dark bulk of his cows littered the pasture. Justice, Jubal, and Annabelle stood together near the fence, dozing. Nothing could look more peaceful than his farm.

And nothing could be farther from the truth of the young woman on his bed, running for her life. And Titus, who would go back into the lion's den as soon as he knew she was safely on her way north. While Zachary lived his peaceful existence on his peaceful farm.

"Why, Lord?" he whispered to the sky. "Why was I taken out of slavery when so many others are still held in bondage?"

There was no answer written in the stars, no voice from heaven, no angel walking toward him with a word from the Lord. No answer other than cricket song and the croak of frogs from the spring that fed the springhouse. He went into his house and checked on his guests. Titus was sound asleep, but the woman tossed restlessly while not waking. Whatever nightmares followed her, he hoped she'd one day overcome them. He stirred the simmering vegetables and sat at the table, resting his head on his folded arms, thinking about his guests. And yet...

He still felt alone.

Daniel had rented stalls from Lawrence, the owner of the livery stable, for the men to live there, then arranged for Lawrence's wife to prepare meals for them twice a day. The men were on their own for supper, but he'd feed them morning and noon to keep them working as much as possible. He'd already decided to build the business before the house, and having everyone across the street was handy. The workers hadn't complained, as they weren't required to pay for the lodging. Even better, Lawrence was reducing the rate to rent his horses and wagons while the men lived in the stable.

Daniel strode to the building site bright and early, whistling a jaunty tune. It was a fine day to begin a new venture. The men were finishing their breakfast when he entered the livery. To give Lawrence his due, the establishment was much more appealing inside than outside. His wife had even hung curtains on the windows.

"Are we ready to begin, gentlemen?"

Isaac, whom Daniel had made foreman because of his knowledge of masonry, stood. "If the lads here can bring the materials to the site, you and I can walk over the ground and talk over the particulars."

"Of course." It took only a few minutes to arrange for the team and wagon and give directions to the rest of the crew, then Daniel and Isaac walked across the street.

"Now that they are out of hearing," Isaac said, "you should know a few things."

"I am listening."

"I will do my best to keep these lads workin' here, but Henry and Will both have a taste for ale. Best to keep them away from the tavern."

Daniel had hired and fired many such men in his business career. "If they work, they will be paid. If they do not, they will be let go. What they do on their own time is their affair."

"Good enough. When I realized we were in a Quaker town, I thought maybe..."

"I am not a Quaker, but I respect these people."

"Another thing you ought to know."

"Just tell me, man, and let us get on with things." He tried to keep the impatience out of his voice, but he was ready to get started, not stand around talking.

"Will and young Jimmy were talkin' about hirin' out as slave catchers before we left the boat."

Slave catchers. Daniel ground his teeth together. Why would a man want to hunt down another human being when he already had gainful employment? Perhaps it was easier work than laying bricks, but even so... To hunt people in search of freedom...

"What you offered is a fair wage," Isaac continued, "including room and board. I will see your places built. But those two, they may go a different way."

It was all *maybe* and *might* at this point. "We shall deal with that problem if and when it arrives."

"You be the boss. Just thought you ought to know." Isaac pointed to the high ground on Daniel's plot and launched into his suggestions for the building.

Daniel told him what he envisioned, but it was obvious the man knew what he was doing. For the first time in a long time, Daniel took a deep breath of satisfaction.

Chapter 14

T HE BARN DOOR SQUEAKED open and Zachary rose, milk bucket in hand, ready to tell Titus he should have stayed in the house.

"Hello, Zachary," said Mark Allen. "Pardon me, I did not mean to startle thee."

Zachary closed his mouth and shook his head. "Thee caught me wool-gathering. 'Tis easy enough to do at this task. One can get lost in the sameness of it, cow after cow." He was rambling, trying to catch his balance at the unexpected, and he forced himself to stop.

"I imagine 'tis." Mark Allen came farther into the barn and looked into the new addition. "Thee are putting in a lower ceiling?"

"Indeed." Zachary stepped away from the cow and set the milk bucket down before joining Mark Allen. "I thought 'twould be warmer in the winter and a good place to keep any young stock or a sick or injured animal."

"I suppose, but thee has lower a ceiling over some of thy stalls already. 'Tis a lot of extra effort to split the logs. How did thee get them up there all by thyself?"

"The simple use of a pulley. Nothing much to it."

"If thee had said something, I would have found time to lend a hand."

Zachary waved away the offer. "'Tis almost completed now."

"So I see." The younger man studied him. "Faye would like a double order of milk this week if thee can spare it. She wishes to try her hand at making soft cheese."

"I should be able to provide that." Zachary took a couple of steps toward the door. Maybe Mark Allen would take the hint. "Is there anything else?" Mark Allen was like a bulldog with a stick caught between the fence rails, unable to move forward and unwilling to let go.

Mark Allen crossed his arms. "Are thee in a hurry to be rid of me?"

"Of course not." Zachary swept an arm toward the cows. "Just busy this time of morning."

"Thee have been busy often of late. And spending too much time by thyself, I think."

How could Zachary explain his need for secrecy without lying or compromising his work? Not that he thought Mark Allen would disapprove or turn him over to the territorial authorities for assisting the fugitives, but as Titus had drilled into him, it was best for people to not know.

"Thee are right. I have not been very social lately. I shall strive to do better." Zachary shrugged. "When thee get to be my age, 'tis easier to sit at home than venture out after a full day's work."

Mark Allen headed for the door but stopped. "I almost forgot. Faye broke her bread bowl." He held up a hand as if to ward off a question. "Ask not, I would be in trouble if I told thee how. Would thee by chance have one she could borrow until I can replace hers?"

"Of course..." Zachary wanted the words back as soon as he'd said them. "I will fetch it for thee and bring it out."

"Let me not take up any more of thy time. Tell me where to find it, and I can help myself."

"I insist." Zachary hurried out of the barn, his heart plummeting when footsteps followed him.

He should have moved Titus and Lizzy to the barn before milking as he'd intended to. But they hadn't awakened, and he'd not had the heart to disturb them. He stomped onto the porch and turned to his friend. "Wait here."

"What are thee hiding, Zachary Brown?" Mark Allen's voice was half-teasing and half-serious.

Zachary would do almost anything for Titus—but lie to a friend? No. He had to draw the line there. He'd walked a thin line while speaking to the slave catchers who'd been after Tess, but he hadn't actually lied. And he wasn't going to start with Mark Allen.

If that made him unfit to help fugitives escape... so be it.

He pushed the door open and ushered Mark Allen in, following him.

Titus sat at the table, facing the door wearing a pleasant smile that was as phony as a wooden egg.

"Thee did not say thee had a guest." Mark Allen turned to him. "I am sorry to have interrupted."

Zachary scanned the room, but there was no sign of Lizzy. However, the rug under the table was off-kilter, so she was likely in the cellar. "This is Titus. Titus, my friend and neighbor, Mark Allen Teed."

Titus rose and stuck out his hand as if he'd been shaking hands his whole life. It was a convincing gesture, considering slaves never shook hands. "Pleasure to meet you." He spoke with almost no slave accent at all.

"Same to thee, young man." Mark Allen looked between Zachary and Titus. "Are thee related?"

The question wasn't without merit, as there were many similarities between them, aside from their skin color.

"No, sir," Titus said. "We are friends."

"Indeed." Zachary took over before Titus ran out of small talk. "Now 'twas a bread bowl Faye needs, was it not?"

"Um, aye."

Zachary pulled his off a high shelf where it had lived since he'd moved in. He'd tried his hand at baking bread once before deciding it was easier to trade milk for it. "Here." He pressed it into Mark Allen's hands. "'Twill need a good cleaning. 'Tis dusty from disuse. And tell her to keep it. As long as I have Gwen to bake for me once a week, I will not be attempting any more bread baking myself."

"Faye will insist on paying thee something."

"All baked goods are gladly accepted in exchange."

"Then I shall let her know." Mark Allen turned back to Titus. "Perhaps I will see thee another time."

"I look forward to it."

Zachary walked with Mark Allen back to his horse outside the barn.

"Thee do look enough alike to pass for father and son." Mark Allen shot him a glance. "Could thee not claim him and keep him safe?"

Zachary sighed. "I wish, but as I am sure thee have surmised, he is in too much danger of being captured."

"I saw the floppy hat on the floor. Faye and I have both seen him before, and I suspect Bran may know something about him as well."

"He does."

"Who else knows?"

"Too many people."

Mark Allen stopped beside his horse. "The low ceiling?"

"Thee are too clever, my friend. I hope others who may come by will be more easily fooled."

"Rub the ceiling timbers with dirt so they do not catch the eye as new. That should help."

"Of course." Zachary shook his head. "I should have thought of that."

"And remember, the slave catchers know not thee or thy barn, so they will not notice a change that a friend would." Mark Allen untied Jughead and mounted. "I will say nothing of this, not even to Faye."

"I appreciate it."

"And if thee ever need anything—"

"I would not bring danger to the door of thy home nor anywhere near thy wife and child."

Mark Allen rubbed the back of his neck. "I had not thought of that."

"I am learning to see things differently." What an understatement. "But now, I must finish milking my cows and then dirty up some timbers."

Mark Allen tucked the wooden bread bowl under his arm, touched the brim of his hat, and rode away.

And so... the first of Zachary's friends knew he was involved with escaped slaves. How many more would figure it out?

What if it put the Friends in danger?

Titus walked across the yard and followed Zachary into the barn. "He someone you can trust?"

"He is a Friend. He will not betray me or thee."

"So all my fancy manners did me no good."

Zachary chuckled. "I was impressed." He went back to the cow he'd left waiting. "Is Lizzy in the root cellar?"

"She is. Scared as a rabbit too. I told her to stay put until I come back." Titus examined the new addition and ceiling while Zachary milked. "You done good on this."

"I do not have a door on the outside yet, but I should have time to get one made and installed later this week, as well as get the rest of the ceiling timbers in place."

"If it be all right, I could shinny up there and work on the floor with a planer, if you got one."

That would prevent splinters for those who used the room. "Hanging on the wall in the workroom."

The boy disappeared into the room and returned with the tool in hand.

"Be careful. I sharpened the blade last week and have not used it since."

Titus gave him a look that said he didn't need to be told and then he climbed the wall and slipped through the open space above. Soon, the *swish* of the planer smoothing wood joined the *schping* of milk spraying into the bucket. It was a comforting combination.

If only there was a way for the boy to stay.

Daniel dusted off his hands and surveyed what they'd accomplished in only one day. He'd bought every shovel the little mercantile had and borrowed another from Lawrence, but even with just those four, they'd leveled the ground and marked out boundaries for the building. Tad and Jimmy had hauled in three loads of bricks, everything the brickmaker had ready to go. These were stacked to the side of the building's layout, ready for when they'd be needed.

The men had left moments ago, heading to the creek south of town to wash and cool off.

But not Daniel. He headed for the livery and the horse he'd rented.

Lawrence must have seen him. He came to the door leading a bay horse.

Daniel hadn't been on top of a horse in a long time, but he'd not forgotten how to ride. Still, he almost regretted letting Arthur, the horses, and the carriage go when he eyed the mount Lawrence held.

He'd stressed the need for a gentle beast, but this one must be older than Methuselah. The swayed back, sunken eye sockets, and grizzled muzzle said it all.

"Are you sure this animal can carry me to Micah and Gwen's and back again?"

"Do not be fooled by King's looks." Lawrence patted the brown neck. "He has a few years behind him, but the blood of royalty still flows in his veins."

"Royalty, eh?"

The other man nodded. "One of his ancestors was shipped over from Egypt, back before the Revolution."

The horse looked old enough to have been in the war. But time was wasting, so Daniel took the reins and mounted, an action that took more effort than he remembered when he was younger. King waited while he fumbled with the right stirrup and settled in the seat. But when he tapped the beast's sides, the old horse moved out.

He remembered the way to the farm, but it had seemed a shorter distance in the doctor's fancy carriage. Bouncing along on top of King, certain parts of his body were complaining by the time he reined the horse into the farmyard.

In the field beside the barn, Micah walked toward him through ankle-high corn using a hoe like a walking stick. Owen clung to his back.

The image brought an unwanted and unpleasant sensation to Daniel's eyes. Though Micah's hair was dark and Owen's fair, and though they shared not a drop of blood between them, they were the picture of a father and son.

Had he ever carried Jonas that way? Not that he could remember. The boy had been with a nanny at that age. Brought down to be fussed over at supper, but otherwise kept upstairs in the nursery. That's what good families—prosperous families—in North Carolina did. He himself had been raised the same way, and he'd not become a slaver and a pirate.

And neither would the boy clinging to another man's back, not if Daniel had anything to do with it. And he intended to have a lot.

Micah raised the hand holding the hoe, the other hand around his back supporting the boy. "Daniel." The word was courteous, if not exactly friendly.

Daniel dismounted, air hissing between his teeth as his feet touched the ground. He'd never imagined riding again would prove so difficult. "Micah. Owen."

The boy peeked at him from behind Micah but didn't say a word. Nor did the man correct him. Well, Daniel could teach him better manners as time went along. After all, this was his first visit to the cabin with Owen here.

"I appreciate Gwen sending word and inviting me to supper."

"We best not keep her waiting." He knelt and lowered the boy to the ground. "Come on. Thee can tie thy horse there." He pointed to the hitching rail. "And wash up with us."

Daniel tied King and joined them at a large basin on the porch. Owen stood on a stool to reach it, and Micah helped the boy wash and dried him with a bit of toweling. "In with thy mother and see if she needs any help."

The boy cast a shy glance at Daniel, then scooted through the doorway.

Micah gestured to the basin, and Daniel washed his hands and then waited while Micah did the same, then scrubbed his forearms, face, and neck.

"That feels better."

"I bet it does." Daniel picked up the chunk of soap and copied the other man's actions. He'd never washed outside in the open before, Margaret would have been scandalized. There was no one other than Micah to see, after all, and after working beside his crew all day, it was refreshing.

"Come inside." Micah led the way.

The cabin was small but tidy inside, and the light from the windows and more from the fireplace made it cozy.

Dinah flashed him a huge grin as she spooned something that smelled delicious into a large bowl.

"Daniel." Gwen put down her spoon and came to greet him. "Welcome to our home. I am glad thee could come."

So he was no longer Mr. Whiteford to her. He hadn't been prepared for that, but in a Quaker community, one should expect it. They didn't believe in giving any type of honor to raise one above any other. "I would not have missed it."

"Owen." She waved the boy over. "Come say hello to thy grandfather."

Blue eyes so similar to Jonas's stared up at him. "Hello."

Daniel squatted beside him. "Hello. I am happy to see you again."

The boy giggled. "Thee talk funny."

"Owen." Gwen scolded then glanced at Daniel. "We will work on that, I promise thee."

"No harm done." He stood. "'Twill take time."

She released a breath—was she nervous?—and ushered him to the table. "Please, be seated. Dinah and I have everything ready."

"I am glad she is a help to you."

Gwen beamed at the girl. "I hardly know how I managed without her."

When they were all seated and through the silent blessing, a practice he was still getting accustomed to, Gwen passed the serving dishes around. Daniel filled his plate with fluffy potatoes, tender ham, green beans, and warm bread. And for once, probably due to a full day of working, he felt he could do it justice.

"Papa says I can get a puppy," Owen said around a mouthful of potatoes.

"Do not speak with thy mouth full, young man," Micah said.

"'Tis all he can talk about these days." Gwen sent Daniel an apologetic smile.

"'Tis good for a boy to have a dog." He leaned toward Owen, who sat on his right. "I had one when I was your age."

"What was his name?"

"Daisy. She was a girl dog."

Owen looked at Micah. "Can I have a girl dog?"

"'Tis hard enough to find any dog, so I think we will have to take what we can get."

The remainder of the dinner was spent talking to his grandson about Daisy. This was far from what he had intended when he'd moved here. He'd thought Owen would be sitting at his table, not that he would be the guest. But he couldn't remember ever having enjoyed a meal more.

Chapter 15

"**O**NE OF MY COWS has gotten too clever for her own good," Zachary told the blacksmith. "I need a different kind of hinge and latch to keep her in." He went on to explain what he had in mind. "And thee might as well make me a spare of the same style, so I have it on hand should I need it somewhere else."

The blacksmith named a price.

His business there finished, Zachary stepped out into the drizzle and turned up the back of his collar. That had been an unpleasant business. He may not have fully crossed the line, but he'd tottered on top of it and as good as lied.

One of the young heifers *had* managed to open a gate—twice—but Zachary had simply tied it shut with a length of rope. The hinges and hasp were for the door to the secret room of the barn addition—things that wouldn't show from the outside and could be locked from the inside.

The blacksmith was a Friend and could be trusted, but it was better this way. By not telling him the truth, Zachary was protecting him and his family from repercussions should he be caught out by the authorities. Even so, being untruthful was a distasteful endeavor, one he hoped not to indulge in very often. He kicked a rock to the side of the street where a wagon wheel wouldn't strike it.

"Well, boys, lookee what we got comin' toward us."

Zachary stopped and looked up.

Three men advanced toward him. He didn't need anyone to tell him what they were after. The coil of rope around the big man's shoulder said it all. These weren't like the first slave catchers he'd encountered by the creek. Everything about this trio said they were dangerous, from the way they swaggered down the street to the easy way the big man carried his rifle.

But what jarred Zachary the most was the third man, who hung behind the other two, holding the ropes of two red hounds. A black man. Just like Titus had said, even black men worked as slave catchers. Likely because they had no choice.

"I think what we have here is a fugitive," said the shorter man in front.

The big man, as tall as Zachary and maybe twenty pounds heavier, spit to the side. "And look at them clothes he be wearin.' He stole 'em for certain."

"I have stolen nothing, nor am I a slave." Zachary made eye contact with the black man. "I have my freedom papers."

The man looked away.

"And you expect we just gonna take your word on that, boy?" The big man moved to Zachary's right and the shorter one to his left.

"Thee should take his word." The blacksmith emerged from his smithy, stepping into the street with his hammer clenched in one hand. "He is part of our community here and has been for years."

"You tellin' me he be one of you Quakers?"

"Indeed, he is." The barber stepped out of his shop and came forward, ignoring the light rain. "As am I. And I can attest to Zachary's claim. He was freed from bondage many years ago."

Two other Friends moved toward them, both brawny young men, and flanked the slave catchers.

"So thee see, there is no reason for thy presence in our town," the blacksmith said. "We do not allow slavery here, so thee will find none in our midst. 'Twould be best if thee moved on."

"We be lookin' for an escaped slave, a gal about so high." The shorter man held up his hand to the exact height of Lizzy.

But the girl was two days gone, and Titus with her. *Watch over them, Lord.*

The big man pointed a finger at the blacksmith, then at each of the other Friends. "Know this, we gonna find that gal. And any other slave masqueradin' as a freeman on this side of the river." He ended with his finger pointed at Zachary. "I got my eye on you, boy."

There were so many words Zachary wanted to hurl back at him, but he held his tongue. Drawing the man's wrath would not help his situation or safeguard those he sheltered. Better to remain silent, to not draw attention to himself.

The black man raised his eyes again, and in them was something Zachary couldn't quite define. Regret, maybe? Sorrow? Misery? Or a mixture of all of that and something more.

The big man turned and shoved his way past his companions, the shorter man following. The black man with the dogs trailed after.

"Good riddance," the blacksmith said.

The barber shook his head. "I knew there would be trouble when Daniel hired those men off the river."

"What did thee say?" Zachary swiveled to face him.

"'Tis true." One of the younger men confirmed. "He said he could not wait for Harold and me or the others to finish our projects, so he hired a crew off the river to start his buildings."

Anger washed over Zachary like a flame. "Where is he now?"

"At the plot he bought, most likely." The barber pointed south. "Across from the livery stable. I hear tell he is working alongside those he hired."

The men continued the conversation, but Zachary barely heard them as he reached Annabelle and swung into his saddle. He reined the mule around and headed south at a gallop, ignoring the drizzle that was turning into a downpour, the rising wind, and the dark clouds looming over his shoulder.

He didn't slow until the livery stable came into sight.

Daniel Whiteford was easy to spot among the workers. He may have rolled up his sleeves, but his waistcoat and breeches were not a workman's clothing.

Zachary vaulted out of the saddle before Annabelle came to a complete stop, dropping her reins.

"What were thee thinking?" he shouted.

Daniel dug the shovel into the ground, dusted off his hands, and frowned at him. "What are you talking about?"

Zachary pointed to the three men working at different places along a building foundation. "Why did thee hire these strangers and bring them into our community?"

Daniel puffed himself up like a partridge. "What possible business is that of yours?"

He took a step closer and forced the answer from between clenched teeth. "When I get accosted in town by slave catchers, and thee have brought strangers into our midst, 'tis very much my business."

"I did not hire slave catchers." The workers gathered in a knot behind Daniel in support of their employer. "I hired these sailors off a barge."

"Who are they?"

"Men who needed work."

"Men thee know nothing about." Zachary jabbed a finger toward the town. "Thee should have hired from the Friends, people we know and trust."

"Your friends would not work for me."

"They would have if thee would have been patient."

"I do not have the luxury of being patient." Daniel grabbed his hat as a gust of wet wind threatened it. "I have a business to get up and running."

"'Tis a twister!" One of the crew pointed north.

Zachary whirled. A dark funnel moved across the landscape, well north of town, debris spinning around it. "'Tis near Micah's place."

Daniel took off at a run toward the livery stable, his crew following him to the shelter.

Zachary caught up Annabelle's reins. The mule shied and rolled her eyes, not happy with the pelting rain and chaos around her as the work crew headed for shelter. He calmed her enough to climb into the saddle and aim her north.

The wind robbed Daniel of his hat as he thumped his heels against King's sides, but he didn't stop to retrieve it. It was just a hat. What did it matter when his grandson was in danger? And not just his grandson, but Dinah, too, and Gwen's family.

He might have gotten disoriented, the driving rain making it difficult to see, if not for the black man on the mule ahead of him. The man who had just accused him of hiring slave catchers.

Anger burned against the worry tightening his middle. His whole life, he'd been against slavery. He'd lost friends over the issue. His one surviving sister would have nothing to do with him. Her husband owned a tobacco plantation, one of the largest around Greenesville. She hadn't spoken to Daniel in more than a dozen years because of his stance on slavery.

But the man ahead of him had hurled the accusation.

Yet he was also racing to reach Gwen's place. If he got there in time—if *they* got there in time—to avert a disaster, Daniel could forgive the man much. The whirling funnel had retreated into the sky, but the wind continued to drive needle-like raindrops into Daniel's face and exposed forearms.

King, ears pinned to his outstretched neck, galloped through the sloppy footing, splashing water and mud in all directions. Perhaps Lawrence had been right about the old horse having noble blood.

The wind had abated somewhat by the time the man on the mule turned to the right. Daniel would have missed the lane had he been on his own. The landscape looked nothing like his last visit. Trees were uprooted, crops flattened. The place looked scoured. And the cabin—

He blinked the water from his eyes.

The cabin was *gone*.

"Owen! Gwen!" Daniel shouted, spurring King for one last burst of speed, which the old horse found from somewhere inside him. Daniel brought him to a sliding stop beside the mule and tumbled out of the saddle, slipping on the wet grass and grabbing the saddle to keep upright.

"Gwen! Micah!" the black man shouted as he rushed to the wreckage that had been the cabin.

Daniel's heart broke like the solid logs that were tumbled in disarray across what had been the kitchen garden of the humble home. Trees too large for a man to wrap his arms around were twisted, jagged shards stabbing at the heavens.

"Owen?" The name came out half-word and half-sob.

If he'd lost the boy, then he'd lost everything.

"Zachary?" He and the black man both turned toward Micah, coming from behind the barn that remained standing despite the shattered cabin.

The black man ran to greet him, and Daniel followed.

"Where is everyone?" Daniel asked.

"In the root cellar." Micah pointed behind him.

"Is anyone hurt?" asked the black man.

"We got there in time." He looked at Daniel. "Thanks to Dinah. She saw the twister coming and alerted Gwen. Together, they got the children to safety. I saw them running and joined them just before it hit."

The black man bowed his head. "Thank thee, Lord."

"Amen to that." Micah turned to survey his farm. "Those we love are safe. The rest we can rebuild. In time."

"May I see Owen?" Not that Daniel didn't trust him, but he needed the reassurance.

"Indeed." Micah headed for the barn. "I should return and let Gwen know about... About our house."

Two wagons careened down the road, one from each direction.

"I will stay and give the good news that everyone is well," the black man said.

"Thank thee, Zachary."

Daniel filed that name away in his memory. He disliked not knowing people by their names. Names were important for a man of business. But more important than anything was the safety of his grandson.

"Gwen?" Micah called as they approached a doorway encased by an earthen embankment beside the barn.

The door eased open, and Gwen appeared, the little girl on her hip. "Is it safe?"

"Indeed. Thee can bring the children out."

She searched his face. "But?"

"The house is gone."

The hand not supporting the toddler covered her mouth, but didn't hide the words. "Oh, no. Micah, what shall we do?" Then she seemed to notice him. "Daniel?"

"We saw the twister from the work site." He half raised his hands and then let them drop. "I came to offer my help, if needed."

Owen and Dinah squeezed around Gwen. The boy's eyes were huge, and he ran to Micah, wrapping his arms around the man's legs.

Micah scooped him up and hugged him. "We are safe. The Lord protected us." He patted the boy's back. "I have to see to the livestock. Stay with thy mother"—he snapped a glance at Daniel—"and thy grandfather."

"I want to go with thee." The boy buried his face against Micah's neck.

"I know, but I need thee to remain with the others." He lowered the boy and tousled his hair. "For now." He headed toward the first wagon that was pulling into the yard.

Daniel bent to the boy's level. "I am very happy that you are safe. You and Dinah and everyone." His voice cracked on the last word, and he cleared his throat. "I was worried." Which was a huge understatement.

"Me too. Dinah said we had to go underground." Owen pointed to the open door of the root cellar. "But it was dark in there. And scary."

The little girl's face puckered and she began to cry. Dinah held out her arms to the child and took her from Gwen, cooing softly.

"Enough talk of scary." Gwen pinned Owen with a look. "Let us see what we can salvage from the house." For all her bold words, her lips trembled.

"Allow me to help," Daniel said.

She looked at him with troubled blue eyes but managed a shaky smile. "That is very kind of thee."

"Was it not you who told me that kindness is something you learned from the Quakers?"

"Did I?" She started toward the house.

"You did." He fell into step beside her. "I remember it well."

"They are wonderful people. I do not know what I would have done without them. Or how I would have managed."

"Gwen." He stopped, and so did she. "I had made the arrangements with Thomas before I offered you the agreement. I would not have turned you out alone with the babe." At least, he wanted to believe that he wouldn't have.

Her smile turned genuine. "Thee gave me the greatest gift that day, and I do not mean my freedom."

"I know. And during many a sleepless night, I regretted it." He held his hand out to Owen and almost burst with joy when the boy grabbed it and held on. "'Tis my intention to do better going forward." He glanced at the ruin of the cabin. "Including helping thee rebuild."

The second wagon had stopped, and Betsy climbed down and headed for them. "Praise God! Thee are all safe."

Daniel followed Gwen, who was almost running to meet the older woman. He followed, dismayed by the wreckage around them, but overwhelmed by this family, this community, that loved one another so well. And the little hand that held firmly to his.

Chapter 16

B Y THE TIME ZACHARY arrived home that evening, the sky was already darkening under a covering of clouds. The cows gathered outside the barn, creating a racket as he dismounted.

"I know, girls. I am late. Give me a minute." He stripped the saddle from Annabelle and turned her out, then entered the barn. Feeble light shone through the open door onto a figure cowering against a stall door.

"The boy, he said I come here. Said I be safe here."

"Thee are safe here." Zachary kept his tone low and gentle.

The boy's teeth flashed in the light, a grin of relief that held uncertainty. He was younger than Titus, thin and ragged. His skin was lighter, his eyes a medium brown with dark circles under them.

"When was the last time thee had anything to eat?"

The boy shook his head. "I doan remember."

"Do thee know how to milk a cow?"

Another grin. "I do."

"Then stand back." Zachary opened the door to the pasture, and the cows flooded in, each one going to her usual stanchion. Once they were settled, he pointed to a dipper hanging on the wall. "Fill that from that first cow and drink as much as thee like." He shook his finger at the boy. "But not so much thee get sick, understand?"

A mass of curly hair bobbed with the boy's response.

"I must milk the rest, and then we shall eat something more."

Zachary started on the line of cows, keeping an eye on the boy. He limped to the nearest cow and milked enough to fill the dipper once, twice, and then a third time. When he seemed to have gotten his fill, he took up another bucket and finished milking the cow.

"What is thy name?"

"Caleb. Momma said it mean bold."

Bold indeed to be out by himself at his age. Zachary finished his cow and stood. "How old are thee?"

Narrow shoulders lifted and fell, but his hands stayed busy milking. "Nobody ever said."

"Where did thee come from?"

"Near Anglin's Ford in Virginia. Massah lived on a hill overlookin' it."

"Thee said a boy told thee to come here."

"Yessuh, he did."

"Did he tell thee his name?"

"Doan nobody give names."

Zachary moved on to the next cow. "Except thee told me."

The thin shoulders lifted and fell again. "You be Quaker, sayin' thee and all. And the boy, he say you safe."

Maybe Zachary was safe, but that very afternoon he'd been accosted on the street by slave catchers. He felt a good deal less safe than he had when he'd left his farm that morning.

He started milking the next cow in line. "Is thy leg injured?"

"My foot."

"What happened."

"I stepped in a trap."

"How bad is it?"

"Bad enough."

The cows had to be finished first, so Zachary focused on milking.

With Caleb's help, it didn't take long to finish. The boy hadn't been boasting when he'd said he could milk a cow. But as Zachary shooed them out on pasture, Caleb sank back on the stool and leaned against the barn wall.

When Zachary got close, he smelled decaying flesh. He pressed his wrist to the boy's forehead. "I must fetch the doctor."

"No!" Caleb bolted upright and almost toppled into Zachary.

"'Twill be fine. The doctor is a Friend—a Quaker. He can help thee." Zachary pointed to the foot wrapped in rags. "If not, thee might lose that foot."

The boy's eyes rounded and he swayed.

Zachary scooped him up and carried him to the house. It would be best for the boy to be in bed, but with slave catchers in the area, it was too risky. He made up a pallet of blankets and laid Caleb on it. "I will slide thee under the bed. There is just enough room." An adult would never have fit, making it an unlikely place for anyone to search. "'Tis best for thee to remain hidden."

Caleb nodded, his eyelids heavy.

"Sleep now. I will return with the doctor as soon as I can." He slid the pallet under the bed. "Thee are safe here, but should anyone else enter, be still and be silent."

"What be your name?"

"Zachary."

"Thank you, Zachary." The voice was muffled with a yawn but filled with gratitude.

"Sleep."

Annabelle had been running hard already that day, and Zachary didn't want to waste time hitching the team, so he caught Justice and bridled him. The black horse would be nearly impossible to see, full dark having settled and the stars hidden behind clouds. He led the animal to the fence and used it to climb bareback on the tall horse because Annabelle's saddle wouldn't fit the big draft. He tapped his heels, and Justice hopped sideways a few steps. He hadn't been ridden in a long time, and the team never liked being separated.

As if to prove the point, Jubal whinnied his protest from the paddock.

Once they were on the road, Justice settled down, and Zachary urged him into a canter. He didn't move as fast as Annabelle, but each stride covered a lot more ground. Zachary pulled him to a halt in front of Paul's house.

Not a single light shone in the windows.

But doctors were used to being awakened in the night.

Zachary slid off Justice and then knocked on the door and waited.

Paul opened it himself after a few minutes, still tucking in his shirt. "Zachary, what has happened?"

"I need thee at the house."

Paul might have been half asleep, but he nodded without question. "Would thee ask Bran to ready my horse?"

"I will." Zachary led Justice around behind the house to the stable, a light already shining from its window.

"Bran?"

The youth emerged leading Paul's horse. "I figgered someone had come to pull the doc out o' bed again." He smothered a yawn. "Who be hurt or sick?"

"Just someone I... found." He used the same phrase Bran had used when he'd brought Titus to the farm.

Understanding sparked in the young man's eyes. "Titus?"

Zachary shook his head. The less said the better.

"Heard tell there was men in town this mornin'."

"Indeed."

"Could be this person need a place to hide. Could be I know of some safe place 'round here."

"Thank thee, Bran. But 'tis taken care of." Zachary led Justice back around the front of the house, and Bran followed with Paul's horse.

"Might not be safe, this person in your house."

"Thee are right, but there is another place."

Bran grunted. "If you need me..."

"I will let thee know."

A sharp nod was the only answer as Paul came out the door with saddlebags over his shoulder. He tied them behind his saddle and mounted. Zachary put his foot in Bran's cupped hands and accepted his help getting aboard Justice.

Once past the houses, Paul asked, "What is the problem?"

"A boy came to my place tonight. His foot is injured."

"How bad?"

"I did not look at it, but I could smell it."

Even in the dark, the grimace on Paul's light face was easy to see. "I do not like the sound of that."

"And he is fevered. He drank his fill of milk and is sleeping under my bed."

"Under it?" Paul shot him a glance.

"There were men in town today—"

"I heard about that. Nasty business."

They let the horses canter, trusting their night vision.

"Are thee concerned?" Paul asked. "With slave catchers in the area? I heard they stopped thee on the street."

"I would be a fool not to be concerned." He studied the woodlot they passed through but saw nothing out of the ordinary. "But I cannot live in fear."

"Thee take chances, my friend."

By helping others? It was true. And yet, inside Zachary welled a sense of purpose such as he had rarely known. He liked helping others. No, it was more than that.

He'd been *called*.

Daniel stalked from the livery stable to the building site. Isaac was instructing Henry and Tad in starting the brick walls on the foundation they'd built.

Will and Jimmy were nowhere to be found, their belongings missing from the livery. They'd left him short of workers, just as Isaac had warned.

He stopped beside his foreman. "Can you and Henry do this while Tad drives the wagon to bring up more bricks? The brickman says they are ready."

Isaac shook his head. "I need to train 'em both or we will get farther and farther behind your schedule."

"None of you saw the other two sneak out?"

The men kept on their tasks, their silence the only answer he would get.

"Fine. I shall return later." Daniel stomped back to the livery and saddled King, a half-formed idea taking shape.

After the twister two days past, Micah had turned down Daniel's offer to put his family up at the tavern until they could rebuild. The Baldwins had opened their home to them, and Micah and Gwen had readily accepted the help.

It had galled Daniel that he didn't have a home to offer.

Micah's corn had been ruined. Not just flattened, but ripped from the ground. Already the middle of June, it was too late to replant. The man needed money to rebuild and would have no crop to sell.

Daniel mounted and pointed King toward the Baldwins' home.

Micah had a fine pair of draft horses, which Daniel had seen at the farm. They hadn't been hurt in the storm. Now, if the young man's wagon had not taken too much damage, he could be very helpful to Daniel. And perhaps Daniel to him.

He stopped in front of the Baldwins', where Betsy rocked on the porch with Gwen's sleeping daughter on her lap. She held a finger to her lips.

"Is Micah here?" he whispered.

She pointed down the street toward the blacksmith and wheelwright shop.

"At the shop?"

She nodded.

He touched the brim of his hat and clicked to King.

The shop's large double doors were open. Micah crawled from under a wagon as Daniel rode up.

He nodded to the vehicle. "Was it damaged in the storm?"

"Nothing that could not be repaired." Gwen's husband set down a pot of grease. "Were thee looking for me?"

"As a matter of fact, I was." Daniel dismounted. "I would like to hire you."

"I have a farm to put back in order—"

"I understand." Daniel lifted his hand. "I would only need you for a few hours a day. I am willing to pay you a wage as well as rent for the team and wagon."

Micah raised a suspicious brow. "Why do thee need me? Did thee not hire off the river?"

"Indeed." Daniel blew out a breath full of frustration. "Yet two of them snuck off in the night."

"I am sorry to hear it."

"I require someone with a wagon and team to haul bricks from the brickman to my building sites, and someone to fetch my deliveries from Roberts Landing."

"I have a house to rebuild."

Daniel rubbed his jaw. "What if I paid you in bricks?"

That hiked the man's brows even farther. "Bricks?"

"For your new house. I could commission the brickman to make them. And if you work alongside my hired man, Isaac, he will teach you how to use them."

"I have no idea what that many bricks would cost—"

"Neither do I," Daniel lied. He needed the help, of course, but he also wanted to help Micah's family—especially Owen. The man would never accept charity, but he should be snapping at the opportunity of honest work. "I need you, young man. And I think you will agree that a brick house is worth the time you would spend hauling bricks and cargo for me."

Micah rubbed his hand on the seat of his breeches, and then offered it to Daniel. "Deal."

Daniel grasped the firm handshake as Thomas came out of the shop, smiling broadly. "I do believe thee have come to a very agreeable arrangement."

"As do I." Daniel mounted his horse, focusing on Micah again. "Can you start tomorrow morning?"

"I will be there."

Daniel wheeled the old horse around and then turned back. "And bring the boy with you whenever you like. 'Tis never too young to start learning."

Micah glanced at Thomas who nodded his encouragement, then back to Daniel. "I will."

Satisfied, Daniel urged King forward. The clouds parted and a burst of sunshine lit his path. As if the heavens were as happy with the results of this arrangement as Daniel was. His building would continue, and he could help provide the house his grandson deserved to grow up in.

No matter how hard he'd tried, Zachary could not find a way to put the hidden door on the barn by himself. Caleb would have tried to help, but he needed to stay off his foot, and Zachary doubted the boy could hold the door fast while he set the hinges. He simply wasn't strong enough.

But he was improving.

When Paul unwrapped the boy's foot, he had feared he wouldn't be able to save it. The infection—which had caused the putrid smell—had been extensive, but not gangrenous. They had caught it in time. They wouldn't have if Zachary had waited for morning to fetch Paul. It'd been that dire.

Zachary turned Annabelle toward Mark Allen's farm. The young apple trees stretched in straight rows, acres of the cider-producing variety called spitters. Zachary had helped Mark Allen plant them two years past, and this summer, they were starting to take shape, although a crop of apples was still two to four years away. Until then, Mark Allen had planted turnips and peas for yearly crops to sell, and Faye kept a large gaggle of geese.

The noisy fowl honked and hissed as Annabelle approached, but the mule ignored them. She'd been there many times and had learned that a well-placed kick would keep the geese at a distance.

Mark Allen emerged from the barn, wiping his hands on a rag. "Hello, Zachary," he shouted over the geese. "What brings thee this morning?"

Zachary lifted the bag holding the hinges and hasps he'd picked up from the blacksmith. "I have a project on the barn in need of an extra set of hands if thee have time over the next few days."

The younger man glanced at the house. "I could come now, if that would suit thee. This afternoon I planned to start pruning the back orchard."

"'Twould suit me fine. It should take no more than half an hour."

"I will tell Faye and be with thee in a minute." Mark Allen trotted through the geese to the cabin and returned shortly to saddle Jughead.

Once on the road, he asked, "What is this project?"

"As thee already know of the space above my addition, thee know I need a secret door on the outside." He jingled the iron pieces in the bag. "I have the hardware, but I need someone to hold the door in place while I secure it from the inside where it will not show."

"Sounds easy enough."

"'Tis easy, but as thee know, 'tis not without its risks."

"Worry not, my friend. I will keep thy secret."

"I have no worries on that front, I assure thee." Zachary nodded to the wooded roadsides. "But we never know when someone will be watching."

"I heard of the men in town the day of the twister."

"'Twas not pleasant, but not as devastating as what happened to Micah's place. I have not been by to see how they are faring."

"Which is very unlike thee."

Zachary shrugged. He trusted Mark Allen above most, but he still didn't want to tell him anything he didn't need to know about—like Caleb.

"Say nothing," Mark Allen said. "I believe I understand." He chuckled. "We shall have to get used to sharing thee with others. We have been selfish in wishing to keep thee to ourselves."

"How are Micah and Gwen doing?"

"Micah is working for Daniel Whiteford."

"What?" Zachary clenched the reins, and Annabelle sidestepped. He loosened his grip and calmed her. "Why?"

"'Twould seem that some of his river men left him a few nights ago. He needed someone who could drive a wagon and load and unload bricks. He even rented Micah's wagon and team, paying for that and his wages with bricks to rebuild his house."

Daniel was providing for Micah and Gwen? Zachary wanted to deny it. He wanted to believe the worst of the man who owned Dinah. The man who'd once owned Gwen. The man who'd given away his grandson.

But Daniel had also raced into the storm behind Zachary and had pitched in and helped Gwen retrieve belongings from the wreckage. He'd comforted Owen. And now he'd hired Micah.

He was making it difficult for Zachary to dislike him.

Chapter 17

I F IT WEREN'T FOR Daniel's current problem, the load of bricks Micah had just unloaded at the building site would have brought him much satisfaction. But instead, the young man was refusing his request. It was yet another obstacle in Daniel's path.

"Thee need another team of heavy drafts." Micah wiped the sweat from his brow.

Daniel almost swore, something he rarely did, but Owen's bright blue eyes kept the words from his lips. "Lawrence has rented out his team for a full week." Which was Daniel's fault. He shouldn't have told the man that he didn't need the horses once he'd hired Micah. Short-sighted of him, that was what it was—short-sighted. And he hadn't risen to prominence in business by being that way.

"Zachary Brown has a good team, even larger than mine, and younger. His wagon is heavy too. Just what thee need. They could make the haul."

The black man who had accused Daniel of hiring slave catchers. Yet inwardly, he winced, because rumors had leaked that Will and

Jimmy had partnered up with those men. So in a way, albeit premature, Zachary had been right.

"He lives two farms out from my place. Thee cannot miss it. He has the prettiest herd of dairy cows thee could ever see. The best in this part of the frontier, for certain."

"Perhaps you could—"

"Nay." Micah shook his head. "The brickman wants the next load moved yet today, and then I must spend the evening at the farm."

Daniel had to hand it to the young man. He was industrious. After he worked hours for Daniel each day, he returned to the farm to tend a field of cabbage and another of potatoes, both planted after the twister. With those fields, he would feed his family and sell the rest as a cash crop.

Which meant Daniel would have to approach Zachary himself.

There was nothing for it. If he wanted to get the order from Robert Landing to Mount Pleasant, he needed a heavy wagon pulled by heavy drafts. And Isaac needed that order to continue setting the bricks.

"Two places beyond yours, you said?"

"Indeed. Only Mark Allen's place is between us."

Mark Allen, who was married to Gwen's sister, Faye. Daniel was learning how everyone in the community fit together. Slowly, but he was learning.

"Would you like to accompany me, Owen?"

Before the boy could answer, Micah did. "I am sorry, Daniel, truly I am, but Gwen requested that I return him after this load." He bumped Owen's shoulder with his elbow. "I hear a trip to the creek has been promised."

The boy bounced on the wagon's seat. "I am learning how to swim! Grandfather is teaching me. Sally Faye cannot swim because she is not big enough." He poked his chest with his thumb. "I am."

Daniel smiled past the hurt of the boy calling another man grandfather. It shouldn't bother him after all these weeks, especially since it was due to his own actions, but it still did. "Perhaps next time."

Owen nodded, and as Daniel walked away, the boy chattered on about swimming and the creek.

After Micah's wagon rumbled off, Daniel saddled King and headed north of town, past Micah's property where the land had been cleared of the old cabin's wreckage. Had it already been two weeks since the twister? July was only days away. His goal of having his buildings up before the frost hinged on getting his supplies delivered.

And that, it seemed, hinged on a man who despised him.

Soon, a barn flanked by a large pasture dotted with cows came into view. It must be the right place, but something was off. A group of men had gathered near the barn, and Zachary's tall figure was framed in the doorway as if holding them off.

Daniel put his heels to King's sides, and as he neared, his heart sank. Will and Jimmy were among the five men. The others were a black man, one short man, and a man as tall and broad as Zachary.

Daniel pulled the old horse to a stop next to Jimmy. "Is there a problem, gentlemen?"

The big one swung around and eyed Daniel up and down. "What business is it of yours?"

"My business is with Zachary here, not you fellows. I shall wait until you are done." He remained on the horse, which gave him the advantage in height, but had no idea what he'd do if things turned ugly. It was the first time he'd faced slave catchers. Men like Jonas. That thought stiffened his resolve to see them on their way out of Mount Pleasant.

"Listen, mister," the short man said. "You should move along. This don't concern you."

"I know him," Will said. "He hired me off the river. He owns a slave."

The big man gave Daniel another searching look. "That true?"

Though the words tasted vile, he said, "'Tis true. A girl I have hired out to help a young mother." Which was shading the truth but might be enough to quell any brewing unpleasantness.

"Then what sort of business do you have with him?" The big guy jerked a thumb at Zachary.

"I have need of his services, as this community has need of the milk his cows provide. Zachary is a member of the Quakers here, and highly respected."

The big man crossed his arms. "You own a slave, but you support the likes of him being free?"

"I do. Especially when I have need of his services."

"Why don't you just buy another slave?"

"Have you any idea of the cost, man?" Daniel let some mock outrage leak into his voice.

That gave the big man pause.

"He be tellin' the truth," Jimmy said. "Mr. Whiteford is a good man."

Such a good man that Jimmy had deserted him and snuck away in the night, but Daniel held his tongue.

The big man glared at Zachary, then turned back to Daniel. "And you willin' to give your word this one has his papers?"

"Indeed." Daniel shifted on the saddle, striking a pose he hoped would make them think he was about to impart some sage advice. "What is more, this community depends on Zachary. They are Quakers and pacifists, to be sure, but not without powerful connections. How else do you suppose they acquired this choice tract of land?" He let that sink in for a moment. "And being pacifists, they would not get involved in anything illegal. 'Tis against all they stand for."

Will shuffled his feet, not meeting Daniel's eyes. "He be right. Quakers don't hold with no law-breakin'."

The big man asked again, "Your word that there ain't no fugitive slaves hidin' in this town?"

"My word." Daniel confirmed it with a single nod. After all, it was true. He'd been here for weeks and not seen or heard of any.

So much could have gone wrong. So much almost *had* gone wrong, and would have if not for the man standing beside him. Together, Zachary and Daniel stood in front of the barn and watched the slave catchers' dust trail until it disappeared.

"Thank thee, Daniel."

"I am glad I arrived before things became unpleasant."

Zachary barked a laugh without humor. "Unpleasant. That is one way of putting it."

"You know what I meant." Daniel's neck reddened.

"I am not laughing at thee." Zachary faced him. "I am very grateful and more than a little shaken by what might have happened."

"Do you think you will be safe now?"

Out here? All by himself? "Only the Lord knows. If 'tis His will, then they cannot hurt me."

"And if 'tis not His will?"

"Do thee believe in the Lord? Are thee a Christian, Daniel?"

"I am."

"And yet, thee owns another person." Zachary almost bit the words back, but they demanded to be said.

"Slavery is mentioned all through the Bible, but not to condemn it." Daniel's brow furrowed. "In fact, slaves are told to obey their masters. Can you explain why that is to me?"

Zachary shook his head. "'Tis one of the mysteries I wish I understood. But I know—from the depth of my soul—that slavery is wrong."

"So do I. On that, we agree."

"Yet thee question the scriptures."

Daniel gazed out over the landscape. "My father kept slaves and used scripture to justify it. I disappointed him when I did not follow in his footsteps."

"But now thee have."

"No." Daniel expelled the word with force. "I never intended to purchase the girl. I simply could not look the other way when those who were bidding had sinister plans for her. She is but a child. If she were not, I would release her today."

The words were simple and sincere. Honest.

Had Zachary judged this man too harshly? Too hastily? Conviction rolled over him, not unlike the twister that had ravished the land. Who was he to sit in judgment of another?

"I owe thee both my gratitude and an apology. I judged thee without knowing thee."

Daniel gave a soft snort. "You saw me as a threat to your friends, someone who kept one of your people in bondage—and someone who hired slave catchers."

"Indeed. Thee are correct on all charges." Zachary spread his hands and humbled his heart. "I hope thee can forgive me in time."

"Nothing to forgive. Logical assumptions on all counts." Daniel coughed, then rubbed the back of his neck. "The fact is, two of those"—pointed down the road toward where the men had disappeared around a bend—"were men I had hired. They deserted me for that life."

Daniel pounded his fist into his other palm. "I should have listened to advice and waited for the Quaker workers to be available, but I had a schedule to keep. A business to open." He gave Zachary a lopsided smile. "And to tell you the truth, I am glad I hired Isaac. He is a craftsman with those bricks, and a good man, as far as I can tell. So 'twas not all bad."

"Maybe he will settle here, then. I believe brickmaking will be a major industry in Mount Pleasant for many years to come. We have raw materials in abundance."

"I will mention the idea to him."

"Now." Zachary took a deep breath and expelled it. "Let us start anew, shall we? What brings thee to my farm this afternoon?"

"Because two of my workmen have abandoned me, I find myself in need of an employee with a heavy draft team and wagon to bring my supplies from Roberts Landing. I had word that they arrived yesterday."

"I heard Micah is working for thee."

"Indeed. But he also needs to tend his farm. 'Twas he who recommended you. He said your team was young and strong. I should tell you, this load will be very heavy."

Zachary certainly owed Daniel a favor. "I will ask Mark Allen if he can milk the cows for me tomorrow evening and the next morning. If the load is that heavy, I will stay the night in Roberts Landing and bring it back the next day so I do not overtax my horses."

Daniel reached into his coat and pulled out a purse. "I will pay your wage as well as the fee for the room and—"

"Nay." Zachary closed his hand over Daniel's purse. "I will bring thy load at no charge."

"I do not expect anyone to work for me without just compensation." Indignation colored the man's tone. As well it might, since Zachary had accused him of being pro-slavery.

"Not as an employee, Daniel." Zachary paused. "As a friend helping another friend."

"A Friend—as in a Quaker?"

"Just as a friend."

Slowly, as if he wasn't quite sure how to react, Daniel offered his hand. "Then as your friend, I humbly accept."

Zachary grasped the hand and shook it.

But a suspicious sheen glistened in the other man's eyes, enough to suggest that he appreciated the offer of friendship more than the work. "Indeed, well." Daniel tucked his purse away. "I have several more things to see to yet today."

"I will see thee in the morning before I leave for Roberts Landing."

Daniel mounted his horse and headed back toward town.

Once he was out of sight, Zachary entered the barn.

"That was close." Caleb popped up from behind a barrel.

"What are thee doing outside the secret room?"

"Them bad guys rode off, and I wanted to hear what that other fella said. Who is he?"

"Daniel Whiteford."

"He own a slave?"

Zachary sighed. "'Tis a long story."

"I caught the gist of it. Sound like he did that gal a good turn to me."

"That is my understanding now as well." He pulled Annabelle's bridle off its peg on the wall. "I need to ride to Mark Allen's and see if he can—"

"I heard."

"When he is here tomorrow, thee must stay in the secret room."

"Won't be here."

"What?" Zachary paused in reaching for the saddle. "Where will thee be?"

Caleb pointed to his foot, wrapped in a clean bandage, then bounced on it a couple of times. "I be good enough to travel. I be goin' on north."

"Are thee sure? A few more days of rest would be prudent."

"Them slave catchers might leave you Quakers alone—or they might not. But they will see me trussed and sent south at the snap of a finger. I need to get north to where I be safe."

Of course he did. That was the whole purpose of Zachary helping fugitives like Caleb, to get them closer to freedom.

So why did it hurt so much when they left?

Chapter 18

WITH A FINAL HEAVE, Zachary shoved the last crate onto his wagon. It was a good thing, too, for there was not an extra inch of space left. And heavy? Even on the well-packed road from the dock, the metal rims of the tall wooden wheels bit into the earth. It would be a slow journey back to Mount Pleasant the next day.

Instead of adding his weight to the wagon, he unwound the reins from the brake and flicked them across the broad backs of Justice and Jubal. "Get up there, boys."

The sturdy blacks leaned into their harnesses and, with a groan of leather and clank of chains, the wagon moved away from the dock. The horses dug in their hooves, heads down, muscles rippling as they pulled the wagon up the steep incline to the town. As he'd pre-arranged, Zachary parked the wagon behind the tavern and led the horses to the livery stable. He unhitched, curried, let them drink their fill at the water trough, and then tied them in stalls where they could enjoy the shade during the hot day. He scratched the ears of the tavern's dog, a pretty black-and-white female with pups somewhere from the look of her. Micah would want to know about those.

Zachary stepped outside, pulled off his hat, and squinted at the sun. Too late for lunch and too early for dinner, but he'd come prepared to relax for a few hours.

He pulled his fishing pole and basket from under the wagon seat and headed back to the river. He walked downstream from the dock, stepping over fallen trees and pushing through thick brush. The pungency of decaying vegetation swirled in the humidity. Mosquitoes and deer flies buzzed around his hat. But he found what he was looking for, an opening in the brush that led to a pebbled stretch of riverbank overshadowed by a large oak tree. The first rock he turned over provided a plump worm, and within minutes, he rested on the damp earth, back against the tree, watching the line of his fishing pole.

And thinking.

Zachary had awakened to the cows already milked, the milk in the springhouse, and Caleb nowhere to be found. It touched him deeply that the boy had done the morning chores before he left as an expression of his gratitude. It would have been better had he left earlier and traveled at night, but the act of sacrifice proved a lot about the boy's character. He would do well in Canada... if he made it that far.

It was not knowing that ate at Zachary.

Had Tess made it? Or Lizzy?

And where was Titus? Zachary had fought the urge to go after the boy more than once. In his spirit, he felt such unease. Titus was in danger, of that there was no doubt, and yet here Zachary sat... fishing.

The pole jerked. It took almost five minutes to wear the fight out of the fish and bring it to shore. The cloudy eyes and dark back of a walleye broke the water's surface. Zachary waded in to grab the slippery fish, careful of the row of sharp teeth in its gaping mouth. He hefted the walleye, which weighed over eight pounds, and grinned. The tavern keeper's wife would appreciate this addition to her kitchen. Perhaps he could catch a few more.

With the prize fish in his basket, and the lid secured with its leather latch, Zachary settled down again. Without another bite, he was in danger of dozing off when the brush rustled behind him. On instant alert, he pressed back against the tree. Whatever—or whoever—was behind him might not see him if he remained still.

The faint creak of leather said something was after his fish.

Would he find a raccoon, a skunk, or even a bear on the other side of the tree?

He rose silently and turned, keeping close against the tree, and leaned until he could see the basket—and the rawboned man stealing his fish. Haunted eyes met his as the man froze, his grip on the fish nearly squeezing it in two in his dark hands.

"Fear not," Zachary said. "I will not turn thee in."

The man's eyes darted left and right, his empty hand fidgeting with the baggy waist of his breeches that he held up.

"I speak the truth. I am here alone, come only to fish. Thee can have it." He nodded toward the fish. "'Twould seem thee are more hungry than I." He pointed to the man's waist. "Thee seem to have lost weight." Which was an understatement. Although he was likely Zachary's age, he looked like he could pass through the eye of a needle.

"If thee would like, I can start a fire and cook the fish right here."

The man shook his head violently, the whites of his eyes prominent.

"Thee fear the slave catchers?"

A nod.

"I understand. But thee must eat if thee are to have the strength to move on."

Another nod.

Zachary left his pole with the line in the water. If he caught another fish, the man would probably eat it as well. Then he took his tin containing flint and tinder from his pocket, and behind the tree in a screen of brambles, he started a small fire, feeding it with dry pieces of wood the other man handed him as it grew. He pulled his knife from its sheath on his belt, scaled and gutted the fish before skewering it, and then placed it on two flat river rocks next to the fire.

The man's eyes remained glued to the knife.

"Where are thee from?" He almost asked for his name, but thought better of it.

"Virginia, near Richmond."

He'd traveled a long way.

Zachary stood and unbuckled his own belt, then he returned the knife to its sheath and handed both to the man. "Thee will move easier and run faster if thee need not hold up thy breeches."

He stared at the belt, then at Zachary. "I stole your fish. Why you give me your belt?"

"Because thee has more need of it than I."

After a long moment, he took it and fastened it around his waist, but he fumbled to remove the knife. "I cain't take your knife."

Zachary held up a hand to stop him. "I have another, so 'tis no hard loss for me."

That earned him a suspicious squint. "How your massah let you have a knife?"

"I have no master. I am a free man. And thee are now in free territory." Zachary sighed. "But not yet out of danger. There are many here in Ohio territory who would have thee returned to thy master. Thee can trust the Friends—the Quakers—but be wary of others."

"You a Quaker?"

"I am."

"How can a black man be a Quaker?"

That question again. "By believing that the light of Christ is available to all men—and women—black and white and Indian alike." Zachary flipped the fish on its skewer, the side closest to the flames sizzling.

"I doan know nothin' 'bout that."

"When thee finds a place to stop running, I hope thee finds a Quaker community. And if thee does, ask them thy questions. They will help thee find the peace thee are looking for—the Lord's peace." How he wished he had time to explain it all, but evening was approaching, and he was expected at the tavern for supper. If he were not to show up, it could raise questions. It would attract notice. And that might start someone poking around to see where he'd been.

"I must go now." He rose. "When thee have eaten, bury what remains of the fire. I wish thee luck and Godspeed." He gathered his pole and empty basket and ambled back to town.

Why was he finding—Bran's description seemed appropriate—so many fugitive slaves? He'd lived in the area for more than three years, and in all that time, he'd only caught a glimpse of Titus in the past. What had changed?

Bran's bringing Titus to the farm, of course, had started things. Titus had brought Tess, and Lizzy, and sent Caleb. But this man? Had it been just a coincidence?

Zachary didn't believe in coincidences.

Long ago, when he'd lived with Eli, an elder had stood during meeting one Sunday and talked about how the Lord often worked through what people called coincidence. The elder had proclaimed that there was no such thing. He'd said that if people could see the hand of God, they wouldn't label it coincidence. They would label it divine intervention.

Despite the heat and humidity, a shiver worked its way down Zachary's spine.

Was the Lord using him to help these people find their freedom?

He wanted to help them, he was sure of that, but he'd thought it was his idea. Knowing, or at least suspecting, that he was part of a bigger plan, part of the workings of men to achieve the will of God... Well, that was going to take some getting used to.

Yet another delay had Daniel grinding his teeth. Things had been going so well since Zachary had brought the supply order the previous week. Daniel paced the aisleway of the livery as the doctor tended Henry's hand, smashed by a stack of bricks that morning. What would Daniel do if he lost a third worker? Unless...

Perhaps the Quaker builders were close to finishing their projects.

Mark Allen was outside speaking to the doctor's young driver, their backs to Daniel.

He fumbled to remember the boy's name but gave up and approached the doctor's carriage.

"I ain't seen him in weeks, and to tell you the truth, I be more than a mite worriful."

"If all thee have told me is true, then he is a resourceful lad. Possibly as resourceful as thee." There was a deep chuckle. "If he has brought other fugitives out before, he should be able to again."

Daniel stopped out of sight of the two speaking. Fugitives? But—

"Titus knows how to remain unseen," the driver said, "but it be his sister this time. I fear 'twill cloud his judgment."

"Then we must pray for him and his sister, but other than that, there is nothing else we can do."

"Until they come across the river."

"Indeed. Once across the river, we can assist."

So, the Quakers *were* assisting fugitive slaves. And Daniel had given his word to those men that they wouldn't. While it didn't sit well that he'd been proven wrong, at the same time, those men had been slave catchers. No better than... his son.

Oh, Jonas, where did I fail you as a father?

Daniel should make his presence known. He wasn't in the habit of eavesdropping, nor did he approve of it. He stepped around the carriage. "Hello, Mark Allen."

"Daniel." The other man startled. "Have thee met Bran?" He pointed to the youth.

"Indeed." He filed away the name. "He drove me to Micah and Gwen's when I first arrived." Daniel nodded to the boy, then faced Mark Allen. "How fortunate you are here. One of my men was injured this morning."

"Not too badly, I hope."

"The doctor is with him now. I was wondering if the Quakers', pardon me, if the Friends' builders are done with their work or even close to it."

"I am not sure, but I can inquire for thee."

"I would appreciate it. Already I am behind schedule and—"

"Daniel?" The doctor called from the livery.

"I must go, thank you." Daniel hurried to the door.

The doctor leaned against a cane. "'Tis not as badly mangled as I first feared, but he will need to rest and keep it clean and elevated for a week. If 'tis healing well with no infection, that should be it." He wagged a finger. "But no work until the swelling is completely gone or he might be laid up even longer."

"I understand." Daniel dug out his purse. "How much do I owe thee?" The doctor named a reasonable fee, which Daniel handed over. "What happened to your leg?"

A dusky blush covered the other man's face. "'Twould seem I dozed off in the saddle while riding home after sitting up all night with a patient. The next thing I knew, I was on the ground, my horse was departing, and my ankle was quite angry with me."

"Liked to scared us spitless it did, when Storm come thunderin' to the house without him." Bran frowned. "Ought to have let me drive him in the first place."

"Indeed." The doctor limped to the carriage and climbed aboard.

"Next time, I will do exactly that."

"Just be seein' you do." Bran closed the door and climbed onto the high seat. He drove the team away from the livery as if he were an old hand at the reins and not a stripling youth.

A youngster who didn't speak with the Quaker thee and thy. Interesting. And one who knew a fugitive slave and his attempts to free more. Was there more to this quiet Quaker community than met the eye? What they were involved in was dangerous. Not only were the slave catchers all too keen on wreaking havoc, but there were laws—fines and possibly a jail sentence.

What if Micah and Gwen were involved?

Was Owen in danger?

"What are thee thinking, Daniel?"

He startled, having forgotten about Mark Allen, who now rested with his back against the wall of the livery. The younger man straightened and joined him. "Thee have a troubled expression."

Best not to ask questions about the fugitives or who was helping them. Not yet, anyway. He needed more facts. "The boy, Bran, does not speak like a Quaker."

"Ah, that one. He is stubborn, but we are working on it." A fond smile softened Mark Allen's features as he watched the carriage disappear behind some buildings. Then he faced Daniel again. "And if thee are intent on settling here, we will be working on thee as well."

Memories of long Sunday mornings in their church box nudged him, Daniel's mind more on the business than the sermon, nudged him. Margaret making sure the children behaved. All of them dressed in their Sunday best. Smiling and shaking hands all the way out the door when they were finished, eager to get home to a fine dinner.

He believed in God, but not so much in church. It hadn't done much for him in the past. But maybe that had been more his fault than the minister's—a thought that left him more than a little uncomfortable. And then there was Owen. If being raised a Quaker ensured that he'd never turn out like Jonas...

"You might have less work to do than you know." He gripped the young man's shoulder before heading into the livery.

"I will check on the builders for thee."

Daniel raised a hand to signal that he'd heard as he reached for his saddle. The building could wait. He needed to speak with Micah. He needed to know that his grandson was not in any danger from the unlawful activity he'd just discovered.

Chapter 19

J ULY'S HEAT ENVELOPED THE land, but Zachary was cool in the spring-house. Two huge willows shaded the building, and the spring that bubbled up into it, the excess water released by a pipe out the side, kept the stone structure at the perfect temperature for storing milk and making butter and cheese. This plot of land had been chosen for its spring, a necessity for a good dairy farm. Zachary had finished his deliveries early, before the intense heat of the day, and now could enjoy the more relaxing work of turning cream into the sharp cheese his customers enjoyed.

It was lonely work.

Where was Titus? He'd been gone for weeks.

And why hadn't Zachary found any more escaped slaves? After the near epiphany at Roberts Landing, he'd assumed he'd be helping scores of people fleeing north. But his secret room had remained empty since Caleb's departure. He only checked it after dark when there was no chance anyone would see him climb the back wall of the barn and lift the secret entrance. Nothing had been disturbed, not the blankets or the stack of clothing he'd left in the chest he'd built to keep the mice out of them.

Maybe it was too secret. Only Titus and Caleb knew about it, and Caleb had gone north, so he wouldn't share that information with anyone. That left only Titus, wherever he was. And Mark Allen, but who would he tell?

Surely, if the Lord intended Zachary to help, He would bring people to the farm.

Annabelle brayed long and loud from the pasture. She was better than any guard dog, announcing visitors without scaring them away. He gave the cheese press a final turn, then wiped his hands clean and stepped out into the glaring sun.

Paul's carriage pulled up in front of the house.

"Hello!" Zachary waved and headed in that direction.

Bran climbed down and opened the carriage door to help Paul out.

"What has happened to thee?" Zachary rushed forward.

"'Tis nothing but a sprained ankle," Paul said.

"Same as he would tell anyone else to stay off of for a week." Bran's tone and crossed arms said what he thought about that.

"Physician, heal thyself?" Zachary grinned at Paul and got a chuckle in return.

"I suppose thee could say that, but there were two emergencies that required my attention." Paul lowered his voice. "And one needs thy help."

"Come into the house."

"Tie the team, Bran, and join us," Paul said.

Zachary brought cool cider from the root cellar and poured three cups, then handed them around. "What can I do for thee?"

"'Twould seem that Bran has found another in need of a place to recover for a few days."

"Paul set him to rights, but he needs to sleep and eat." Bran shrugged. "Maybe eat a lot."

"A man then?"

"Just about." Paul took a long drink of his cider. "I would guess maybe seventeen, and Bran is right. What he needs the most is food."

"My cows are producing enough to share, and the kitchen garden too. 'Twill be no hardship to see him fed well."

"Thee are a blessing, my friend." Paul's brow creased. "But after the men accosted thee in town, I hesitate to ask thee to house him here."

"Worry not. I know the consequences of my actions—probably better than thee—but I feel led to do this. 'Tis more than a wish, I feel 'tis a calling."

Silence stretched between them while Paul considered his words.

"I don't understand," Bran said. "What is a calling?"

"'Tis when thee know that the Lord is calling thee to do something." Zachary chose his words with care, because the boy had yet to join them, even after three years living among them. Nothing would please him more than to welcome Bran into the Society of Friends. "Sometimes, 'tis a single thing He would have thee to do. Or it could be something short-term like a journey or season. And sometimes 'tis a life calling, a vocation."

Bran scratched his head. "You think God is tellin' you to help them slaves?"

"I do."

"How do you know?"

Zachary pressed his fist to his chest. "Because I feel it in here. Because the light of Christ lives inside of me. He speaks to me, not in words, but by something deeper. More intimate." Zachary shook his head. "I wish I could explain it to thee better, but 'tis something thee must experience. And thee cannot experience it until thee accepts Jesus for who He is."

Paul remained silent. Perhaps he'd already had similar words with the young man. It was like that with many people. They needed to hear about Christ from many different sources before they were ready to accept Him as their Lord.

"Do you think...?" Bran's words trailed off, and he looked out the window.

"Think what?" Zachary asked.

Troubled gray eyes met his. "You think God be usin' me?"

Oh, Lord, give me the right words. "I think the Lord uses all of us to accomplish His will. But some, we know from the scriptures, are set apart. 'Tis a promise of sorts, like with the prophets."

"But their lives was hard," Bran said.

"The Lord never said He would make our lives easy. And if thee think about it, how often is the easy thing the satisfying thing?" Zachary asked.

Bran crossed his arms and leaned back in his chair, eyes on the floor.

"If thee are called to do this, then God bless thy efforts." Paul rose. "We will bring him by after dark. Bran has him in a safe place for now with a hamper of Bridget's best biscuits and ham. Come Bran, we have another stop to make, and then I believe I shall get off this ankle for the remainder of the day."

"Wise counsel, indeed." Zachary chuckled.

Bran said nothing more as he helped Paul into the carriage and climbed onto the seat. He gave Zachary a long look that ended in a nod and then clicked to the horses.

Had Zachary said enough? Had he chosen the right words? He hoped so, but only time would tell.

Until then, he had another guest to prepare for.

Of all the days for Micah to be off harvesting cabbages.

Daniel urged King for more speed. Even now, his grandson could be in danger.

His initial alarm from overhearing Mark Allen and Bran at the stable was churning into anger.

Anger that Owen might be in danger. Anger that Daniel's building project was taking too long. And anger that he seemed to have little to no control over any of it.

Deep down, a lingering anger at his children for their inexcusable behaviors.

And that Margaret had died and left him all alone.

Except for Owen. And now he must make sure that Owen was safe.

The horse's hoofbeats pounded to the cadence of *keep Owen safe, keep Owen safe*.

Micah's farm came into view. His team was hitched to the wagon, and he and Gwen were bent over in the field cutting cabbages and setting them in the wagon's bed.

Where was Owen?

The already simmering anger exploded.

Pulling King to a stop so suddenly that the old horse reared, Daniel half-fell and half-dismounted, then dropped the reins and stalked toward Micah.

"Daniel, what is wrong?" Alarm colored Gwen's voice.

"Where is my grandson?"

"What has happened?" Micah moved in front of Gwen, blocking her from Daniel's view.

"Where is he?"

Micah planted his feet, one hand clenching the harvest knife and the other balled into a fist. "At the creek with Dinah. Now tell me what this is about."

"You left my grandson alone with a slave when there are slave catchers in the area?" Daniel shook with the intensity of his emotions. "How can you be so irresponsible?"

"Now, wait a moment—"

"I will not wait. Only today I learned that people in this town—Quakers—are assisting the runaway slaves. What happened to your pacifist ideals?" Daniel practically shouted the question.

"Daniel." Gwen stepped around her husband and got between him and Daniel. "We are pacifists. We do not fight." She glared at Micah, then turned back to him. "But that does not stop us from helping those in need."

"So you admit to helping runaway slaves, to breaking the law?"

"Now see here—" Micah stopped when Gwen pressed her hand to his chest.

"We have not," Gwen said. "For we have not had the opportunity. But should one such as Dinah come to our door, they would not be turned away."

"That is against the law. You could be arrested, fined"—he jabbed a finger at Micah—"even jailed. And then what would happen to your wife and children? To Owen?"

Micah's face was red with fury.

Gwen spoke before her husband could. "Thee are angry over something that has not happened and might never happen." Gwen stayed firmly between them. "'Tis time to step back and talk about this calmly."

"Calmly? While my grandson is in danger?"

Micah took a step closer, almost squeezing Gwen between them. "*My son* is not in danger. He is at the creek with Dinah and Sally Faye."

"And I expect we shall see them shortly with all this shouting," Gwen said. "Let us speak respectfully to each other before they arrive. I do not wish the children to be upset."

As though summoned by her words, the children came through the tree that lined the creek.

"I will lower my voice, but heed my words." Daniel retreated a few paces. "If Owen is in any danger, I will come and take him away."

"Thee have no right." Micah advanced into the space Daniel had opened, ignoring his wife's tug on his arm. "Thee gave that up when thee gave *him* up. When thee cast him *away*."

Each word hit like a blow from a hammer.

"Please," Gwen pleaded, "both of thee, not in front of the children."

And she was right. Even from across the field, Owen's round eyes and pale face were plain as he clutched Dinah's hand.

"Do you swear to me"—he lowered his voice—"both of you, that you have not shielded any runaways?"

"We have not," Gwen answered.

"I will tell thee this, and one time only." Micah's voice was hushed but menacing. "My son's safety means more to me than it ever could to thee—the man who gave him away. Never question that again. Never question my ability to keep my family safe."

"Please, Daniel." Gwen's blue eyes held no censure—only the pleading of a mother trying to prevent distress to her children. "If thee cannot let go of thy anger, please leave before the children arrive. 'Twould do thee no favor to make a reason for Owen to be frightened of thee."

Micah's rigid stance, the way he gripped the knife, the fierceness in his eyes that held nothing of a pacifist, was the reaction of a man willing to fight for and protect his children.

The reaction of a father.

Owen's *father*. Proven now in front of Daniel's eyes.

The anger drained from Daniel, and he bowed his head, resting his forehead on his hand. "What have I done?" He'd panicked. Assumed the worst. Not even given these good people a chance to defend themselves. Shame washed over him.

Gwen's fingers wrapped around his forearm. "Thee imagined a danger to someone thee love, and thee reacted in haste."

He glanced up to her gentle smile.

"I did not imagine it. I have seen the slave catchers. Today I overheard two of the town's people discussing helping fugitives." He pulled his hand down his face. "And I let fear push me to the wrong conclusions. I hope you can accept my apology."

Micah slid the knife into its sheath at his belt and crossed his arms. "Gwen spoke the truth. We know nothing of anyone assisting the fugitives, but I can see how this would frighten thee."

"You are both gracious."

"Nay, Daniel." Gwen's smile was genuine and lovely. "We can offer thee grace because grace has been given to us."

"Papa!" Owen broke from Dinah's hand and rushed to Micah's side. "What happened?"

Micah swung the boy high and settled him on his hip. "Nothing to worry thee, my little man."

Owen looked at Gwen.

"'Tis true. Just something troublesome in town, but it does not concern us."

Then he looked at Daniel, seeking reassurance. How good it felt to be included in this little family—something he'd almost ruined. "Your parents are correct. 'Tis nothing for you to worry over."

The broad grin he received in answer was only topped by the little arms that reached for him. Daniel's heart nearly burst with love—and relief—as he took the boy in his arms.

Zachary doused the lantern and then opened his door.

Bran stood in the shadows with a taller shadow behind him. "His name be—"

Zachary raised a hand to stop Bran. "'Tis better if we know not. That is one thing Titus drilled into me."

The young man gave a sheepish look. "Me too. I should have remembered."

Zachary turned his attention to the living scarecrow behind the young man. "Welcome. I am glad thee are here. I will return the favor of not sharing my name."

"You a Quaker?" Disbelief was thick in the man's deep voice.

Zachary suppressed the sigh that threatened and offered a smile.

"The Friends are open to all who follow Christ."

"Even me." Bran shrugged. "I ain't there yet, but I can see the light."
Thank Thee, Lord!

"Let me show thee the secret room." Zachary led the way through
the darkness. "'Tis a bit awkward to get to, but that makes it a good
hiding place. Inside, thee will find a trunk filled with clothing. If thee
needs something, please, take it. There is also a pail of fresh water
and a slop bucket with a lid. I will send Bran up with enough food to
see thee through until tomorrow night. Stay in the room while the sun
shines. Rest and regain thy strength before leaving, no matter how long
thee need."

"How can I ever repay you?" There was a raspy quality to the man's
words that proved their sincerity.

"By reaching freedom. I am only sorry thee must travel so far to find
it."

The man ducked his head. "I believe in God, too, the God of the
Bible. If He wants me free, ain't nobody gonna stop me."

Zachary paused and faced the man.

"And if He allows thee to be captured?"

"I reckon if I be captured, that be His will too, and I gotta live with
it." He snapped his head up with eyes that were clear and determined.
"But I had to try. I had to give it my best effort."

"I am proud to help thee." Zachary swallowed the lump in his throat.
"Just as someone once helped me."

"If I get free, I gonna be helpin' others too."

"I am glad to hear it. I think, if enough of us work together, we can
change this country."

"Amen," said Bran.

"Show him how to climb the wall, then come to the house for the
food," Zachary told Bran before facing the man again. "Rest easy. Thee
are safe here."

"Bless you, suh."

He wasn't used to being called sir, Friends didn't use such titles,
and he'd never been treated as an equal, much less a superior, in his
former life, but the respect in the other man's eyes was unmistakable,
so Zachary didn't correct him. And it felt good to hear it. He'd have
to repent of that bit of pride during his evening prayers, but for the
moment, he let himself savor it, knowing he'd been able to help this

man.

Knowing he was doing what he was meant to do.

Chapter 20

"**B**ACK, JUSTICE. BACK, JUBAL." Zachary urged his team until they had squared the wagon with the dock. Daniel had hired him to fetch another load of supplies because Micah hadn't been able to fit everything on his wagon earlier in the week.

The skinny man had left the secret room after a five-day stay, so it suited Zachary to come.

Since it was a partial load, he'd stopped by several places to see if anyone else needed goods brought back from Roberts Landing. He had lists from Faye, Betsy, and Bridget to fill. It would be helpful once Daniel opened his business. They wouldn't need to make the trek to the river for supplies the mercantile didn't have room to stock.

It took him half an hour to load the crates of supplies. With the wagon half full, the team had no trouble pulling it up the incline. Zachary parked and did his shopping, then stopped at the tavern for lunch before returning to Mount Pleasant.

He entered by the back door, which opened directly into the kitchen.

"Zachary!" Mary, the tavern keeper's wife, turned from the hearth, surprise lifting her brows under her ruffled cap. "'Tis good to see you back so soon."

"'Tis good to see thee as well."

"Are you hungry?"

"Even if I were not, the aroma from that pot would make me so." Mary was one of the best cooks in the territory, and he never missed having a meal there, even if he was restricted to eating in the kitchen. Not that Mary or her husband would turn him away from a table out front, but their regular customers were a split between those against slavery and those for it. Zachary ate in the kitchen to prevent any unpleasantness from coming to the tavern owners.

"Sit yourself down. I'll bring you a bowl." She bustled back to the stove to fetch his meal when a series of yips and the scrabbling of toenails announced the arrival of five black-and-white pups. "Nathaniel!" she yelled through the door now open to what must be their living quarters. "Come get these animals out of my kitchen!"

A tow-headed boy appeared. "Sorry, Ma."

"Child, you need to find homes for these pups."

"Aw, but..."

"They are underfoot and eating us out of house and home."

Zachary knelt on the floor and one of the pups rushed to him, body wriggling like a worm on a hook, pink tongue washing his hands. Its face was split right down the middle, half white and half black. "How much for this one?" He looked up at Mary.

"That be the only female in the litter. My husband was hoping to get a dollar for her."

Daniel had insisted on paying Zachary for this delivery, so he fished the money from his pocket. "Nathaniel, could you spare a short length of rope so I can tie her in the wagon?"

The boy nodded, then herded the rest of the pups away.

Zachary ate his stew with one hand and held the squirming pup with the other. He left a small amount in the bottom of the bowl and set it and the pup on the floor. She'd need something in her stomach for the trip home.

He fashioned a tether from the rope the boy had brought him, then dug in his pocket to pay for the meal, but Mary waved it away.

"You do me a service, taking that pup off our hands. The stew is on the house."

He thanked her and stepped out into a drizzling rain, glad that he'd brought an oiled tarp and had wrapped the ladies' purchases in it.

"I hope thee enjoys getting wet, little one." He climbed onto the seat, tied the pup's tether to the brake handle, then gathered the reins. "Hup, boys. Take us home."

The road remained firm, having been baked solid under the summer sun. The pup curled herself under the seat and out of the worst of the drizzle. Zachary pulled his hat low over his eyes. Getting wet wasn't too bad. At least it brought some relief from the heat.

Had the skinny man found a dry place to wait out the day?

Zachary took a deep breath and blew it out. He'd done what he could. After that, those running for their freedom were beyond his help. He needed to learn to let them go. In an odd way, it was easier this time. Perhaps because he didn't know the man's name. Or maybe because he was a man, not a child or a woman. Pondering such thoughts occupied the first hour of the journey.

"Zachary!"

The call came from a voice he knew well. He hauled back on the reins, searching the grove of trees the road cut through, heartbeat racing.

A floppy hat in a tangle of brambles was his first glimpse, and then Titus, bent nearly double, crawled out after it.

"Titus, thee are a sight for sore eyes."

But the boy didn't smile. "I need your help."

Zachary set the brake, jumped to the ground, and rushing to Titus. "What is wrong? Are thee injured?"

"Not me." Titus turned back to the brambles. "Come on out."

Another boy, younger than Titus, crawled out. His left arm was wrapped in moss and hung at an unnatural angle. His dark face was lined with pain, and his eyes were cloudy. How had the boy made it this far?

"Help me get him in the wagon."

Titus pulled on his sleeve. "You should know, was a dog what done this, and they ain't far behind us."

"The rain should help dissipate the smell." Zachary tried to remember what he'd heard about tracking dogs.

The puppy whined from the wagon.

Would the dogs pick up her scent and follow it instead of the boy? It was worth a try. "Titus, untie the pup and give me her rope. Then drive the wagon forward, slowly, while I carry the boy and let the pup walk beside us. I shall move back and forth across the road several times to make the trackers think the dogs are confused."

Titus scrambled onto the wagon, while Zachary knelt by the boy. "'Tis going to hurt when I lift thee, but do thy best not to cry out."

Dark curls bobbed in reply.

As gently as he could, he lifted. The boy swung his good arm around Zachary's neck.

"Okay, Titus, drive on—slowly." Zachary waited for the wagon to pass, then tugged on the pup's tether. "Come on, girl. Let us confuse the beasts behind us." And he didn't mean just the canines.

He crisscrossed the road three times, then asked the boy, "Do thee think thee could ride on my shoulders?"

He got another nod, so he grasped the boy's waist and settled him higher, leaving the pup to walk a bit more.

Before they left the grove and the road entered open countryside, he told Titus, "Stop the wagon." Then he lowered the boy onto the bed behind the seat where the oilcloth kept his purchases dry. "Slide under the tarp and keep out of sight."

Then he turned to Titus. "Drive forward but stop before leaving the trees." He tugged on the pup's tether and had her cross the road two more times, then he walked her deeper into the woods where he lifted her to his shoulders, getting his face thoroughly washed by her tongue, and returned to the road and his wagon. It was the best he could think to do to confuse the hounds.

Please, Lord, let it be enough.

As he climbed to the seat, he ordered Titus to join the boy under the tarp, tied the pup again, and lifted the reins as the heavens opened wide. Water poured as if from an upended bucket.

Thank Thee, Lord.

What his puny efforts couldn't hide, the rain would wash away.

But there were slave catchers out there.

Zachary didn't pull in a full breath until the buildings of Mount Pleasant came into view. The downpour had settled back to a steady drizzle. Instinct urged him to go straight to Paul's house, but caution said not to do anything to draw attention. So he headed to the building site. Daniel and two of his workers emerged from the livery to help unload.

"All thy supplies are in the crates," Zachary said as he climbed from the seat. "Do not disturb the tarp. I have purchases for the ladies under that keeping dry."

"Thank you for doing this." Daniel pulled up the collar of his coat. "'Tisn't the best weather in which to travel."

"'Twasn't a problem. Oh, I have something else for thee." Zachary untied the pup and handed it to Daniel. "I thought thee might like to be the one to deliver her to Owen."

The older man took the wet pup and let it lick his face, earning a wide smile. "He will be so pleased. 'Tis a girl dog?"

"Indeed. The only one of the litter."

"What do I owe thee?" Daniel asked, but couldn't seem to take his eyes off her.

"A dollar."

"And worth every penny of it." Daniel fumbled to get his purse out of his wet waistcoat while the pup wiggled and squirmed. "She is a darling thing." He handed over the money. "Owen will love her."

"I thought the same."

Pleasantries out of the way and the wagon unloaded, he turned the team to Thomas and Betsy's to deliver his purchases there, then to Paul's house with the things Bridget had requested. She rushed out of the house to get them, all smiles.

"'Tis perfect timing. I can use some of this for supper. Thank thee, Zachary."

"Happy to oblige." He pulled the last package out from under the tarp, ignoring the hand that pushed it toward him. "Would thee ask Paul to stop by the farm?"

"Are thee ailing?" Concern crinkled her brow.

"'Tis a minor thing, but a long ride on this wagon has... brought it to light."

She pressed her fingers over her mouth. "I shall ask no more questions."

"'Tisn't the type of condition one wishes to discuss." He shrugged as if embarrassed.

"I'm sure 'tis not." She headed for the house but called over her shoulder. "I will send him out directly when he returns."

Better she believe he had a boil on his backside than to make her worry unnecessarily. In keeping with the ruse, he made a show of settling himself on the seat before clicking to the team. Knowing they were close to home, they stepped out smartly.

How easily the half-truths and now an outright lie had slipped from his tongue. If he were truly honoring God's call on his life, shouldn't he be able to do it without deceit?

Rahab.

Zachary didn't hear the word, but he felt it in his spirit. Rahab the harlot had lied to protect the spies of Israel in their time of need. And she was in the lineage of Christ. Not that Zachary would ever be anything like that.

But it gave him a measure of comfort.

With it too wet to work, Daniel saddled King. He mounted with the pup secured under one arm and covered by his coat. The pup snuggled close and fell asleep. She must be exhausted after her long journey. Daniel grinned and clicked to get King moving. How happy his grandson would be to get such a fine animal with obvious collie breeding. The weather would probably have kept Gwen and the children at the Baldwins' house, so he reined King in that direction. Clouds still hung heavy above, but the rain had finally dried up.

He tried not to begrudge the delay in the brickwork. The farmers needed the rain, and they all needed the farmers' crops. But it was hard when he wished to be settled in the business.

He pushed aside all thoughts of industry when he turned the corner and spied Owen on the Baldwins' front porch. He was seated next to Dinah, feet swinging from the bench. When he saw Daniel, he hopped down and waved.

"Grandfather!"

Daniel's heart swelled at the word and the note of excitement it carried. It'd been four months since he sold everything and began his move to the northwest. Months of frustration. But the joy of hearing his grandson eagerly call to him erased all that.

"Is your mother in the house?" he asked. After all, he couldn't give the boy a puppy without her permission.

Owen nodded.

"Run and fetch her for me. Tell her 'tis important."

He scampered inside.

Daniel dismounted while keeping the sleeping puppy concealed. "How are you doing, Dinah?"

"Jus' fine, Mr. Whiteford." She balanced a bowl in her lap while snapping beans from a bucket beside her on the bench.

"Everyone is treating you kindly?"

"Yessuh."

"Is there anything you need?"

She lowered her face but peeked up at him. "I could use some cloth for another apron. It be a chore, keepin' this one clean every day."

"I will send some straightaway."

Dinah flashed him a brilliant grin. It was so easy to please her, and it pleased him to do so. Had he treated Jonas and Constance so kindly? Or had he been too wrapped up in his business to notice them as he should have?

Gwen appeared in the doorway, breaking off his thoughts. Owen clung to her hand on one side and little Sally Faye on the other, while the bulge of her apron said the next child wasn't too far off. "Daniel, are thee looking for Micah?"

"May I have a word with you without the children?"

She told the children to wait inside, then closed the door and approached. "Has something happened?"

"Not at all." He smiled to put her at ease. "I did not mean to alarm you, but I need your permission to gift Owen with this." He opened his coat enough for her to see the sleeping pup.

"Oh, Daniel." Gwen's smile removed all traces of worry. "What a precious puppy. Owen will be thrilled."

"Then I have your permission to give it to him?"

She cocked her head at him. "Thank thee for asking."

He cleared his throat. "Well, you are his mother. 'Twas I who made sure of that. So 'tis only right and proper that you approve the gift." And he meant it. She was Owen's mother in every way that mattered. In every way that Constance never could have been. The pup was as much an olive branch to her and Micah as it was a gift for Owen.

"Thank thee for that, as well." She turned to the house. "Come out,

Owen and Sally Faye."

The words had barely left her lips before the boy barreled out the door and raced to them. The girl clung to the doorway. "Can thee stay for dinner, Grandfather? Betsy said I could ask."

"Maybe another time." Betsy may have given her consent, but it would have been grudgingly. That one had still not warmed up to him.

Owen pulled a face, but Daniel knelt beside him. "And you will be too busy to visit with me."

His blond hair flew as he shook his head. "I am not busy."

"Because you have not seen her yet."

"Who?"

Daniel opened his coat and the pup stirred awake, mouth gaping in a huge yawn, pink tongue lolling out to curl at the end.

"A puppy!"

Gwen smiled at him as he handed the fuzzy black-and-white bundle to Owen. Soon, the air was filled with Owen, Sally Faye, and Dinah's giggles.

The pup hardly knew where to lick next.

And Daniel couldn't have been happier.

Chapter 21

Z ACHARY STEELED HIMSELF FOR what Paul was about to say. The doctor's grim expression warned him he wasn't going to like it. He handed the doctor a cup of cider and joined him at the table.

"I did my best, but I cannot guarantee I saved his arm." Paul took a long drink, then cradled the cup in his hands. "I will return to check on him in the morning, and probably every day for a while. I will come at different times and from different directions so not to draw attention."

"So he could still lose that arm?"

"Indeed. 'Twould not surprise me in the least. The damage done..." He frowned into the cider as if it had sprouted thistles, then up at Zachary. "How can any man allow such a thing to happen to a boy? Just a child?"

Zachary looked away, forcing himself to face long-buried memories. Memories he'd worked hard to unremember. Painful memories. Paul waited, as if he understood. He couldn't, of course. Not really. Nobody—white or black—who hadn't lived as a slave could truly understand.

"They do not see a boy or a child when they look at him. They see a thing to be owned and used or sold if they wish. A beast—not a person. Not a human being." The memory that hurt the most shattered his heart all over again. "When my oldest brother tried to run, they caught him. They whipped him. And then..." He rubbed his sweaty palms on his breeches and swallowed the bile inching up his throat.

"Go on." Paul's voice was a murmur of compassion.

"They cut the tendons in the back of his legs so he could not run again."

Paul set his cup aside and dropped his face into his hands. "That is the most horrendous thing I have ever heard of."

"It might have been—if they had stopped there."

Paul's head snapped up, mouth open.

"Then the master sold him. Pulled him from our sobbing mother's arms, still bleeding from the lashes as well as his legs."

"And that is..."—Paul seemed to flounder for the right words—"the most barbaric thing I have ever heard. Did thee ever see him again?"

Zachary shook his head. "We know not if he survived, or if he bled to death on the way to the sale."

"How old were thee when this happened?"

"Five." Barely old enough to remember, and as hard as he'd tried not to, the images, sounds, and smells came rolling back. He didn't tell Paul the rest, about how his father had also been whipped for trying to protect his son. Whipped until the blood ran from his back and he couldn't stand. Then he was left to lie in the dirt under a scorching sun until he could crawl to the slaves' quarters, nobody allowed to help him.

He didn't tell how his mother had grieved for months, years. If she still lived, she probably still grieved for her son.

"I cannot imagine how thee survived such a traumatic event at such a tender age."

"I had no choice. None of us did. 'Tis what it means to be a slave."

"How thee must have hated the man who ordered that done."

"And the man who did it, the overseer." Zachary grimaced at the bitter thoughts of that one. "I had to learn to forgive them as Christ forgave me."

Paul closed his eyes and drew in a deep breath, then released it and looked at Zachary again. "I know not if I could have done it."

"With His help, thee could have." It had taken years of tutelage under the very patient Eli. Zachary had finally come to grips with his own sin—which he still considered minor in comparison to his master's—and knew that he had to forgive even his old master and overseer if he was committed to the One who had forgiven him. And since that day, he'd done his best to bury the memories.

But maybe it was time to unbury them. Maybe it was time to tell his friends about the horrors. And maybe, if he did, they would step into the breach and help the fugitives fleeing slavery for the freedom the Friends took for granted. It would mean dredging up more pain, but strangely, speaking of it to Paul hadn't left him shaking and angry. It hadn't reared all the old hatred and thirst for vengeance. Instead, he felt as if his friend now shouldered some of the burden.

Maybe he was ready.

Is this my next assignment, Lord?

It was Sunday afternoon and Daniel hadn't been to see Owen since he'd delivered the puppy five days prior. Not that he hadn't wanted to go, but being short-handed, he'd been working from sunup to sundown right beside Isaac. At first, he'd found it hard to take directions from the other man, since he was used to being the one giving orders. But he didn't know bricks and Isaac did.

Daniel rotated his aching shoulders. The physical work was tiring, but his breeches were fitting looser and his waistcoat buttoned easier. Other than the muscle aches, he felt better than he had in years. Perhaps he ought to keep doing more physical labor, even after the business was up and running.

He hefted the saddle onto King's back and cinched it, then bridled the old horse and led him out of the livery. It was an overcast day with a refreshing breeze. Owen and the puppy would enjoy a long walk along the creek. They could take off their shoes and cool their feet in the spring-fed waters.

Micah would not be working, it being the Lord's Day, but he'd mentioned they would be at the farm for the weekend, so Daniel started King down the road leading in that direction. When he turned into the farm's lane, his tow-headed grandson ran toward him, the black-and-white puppy at his heels.

"Grandfather!"

Daniel stopped King, and the steady old horse made no fuss over the puppy gamboling around its hooves. "Would you like a ride back?"

"Yes, please." Owen raised his arms, and Daniel lifted him and settled him on his lap while the puppy yapped its dismay at being left behind.

Daniel nudged King forward. "What did you name your puppy?"

"I wanted to name her Rock because I like rocks, but Momma said that was a boy's name."

He hid his amusement because the boy was so serious. "I think your mother is correct."

"So I named her Blossom because Momma likes flowers when they blossom."

"Blossom is a fine name, one she can be proud of."

Owen beamed. "I think so."

Gwen was cooking over a fire near the wagon and waved them over. "Greetings, Daniel. Will thee share dinner with us?"

"I would love to." He lowered Owen to the ground and then dismounted. "I confess I came prepared to contribute, in hopes I would be invited." He retrieved a linen cloth from his saddlebag and handed it to Gwen. She peeled back the fabric and exposed two long loaves of bread. "Eliza baked them yesterday."

"Thank thee. They will go perfectly with the fish chowder."

Micah approached, Sally Faye riding on his shoulders. "Will she miss them?" He pointed to the bread.

Daniel shot him a sharp look. After all, he would never steal, but the grin on Micah's face had him laughing along with the joke.

The afternoon passed all too quickly until evening darkened the edges and the children had been tucked away under blankets spread beneath the wagon. He'd come to cherish days like this already. Mounting King and turning for town, he envisioned many more. And not just with Owen. He'd enjoyed the time spent with Micah and Gwen as well. And Dinah, who had entertained Sally Faye and helped Gwen with the dinner. The slave girl had blossomed under Gwen's care.

He smiled at the word that matched the puppy's name.

"You there!"

The shout jerked him from his happy thoughts.

It was the same group of men who had been at Zachary's farm weeks ago. All except Jimmy. Good. Maybe the young man had smartened up and left the disgraceful work. But Will was still with them.

"What do you want?" He brought King to a stop.

"You were the one who told us these Quakers would not assist slaves, right?" said the big guy.

"I said that, yes." And he'd believed it. But now things were different. Now he knew the truth.

"We followed a boy down the road to this town five days ago," the big guy continued. "We lost his scent in a downpour. But we rode on because of what you said."

"Yeah," the shorter man said. "And the boy ain't north of here. He must be around this place still."

"Gentlemen." Daniel leaned leaned forward on King's neck. "I am a man of commerce, and I have chosen this town in which to start a new business. Do you know why?"

They shook their heads, all except the black man holding the dogs. That one just stared at him.

"Because these people are good, God-fearing, law-abiding citizens. They are the kind of people I want to do business with." He sat back. "Now if you get them stirred up with a bunch of nonsense about someone harboring or helping slaves escape, that is going to impact my business."

The big man spit to one side. "That ain't our problem."

Daniel opened his coat and withdrew his purse. "I am willing to make an investment in my business right here and now." He looked at the big man first, then the shorter one, and then Will. "I will give you twenty dollars in gold apiece—which I gather is more than you would receive for returning a slave boy—if you will ride out of Mount Pleasant and leave these good people alone."

"Twenty dollars apiece?" Will's tone was filled with awe. "Gold?"

"Not a penny more, and only if you ride on."

Shorty looked at the big man, who was obviously the one in charge.

"You would pay us sixty dollars to ride out of here?" the man asked.

"To ride out and not *return*." Daniel stressed the last word.

The big man scratched under his scraggly beard. "I guess we could do that."

"Splendid." Daniel made a show of emptying his purse, because there were just three twenty-dollar pieces in it. He didn't usually carry that much money with him, but he'd planned to send Micah to Roberts Landing for more supplies the next day. Now that would have to wait. But it was worth it to safeguard the town and thus safeguard Owen and his family.

He gave the purse one last shake to show it was empty, then handed the coins over to Will, who was closest. The big man stuck out his hand, and Will gave them over. All three coins. Would Will and Shorty get any of it? Not that it was Daniel's concern.

"Nice doin' business with you." The big man laughed as Daniel heeled King into a canter.

Had he done the right thing?

It was dark under a cloudy sky devoid of stars. Zachary was waiting on the porch when Titus arrived and handed him the empty bucket. The bread, cheese, raspberries, and garden greens he'd sent up to the secret room were gone.

"'Tis time I head south again." Titus rubbed his belly. "You got me all fed up and ready. And I know Prince be in good hands."

The young slave boy was named Prince, as one would name a dog or a horse. Zachary would have preferred not to know his name, but he'd picked it up during conversations in the week that Paul had been coming every day. It was one thing to not know the name of someone passing through. But Prince would be in the secret room for at least another fortnight. It would have been awkward, and dehumanizing, to call him nothing but boy.

Paul was hesitant to call it a miracle yet, but so far, he'd saved the boy's arm. It would be horribly scarred for life and never regain its full strength, but it would be functional for most things. He'd be able to have a normal life.

If he made it to Canada.

While Titus was set to move south again, into the dragon's lair. Into the teeth of danger.

"Must thee go back?" Zachary needed to ask, even though he knew the answer.

Titus nodded. "I know where Miriam lives. I just need the opportunity to get her out. They watch her close, her being in the house and all."

Her being *in the house* meant that she slept under the eaves, not in the slave quarters. She would be outside only during the day, and then infrequently. Freeing her would entail a daylight run—the most dangerous of attempts.

As much as Zachary wanted to argue with Titus, to demand that he not go back, if Zachary knew where even one of his brothers was, he'd be on the boy's heels across the river to try to free him. But they'd been sold off long before him since he was the youngest. And Momma, did she yet live? If so, she'd be an old woman, bent and frail, too old to run.

"I best be on my way." Titus took a step.

Zachary grabbed the back of his shirt. "Fill a sack with cheese, dried apples, and those carrots I pulled this evening."

"I doan wanna take all your food. You already done so much."

"God has provided for me, more than enough to share with thee and the others."

Titus cleaned his ear with a finger, then looked back at Zachary. "You believe that?"

"Indeed. God has always provided for me. In His time and in His way."

"He let you be a slave."

"He did. And He brought me out of slavery."

"You said Eli done that."

"At the urging of the inner light of Christ, Eli let himself be used by God."

Titus faced him fully, and did he stand a little taller? "You reckon He might be using me too?"

"I would not doubt it." If anyone was a modern-day Moses, it was Titus. He might not be leading a multitude to freedom, but one by one, he was bringing others out of bondage. While Zachary provided them with food and shelter, which wasn't without its own set of dangers, especially for him, a freed slave.

He still felt like there was more he could do. He'd almost spoken out at meeting that morning, but something had held his tongue. Maybe next Sunday, if he felt so led, he'd begin the next part of his mission.

But he'd wait until he knew it was God's leading and not his own desire.

According to the tavern's calendar, it was Monday, July 11. They were set to begin the roof on Daniel's business, its brick walls tall and straight and almost glowing in the early morning sun.

Daniel needed to order the glass for the windows, but that would have to wait another week. By then, Henry's hand would be healed enough for him to return to work, and Daniel could take a day to place the order in Roberts Landing.

The tromp of boots on the dusty ground drew his attention away from the building. He turned to greet the men, but it wasn't Isaac and Tad alone. Behind them, coming down the road, was a gang of seven burly Quakers with tools in their hands. Two carried a ladder, and all wore friendly smiles.

"Greetings, Daniel." The one in the lead called.

Daniel had met him before but couldn't remember his name.

"We hear thee are putting on a roof today. Could thee use a few more hands?"

It wasn't really a question, since he obviously needed help, but Daniel answered anyway. "Indeed, we could." The *we* slipped out before he thought about it. When had he started thinking in terms of we instead of I?

The Quakers stopped to admire the work already done.

Conversation flowed between Isaac and Tad and the newcomers, with Daniel relegated to a listener for the most part. When good men were doing what they excelled at, it was wise to stand out of their way. He'd learned that early in his business career—hire men who knew what they were doing and then allow them the freedom to do it.

Within minutes, four of the Quakers and Tad started on the roof of the business, while Isaac and three more Quakers walked to the other building site to begin work there.

Daniel followed them to mark out the boundaries of his new house.

"I appreciate you gentlemen coming to work for me," Daniel said to Timothy. He'd remembered the man's name when someone else had said it during the discussion.

"We are not working *for* thee today." Timothy grinned at him. "Today we are helping a member of our community who ran off the slave catchers."

Daniel stopped. "How did you know?"

"When thee pays a sum of money to men such as those, they will spend it on drink that loosens their tongues." He fell into step with the others who had passed them on the road and pointed to the man in the lead. "He heard their talk in Roberts Landing on Saturday."

"I hope what I did was right." Daniel harbored more than a few doubts. After all, the men could break the agreement and return. Nothing was binding about it. It was a gentleman's agreement, and he doubted the gentlemanly character of anyone who would work in the slave trade.

Even Jonas.

"Can assisting others ever be wrong?" Timothy's grin said he didn't need or expect an answer.

But Daniel pondered the question as he walked. According to the law, it was wrong. But who wrote the law? A bunch of men sitting in a stuffy room with pipes in their faces and buttons groaning against their waistcoats, half or more of whom owned slaves.

There must be a higher law.

The men walking ahead of him believed so. Maybe it was time for him to explore more about what they believed. They worshipped the same God he'd always worshipped, or at least he'd listened to the Sunday sermons about that God. He vaguely remembered a sermon about a higher law, but from many years in the past.

Perhaps he'd consult Thomas about it. He was an elder and respected in the community. What would it hurt to ask?

A wagon rumbled into the farmyard.

Zachary straightened from hoeing his kitchen garden and wiped the sweat from his brow as it came to a halt. "Micah, 'tis good to see thee."

"Always good to see thee as well, but my visit is not social." He set the brake on the wagon and hopped down.

Zachary leaned the hoe against the fence and joined him. "What has happened?"

"There is a man in the trees near the creek. Dinah discovered him an hour ago."

"A fugitive?"

"'Twould appear so, but he will not speak to me. His foot is injured, but he will not let me see to it." Micah rubbed the back of his neck. "I thought to fetch Paul but decided to come to thee instead." He shook his head. "I am not sure why, except perhaps the man will speak to thee."

"I will saddle Annabelle—although we may need to move him. Let me hitch the team instead."

"We can use my wagon."

"Nay, Micah. Thee have a wife and children to protect, and there are slave catchers in the area."

"Have thee not heard?"

"Heard what?"

"Daniel paid them off."

The words were there but made no sense. "Paid them off?"

"'Twould seem they accosted him on the road over a missing slave boy and accused him of misleading them the night he met them here. He paid them to leave the area and not return."

Daniel had done that? Daniel, who *owned* Dinah?

No, that wasn't fair. He'd explained how he'd come to own her. He'd saved the girl from a much worse fate. In fact, Dinah had come out of her shell under Gwen's care. He'd not have recognized her at meeting the other day, all dressed in plain clothing with a new apron and sitting with the other girls, if not for the color of her skin. She sat straight and tall with a natural grace and confidence that hadn't been beaten out of her. Or maybe it had been lovingly restored by Gwen's gentle care.

But paying off slave catchers? That was a fool's bargain. Once the money was gone, they would return.

"'Twas good of him to try, but I doubt 'twill remove them for long. They are too greedy and ruthless."

Micah sighed. "I fear thee are correct."

"So I will hitch the team and follow thee, then let me handle it."

"I know thee are right, but it seems like I should be doing something to help."

"Thee can go to Paul and tell him to come to my place, that thee have *found someone*—use that phrase. And do not hurry or do anything that will draw attention to thee. Remain calm and deliver that phrase. Paul will understand."

"I will do as thee say."

Zachary fetched the team from the pasture, and Micah helped harness and hitch them.

When they arrived at the creek, Micah pointed to the right location, then touched the brim of his hat and drove his team toward town.

Zachary halted Justice and Jubal, set the brake, and climbed down. No doubt the fugitive had already seen him, so he began speaking.

"Thee are among Friends here. Quakers. There is nothing to be fearful of from me. I know what thee have been through. I was there once myself." Funny how it was becoming easier to talk about his past after years of avoiding it. "'Twas a Quaker who helped me, and now I am a free man."

Movement in the bushes ahead preceded the man standing. He gripped a tree trunk for support, thin as a buggy whip. But then, they all were. What was left of his shirt hung in tatters from the armpits down, and one sleeve was missing. His face was covered with several weeks' worth of whiskers, but still visible were angry scratches as if he'd tangled with brambles and lost. Or a mountain lion. His eyes were recessed and wary.

"My friend says thee have an injured foot that has stopped thee here at the creek."

A single nod.

"I have a secret room at my place, where thee can hide and heal." Zachary took a few steps closer, but the man shrank back as if intending to run, so he stopped. "And I have plenty of food for thee to eat."

Something gleamed in the man's light brown eyes. Was it hope? Or was it simply a primal reaction to the offer of food? Whichever it was, he no longer looked on the verge of flight.

"Let me assist thee onto my wagon. I have a tarp in the back to conceal thee."

Another single nod, but the man didn't move, so Zachary continued his approach, one hand outstretched. When he was close enough, the man grabbed it in a crushing grip and then collapsed.

"Easy there." Zachary eased him to the ground. He was breathing, but it was shallow, and his eyes had rolled back. Zachary scooped him up as one would a child. He weighed almost nothing, his hip bones jutting out like handles on each side.

With great care, Zachary got him into the back of the wagon. He positioned two round nail kegs he kept there and draped the tarp over it all. Instinct said to rush to the house, but he restrained the horses at a steady trot, one that wouldn't draw attention. Halfway between Micah's place and his, he passed a couple of Friends in a buggy and waved as if it were any other day, any other trip back from some mundane errand.

He pulled the wagon into the farmyard and around behind the barn. Ideally, he didn't open the door to the secret room during the daylight hours, but this man was in trouble. He didn't have time to waste.

"Prince!" he called as loudly as he dared. "Prince, open the door. I need thy help."

The door opened, and Prince stuck his head out.

"I have a man in the wagon." His voice lower, he added. "He has passed out. I will need thy help to haul him up."

"But my arm—"

"Thee will have to rely on the other. Toss down the rope." Zachary kept a long rope in the room secured to a beam so that a person could slide down and make a hasty exit.

He turned the wagon until the back was toward the barn. "Back, Justice. Back, Jubal." The well-trained team brought the wagon's tailgate directly under the hidden door. Zachary set the brake before climbing over the seat into the wagon's bed. He removed the tarp and knelt beside the man.

It took a moment to register what he was seeing.

Lifeless eyes stared back at him. No breath raised and lowered his chest. A gentle touch at the neck brought no beat against his fingertips.

Zachary sat beside the body, fighting a flood of grief and helplessness, then looked up at Prince. "Haul up the rope and secure the door. I will bring thee fresh water and food come dark."

"He dead?"

Zachary nodded, all energy draining from his limbs.

Prince's face pulled into long lines of sorrow. "He got so close."

"He did."

The rope disappeared, and the hasp slid into place above him with a *snick*.

Zachary covered the body with the tarp. For a long time, he sat with his knees pulled up, arms wrapped around them, head resting on top.

He'd failed this one.

That wasn't logical, of course, but it was how he felt. When he'd decided to help the fugitives, it had never occurred to him that some of them might die in his care. He wasn't prepared for this.

Jubal snorted and shook his head, his bridle jingling. When that didn't get any reaction, the large black horse pawed the ground.

"I hear thee." Zachary unwound himself and climbed into the seat. He drove the wagon into the shade on the east side of the barn, then unhitched the horses and turned them out. He'd hung the last piece of harness on its peg when hoofbeats reached him. From the doorway, he shaded his eyes and watched a horse coming from the west.

Paul.

He walked out to greet him. "I am sorry to have brought thee all this way."

"Micah said he found someone?"

"He did, and I brought him here." He wiped his hand across his face. "But he did not survive the short journey."

Paul dismounted and tied his horse to the hitching rail. "Where is he?"

"In the wagon. I will bury him in the woods after dark."

Paul followed him and climbed into the wagon. He poked and prodded the body for a few minutes.

"He had an injured foot."

"I saw that. A nasty gash. Very deep." Paul stood and covered the body before climbing down. "I suspect he bled heavily from that wound and grew weaker than he already was in that emaciated state."

"He looked more than half starved."

"Indeed. Even without the wound, he could not have survived much longer."

"But 'tis summer, when food is easy to come by. He should have been able to forage."

"Did thee notice his hands?" Paul asked.

"Not particularly."

"No calluses. He was a house slave, I would guess. He may not have known how to forage, or what foods were safe to eat." Paul wiped his hands on a handkerchief and then stuffed it in his pocket. "The field slaves are better equipped to run."

"But he got so close." Zachary echoed Prince's words.

"'Tis a shame he did not make it."

"I wonder how many others have left their bodies littering the landscape, unseen and unmourned."

"I believe all of them are mourned." Paul started toward his horse. "One needs not to see death to feel its sting." He untied the horse and swung into the saddle. He turned the horse but paused. "Zachary?" He looked back. "Bury him not on thy property. Bury him on the other side of the brickworks. That land is rocky with little growing other than shrubs. 'Twould be easy to conceal a fresh grave there."

"A wise suggestion."

"I will be back after dark to see Prince, although thee may be away then."

Zachary nodded, and Paul rode off.

With a heavy heart, he resumed his farm chores, filling the hours until he'd have to dig a grave.

Why did Thee bring him this far, Lord, only to let him die? Why did Thee not allow him to taste freedom?

Only the Lord knew those answers—certainly not Zachary Brown.

Chapter 22

D ANIEL HAD HOPED TO make the trip to Roberts Landing himself, but with two crews working now—he'd hired the Quakers after the first day, when they'd volunteered to help—he needed to remain on-site to answer questions or deal with any issues that arose with the house. King's steps were muffled on the dew-drenched grass as he walked up to Zachary's barn that early morning.

Daniel dismounted and entered the open doorway, where Zachary hunched on a three-legged stool beside a large brown cow, head resting against its flank, hands stripping milk into a bucket.

"Hello."

Zachary startled and stood, scanning the barn's interior before focusing on him. "Daniel, I did not hear thee."

"Pardon me, I did not mean to interrupt. 'Tis perhaps too early."

"Not at all." Zachary moved the bucket away from the cow. "What can I do for thee?"

"I hesitate to ask, but could you drive to Roberts Landing today and deliver an order for me? With so many workers, I need more materials, and quickly. Micah is needed to haul bricks to the house site today."

"I can go after I finish the milking."

"Let me pay you upfront." Daniel pulled out his purse, but fumbled and dropped it. He bent to pick it up. As he started to rise, movement caught his eye. A black boy was hiding in front of a cow in the stanchion. "Zachary?" he whispered. "Did you know someone is in with your cow?"

"I wish thee had not seen him." Zachary's tone was heavy with regret. "I know thee swore to the slave catchers that there were no fugitives in Mount Pleasant, and I have heard that thee paid them off to leave this area."

A fugitive slave. It was one thing to know they were in the area, but quite another to see one himself. "At the time I swore to them, I did not know, but when I paid them, I had come to know that slaves are escaping through Mount Pleasant."

Wrinkles creased his dark brow. "But thee paid them anyway?"

"It seemed the easiest way to be rid of them, at least for a time."

"They will return." There was finality in the flat words.

"Probably, but I do not regret it, even if it keeps the area safe for only a short while."

Zachary cocked his head. "Thee are a complex man, Daniel Whiteford, and one I misjudged badly."

Daniel shrugged. "I understand why."

"Come out." Zachary waved the boy forward and turned back to Daniel. "He was badly injured by dogs but is almost healed." Zachary put his arm around the narrow shoulders. "Show him."

The boy pushed up his sleeve and held out an arm crisscrossed with red scars, puckered flesh, and faded bruises. Another long scar rose above his collar and ended below his ear.

Daniel's stomach churned. "How horrible." There were no other words.

"He is well enough to travel. Soon he will move on, move north."

"A boy? On his own?" The memory of Dinah on the auction block came tumbling back, a girl on her own. It was madness, this practice of slavery.

Zachary rubbed his chin, studying Daniel as if seeing him for the first time. Then he glanced up before back to Daniel. "The Lord will guide him or send someone to help him."

"How can you know that? Did you hear from God?" He wouldn't put it past a Quaker to claim that.

"Not a voice, but a feeling—a certainty."

"I feel it too," the boy said.

Well, Daniel didn't. He didn't feel anything other than anger that someone had abused the child. But the germ of an idea sparked. "Maybe I can do something."

Two sets of dark eyes fixed on him.

"That order I need taken to Roberts Landing is mainly for glass. 'Twill come shipped from the glassworks in Steubenville. I know 'tis a long journey, but if you were to go directly to Steubenville, the boy could accompany you. 'Tis still on the river, but farther north and east."

The boy looked up at Zachary. "Titus told me to go to Steubenville next."

"He did?" After the boy's nod, Zachary faced Daniel. "I assume thee brought the order?"

"Indeed, along with a note for payment to go to my steward." He withdrew both from his coat pocket and handed them over. "When can you leave?"

"After I finish milking, I will ride to Mark Allen's place to see if he can milk the cows for the next three days. 'Twill take that long to travel there and back. It must be all of twenty-five miles, and bringing glass back, I must travel slowly and carefully."

"That sounds about right." Daniel opened his purse and handed over a fair wage for three days. "Please do be careful of the load coming back. Glass brings top dollar out here." He pulled another coin from his purse and extended it to the boy, who took it, staring with wide eyes. "And take special care that this one arrives safe and unseen. Keep the coin hidden, lad. You might need it down the road. I would give you more, but 'twould make you suspect, I believe."

"'Tis true. Someone would think him a thief." Zachary ruffled the boy's hair. "He is anything but. He should have stayed hidden, and yet he insisted this week he must help with the milking to earn his keep."

"Good lad. Work hard for what you want, and you will earn the respect of others." Daniel stuffed his nearly flat purse back into his inner pocket. "Thank you, Zachary."

"I will bring thy glass back in good condition."

"Very well." Daniel strode out of the barn and mounted King. Satisfaction at getting his glass had somehow been eclipsed by knowing he'd assisted the child on his journey north.

He'd broken the law.

But in his heart, he couldn't regret it.

Nothing woke a person up any better than the scent of bacon sizzling in a skillet. Zachary inhaled the aroma, and Prince roused from his blankets under the wagon.

"Come on, sleepyhead. Rise and shine."

Prince crawled out from under the wagon and stood, stretching, his good arm flung wide. The other didn't fully extend, but he hadn't lost it, and that was due to Paul's skill as a doctor. Watching him improve went a long way to ease Zachary's lingering pain over the death of the man from the creek.

"Ain't even daylight yet," the boy mumbled around a yawn.

"We still have a long way to go." And he wasn't sure how long he'd have to spend in Steubenville to get the glass and start the journey back. Without Prince. As with Titus, the boy had inched his way into Zachary's heart. If he had his way, he'd keep both of them close. But to try to do so would only endanger them. Far better that they reach Canada. At least there, they could stop looking over their shoulders for the next man who would try to capture and return them to slavery.

"Thee are sure thee know the place to go?"

"Titus give me directions."

"I wish thee would share them with me."

"He told me not to." Prince didn't look happy about that. Perhaps he'd grown fond of Zachary as well.

Zachary forked the bacon onto two tin plates, then added biscuits he'd brought from home and a thick slice of cheese. "If anything happens to Titus—and I pray daily that nothing will—who will guide the next person to the proper place?" He handed over a plate. "How will I help the one who comes after thee?"

Prince didn't tear into it as he used to do with his food. Wearing clothing from the chest that wasn't new but fit him well, the boy barely resembled the emaciated and mangled child who had shown up with

Titus. His eyes were clear, free of hunger and exhaustion, but his face was too old for a boy his age. He'd seen too much. Survived too much. Yet there was a certainty in Zachary's spirit that this one, at least, would make it to Canada and achieve his dreams.

Thank Thee, Lord, and let it be so.

Chewing on a mouthful of biscuit, Prince pointed a piece of bacon at him and swallowed. "You be right, I think. And Titus, he just be trying to protect you."

"Titus wants to protect everyone. 'Tis his nature."

Dark curls bounced as Prince shook his head. "You be special to him."

Was he? A warm flush washed over him.

"He talkin' and talkin' 'bout you. Zachary this and Zachary that. Truth, I had trouble believin' anyone could be as good as he say you are." He ripped off a bite of the bacon. "But he be right."

"Well, I am very fond of Titus as well." Zachary nudged the boy's shoulder. "And now thee."

"How come you doan have no family of your own?"

And there was the question Zachary never wanted to answer. In the past, it had made him uncomfortable, irritated, and even angry. But there was no judgment in Prince's expression, just child-like curiosity.

"'Tis difficult, being a black man and a Quaker."

"Because they ain't no black women Quakers?"

"None that I have met, but I have heard of a few in Pennsylvania."

"Then maybe you"—he jabbed his last piece of bacon at Zachary—"need to go to Pennsylvania and find one."

He'd thought of that many times, but with the dairy herd, being gone meant someone else would have to take on the daily work of milking every morning and evening. Mark Allen was willing to help, but he had his orchard to tend and a wife and baby at home. Zachary wouldn't impose on him too often or for too long.

"Someday, maybe."

"Doan you ever get lonely?"

Why that question? Answering it was like picking at a scab. "I am often lonely." He smiled to remove any sadness from his words. "But then someone like thee comes along and eases the loneliness."

"You know what I'm gonna do?"

"Tell me."

"When I get to Canada, I gonna learn to read and write so I can write you a letter and you doan be lonely."

Suspicious dampness gathered in the corners of Zachary's eyes, but he blinked it away. "I would like that, very much."

Prince leaned against Zachary and told him everything Titus had shared about the safe house near Steubenville. Zachary repeated it back to him to commit it to memory. He lingered there by the fire, enjoying the boy's closeness as the sun colored the eastern horizon.

He might never see Prince again, but now he had hope that he might hear from him sometime in the future.

They topped a rise in the hilly country next to a large rock beside a twisted oak several yards off the road. Steubenville spread out before them. As a town, it was only a few years older than Mount Pleasant, but being right on the Ohio River, it had grown much larger, much faster. Buildings several stories high rose toward the sky. Docks jutted into the river, and sheds and shanties and every sort of building gathered around their bases, while boats and barges of all shapes and sizes bobbed along their lengths. The streets were dotted with horses, wagons, and carts. Pedestrians moved along a boardwalk. A scene busy enough to make a man dizzy.

"This be the right place?" Prince stood from behind the seat and looked over Zachary's shoulder.

"Aye. The tree and rock are just as Titus described to thee. And that is the town ahead." Zachary suppressed a sigh. They'd made good time. Too good. It was here they would part ways forever. He set the brake and climbed down as Prince scrambled out of the wagon's bed.

Zachary pulled a sack from under the seat that he'd filled with food for the boy's journey. Prince took hold of it, but Zachary didn't let go. At the boy's quizzical expression, he asked, "What was thy real name? The name thy mother gave to thee?"

Prince let his hand fall from the bag and looked away. "I doan know. Never knew my momma. She died when I was too young to remember her."

"Who named thee Prince?"

The thin shoulders lifted and fell, and he studied his toes in the dirt before looking up at him. "Why?"

"Because Prince is a name one would give to a dog or a horse." Despite Zachary's intentions, his words came out harsh. "I did not mean that to sound like a condemnation of thee. 'Tis just that thee deserve a man's name—not an animal's."

"Guess it doan much matter."

But it mattered to Zachary, and he sensed that it mattered to the lad as well, even though he didn't want to admit it.

"I reckon if the good Lord had intended me to have children, He'd have given me a wife by now." Zachary grasped the thin shoulder and gave it a little shake. "And maybe a boy like thee. My father's name was Darius. 'Tis a good name. A strong name. A man's name. 'Tis a pity I have no one to pass it on to." He waited until Prince raised his eyes. "Unless thee would like to take it as thy own."

"Me?" Surprise squeaked in the boy's voice, but also something else. Joy. And it was accompanied by a huge grin. "You give me your daddy's name?"

"I would be proud—honored—if thee would take it."

Arms came around him so fast and with such force that Zachary nearly lost his balance. But he steadied them both and returned the hug, savoring the moment. "Just do me one favor, Darius."

"Anything." The word was muffled by Zachary's coat.

"Do as thee said. Learn to read and write and send me a letter when thee can. Let me know that thee are in Canada and doing well."

Darius stepped back. Wet rivulets streaked his cheeks, but he nodded. "I will. I promise. And I gonna learn to talk real good, like you."

"Find a community of Quakers if thee can. Let them teach thee more about God than I had time to, so that thee will come to know the inner light of Christ. That would make me happiest of all."

"I promise that too."

"Then." Zachary pressed the sack into Darius's hands. "Go in peace, Darius, and go in safety with the Lord's blessing on thee."

Fresh tears cascaded down his cheeks as Darius nodded, gripped the sack, and walked away, following the path Titus had explained so well.

Taking a large piece of Zachary's heart with him.

Chapter 23

"Twill be fine, I just need to sit down for a moment." Daniel allowed the two men to assist him to a bench they'd built under the huge oak tree in what would be his front yard. Allowed them? He'd never have made it that far without their help.

"I think someone should go for the doctor," Henry said.

Tad practically lifted Daniel onto the bench. "I will."

"I do not require a doctor." But he might as well have been talking to himself.

Henry unbuckled Daniel's shoe and worked it off the injured foot while Daniel did his best not to cry out. Of all the clumsy, stupid things to do. He'd dropped his end of the timber they were getting ready to raise to the roof—right on top of his foot.

Henry peeled off his sock next, and Daniel's vision swam against the pain.

Maybe the doctor was a good idea, after all.

Tad was already striding in that direction when Micah appeared in the wagon with another load of cedar shakes. The two men spoke, and then Micah turned the wagon around and headed into town.

"It don't look good." Henry stood.

Tad joined them. "Micah will fetch the doctor."

"No need to stop working on my account." Daniel waved them away. "I will be fine until the doctor arrives."

Henry pointed at the bench. "Stay there. Some of them toes are broke. Don't be moving 'em until the doctor binds 'em up." He stalked off, Tad following.

Daniel squirmed to get more comfortable, his back against the tree. Another delay in the building. No, that wasn't true. Losing one of the others would be a delay. He was assisting, but he wasn't a builder, especially now that the Quakers had hired on. The business office building was completed, and Isaac and the other crew were erecting a storage building for it while this crew was putting the roofing timbers in place. They would put up the milled boards next and start setting the cedar shakes soon.

It was the middle of August, and at the rate they were going, he'd be moved into his house in a fortnight. Or whenever he managed to get some furniture delivered. He'd sold everything with the house in Greenesville. Every. Single. Piece. He'd wanted a fresh start in a new place to build new memories.

His foot throbbed.

His new house would be empty without Owen in it. He'd resigned himself to the fact that Owen needed to stay with his family, for there was no doubt he was loved by Micah and Gwen and little Sally Faye. Even Dinah doted on the boy. He'd thought about bringing Dinah here to keep house for him, but Gwen needed her help, and Dinah needed Gwen. She'd blossomed under the woman's gentle and loving care.

He'd need someone to keep house for him, though. He could do many things, but cooking and cleaning and laundry were not among them. He should ask if there was a widowed Quaker woman in need of a position who would live in the servant's quarters he'd designed. Not under the rafters as was the norm, but a bedroom and sitting room beyond the kitchen pantry, where a housekeeper would have privacy. The sitting room even had its own outside entrance. A woman should enjoy living there. An older woman, of course, would prevent the wagging of gossipy tongues, but a younger woman with children would bring a bit of cheer into the house.

Maybe it was best to pray that God would bring the right woman at the right time.

Where had that thought come from?

Daniel rubbed his eyes. All this time spent with the Quakers was shaping his thinking. Next thing he knew, he'd be *theeing* and *thying*. That would make Owen laugh, and he dearly loved the boy's laughter.

What was it Timothy had said at meeting last Sunday? "A merry heart doeth good like a medicine." Daniel didn't remember the rest, but he'd liked that part. Oddly enough, he'd enjoyed attending the Sunday meetings for the past month.

The rhythmic pounding of hooves pulled him out of his thoughts, which was a shame because they had distracted him from the throbbing in his toes.

Paul dismounted and tied his horse to a branch of the tree. "Micah said thee were injured."

"'Tis only my foot, but painful enough."

Paul squatted in front of the bench and examined the foot with gentle fingers, but still Daniel winced. "'Twould appear thee have broken two toes, but they are the middle two, so I can bind them. However,"—Paul gave him a warning stare—"thee will need to stay off this foot for at least a week. A fortnight would be better, but I know how driven thee are to get thy house and business in order."

"A man of business must have a business to manage."

"One must also allow time to heal." Paul wrapped the toes with a bandage.

Daniel gritted his teeth against the pain.

"No more walking than thee must to see to the body's necessities. No wearing a shoe on that foot. And keep it elevated as much as possible." Paul stood. "The bruising will hurt as much or more than the broken bones. Do not rush things, I beg of thee."

"I will be good, doctor, you have my word."

Micah pulled up in the wagon. "Is he all right?"

"He will be." Paul stowed his medical bag behind his saddle. "If he listens to me. Take him to the tavern, for he cannot walk on that foot. And he will require assistance up and down stairs for a few days if thee cannot convince him to stay abed." Paul mounted. "Now I must check on a few other patients. I will see thee again tomorrow, Daniel." He reined his horse around and left.

"Do thee wish to go to the tavern now?" Micah asked.

"I think not." Daniel leaned back against the tree. In truth, he didn't want to move his foot until he had to. "I will observe from here for the rest of the afternoon."

Micah drove the wagon near the house and unloaded the crates of cedar shakes as Daniel's eyelids drooped. It was the heat, of course, and the trauma of his injury causing his drowsiness. Soon enough, he lost the battle to keep his eyes open.

Weeks had passed since Darius's escape, and Zachary had made the same trek to Steubenville three more times with other fugitives who'd been told about the secret room. All three claimed to have been sent by someone resembling Titus. By their accounts, Zachary had a good idea of where the boy was, or at least where he'd been when he met those others.

Deep in southern Virginia.

It might not be the most dangerous place for a runaway slave in the South, but it was close enough.

The urge to saddle Annabelle and ride south was strong, maybe the strongest it'd ever been. Was the Lord leading? Or was it his own loneliness spurring him to find and rescue the boy—who'd proved more than once he didn't need it?

Zachary missed Titus. As he also missed Darius. How had those two so wormed themselves into his heart?

Because there wasn't anyone else. Just him and the livestock, day after day. The solitude was oppressive at times.

"Hup, Justice. Hup, Jubal." Zachary jiggled the reins just enough to keep the team's feet moving in the stifling August heat. The wagon was loaded with dried hay to be stacked near the barn. This was the final load and they were all tired. Zachary's skin was coated with an itchy mix of sweat, dust, and hay chaff. The horses hadn't escaped it either, their coats looking more gray than black.

He stopped the wagon and unhitched the team, and turned them out on pasture before grabbing his hayfork and pitching the pungent hay onto the stack he'd already started.

Justice and Jubal rolled in the dust near the barn before lurching to their feet, shaking the excess dust from their backs, and snorting.

"Go ahead, enjoy thyselves while I labor for thy winter provisions." He tossed a forkful of hay as Justice blew another long snort. Zachary worked until the stack was shaped and packed to allow water to run off it and keep the interior dry and mold-free. The health and well-being of his livestock depended on a good supply of properly stacked winter hay.

The angle of the sun said he had time for a swim before the cows needed to be milked. And nothing sounded more appealing. He barely got the hayfork on its hook before he strode toward the creek. The spring that cooled his springhouse wasn't large enough to swim in, and even in this sweltering heat, it was too cold. But the creek wound its way across the back of his property through a grove of trees that also sheltered a patch of blackberries. Those would be almost as refreshing as the swim.

On the bank, he stripped to his smallclothes before walking into the water. It wasn't above his head on this section of the creek, but he could swim once it reached his waist. And he did. Plunging in, he let the cool water soak his head. He rose and shook, water spraying around him, and blew out a long sigh, not unlike the horses had in the pasture's dust. That thought made him grin. He'd take a cool creek over a dusty wallow any day.

He floated on his back, watching the puffy clouds until a *whuff* caught his ear.

A familiar if unwelcomed sound. It meant he wasn't the only one who'd come to enjoy the blackberries and maybe a swim. He lowered his feet to the pebbly creek bottom and searched for the source of the sound.

Bushes and brambles moved beneath the trees, and then a black head poked up, its nose in the air. *Whuff.*

Zachary remained still.

The bear had caught his scent but didn't know where he was.

It wasn't a huge bear, but any bear presented a threat, especially while it and the berry canes were between Zachary and home.

Whuff.

Why was it so insistent on sniffing—

Zachary resisted the urge to smack his forehead. On the bank were his sweaty clothes. His pungent, sweaty clothes.

The bear rose to its hind legs, head swinging from side to side, nose wrinkling in the air.

He could hardly blame it.

Lumbering forward on all fours, it approached the pile of clothing with a few more *whuffs* and a whole lot of caution.

And then a man jumped out from behind a tree, a long stick in each hand, legs braced as if to fight the bear.

He yelled something, words Zachary had never heard before, and held the sticks crossway to his body. His skin was black as coal and glistened in the sun. He was bare to the waist, and his long legs extended from a ragged pair of breeches over bare legs and feet. He never took his eyes off the bear as he spoke more of the strange words.

The bear rose on its back legs again, front paws spread, wicked claws flashing in the sunlight, teeth exposed as it roared in response.

The black man didn't move, just spoke more of the words.

Maybe the bear understood, or maybe it was as confused as Zachary, but after several minutes of staring at each other, the bear dropped to all fours, grunted, and ambled away.

The man picked up and clothing and glanced at Zachary. "He say, you stink." The words were heavily accented, as if he came from another country.

Zachary started for the shore. "He would be correct. I did before my swim."

"You work hard." The man mimicked forking hay. "I watch."

Zachary reached land and took the fabric from the man's out-stretched hand. "Thank thee for saving my clothes. 'Twould have been an inconvenience to replace them."

The man cocked his head.

"Hard to get new clothes."

At that, he nodded.

"Are thee hungry?"

The head cocked again. "Thee?"

Zachary grinned. "'Tis Quaker speech. Means you."

"Thee—you." He said the words as if tasting them.

"Hungry?" Zachary motioned eating.

"Hungry. Eat berries until you—thee—come."

"Come to my house, and I will make thee something more filling than berries." Zachary motioned. "Come." The importation of slaves had been banned for years, but pirates still smuggled them in. This man had a story, and probably not enough English to tell it. But he would leave with a full belly and another set of clothing to keep him warm in the colder climate up north before he moved on.

And tonight, Zachary wouldn't eat alone.

Chapter 24

Z ACHARY USHERED THE LAST cow out of the barn and shut the gate, leaning against it and staring into the darkening sky. The sun wouldn't set for another couple of hours, but a storm was blowing in, and it looked like it might be a wild one. Fall storms rarely brought tornadoes, but the memory of the one that had leveled Micah and Gwen's house was still fresh. Zachary closed up the barn and secured anything that might blow away. The cows and horses would be safer on pasture, so he'd leave them there.

In the house, he closed the shutters and barred the door before starting a fire in the hearth. It wasn't cold, but the light would be cheery, and he could put together a simple soup for his supper. He was shaving cuts off a smoked ham into a pot of water when the wind hit. The house shuddered against the first blast, and the fire danced in the hearth.

The temperature plummeted on the heels of the wind, cool air slithering under the door. But Zachary was safe and snug as he added potatoes, carrots, and onions from his garden to the pot and swung it near the flames to simmer.

As often happened with summer storms, it settled into a steady rain after its turbulent start, sending an occasional gust of wind. The patter of rain on the roof lulled Zachary into a doze while his supper cooked.

Wild pounding on his door jerked him awake.

"Open up. We got a hurt man here." Someone pounded on the door hard enough to rattle its hinges.

"Coming." Zachary unbarred the door and pulled it open.

The slave catchers huddled under the roof of his porch, including the black man, dripping like they'd been swimming in their clothes, their hounds with them.

"Let us in. George be in a bad way."

Everything in Zachary wanted to slam the door and bar it again, but everything the Bible taught otherwise. He opened the door wider. "Bring him in and put him on my bed."

The two shorter men wrestled the larger man—who must be George—through the door and onto the bed, lifting his legs last.

"What happened?" Zachary asked.

"Tree came down in the wind and whacked him on the head," the shortest one said.

Zachary grabbed a clean rag and wash basin and knelt next to his uninvited and unwanted guest. He cleaned the dirt, debris, and blood from George's hair.

"Do you know anythin' about doctorin'?" the short man demanded.

"Some." Zachary offered the rag to him. "Would thee rather do this thyself?"

The man backed hastily away. "No. I was just askin'."

Once he cleaned everything away from the wound, Zachary sat back on his heels. "Someone must fetch the doctor." He secured another rag as a bandage and turned to the four men watching him. "This is beyond my skills."

The short man poured forth a lengthy expanse of profanity.

"I will go." The man who'd worked for Daniel for a short time headed back out the door. "I know where the doc's house is."

"Take the boy"—he jerked his head at the black man—"and the hounds. You might cross a scent."

They left, shutting the door behind them, leaving Zachary with the unconscious George, the short man, and the silent one.

"Did thee not come to an agreement with Daniel Whiteford about leaving Mount Pleasant and our people alone?" Zachary asked. Not that he was surprised to see them. If anything, he was surprised that it had taken them this long to return.

"What business is that of yours?"

Zachary rose, took the dirty water, and flung it off the porch before returning. "As I am a member of the community and a free black man, I suppose it concerns me as much as anyone."

"Don't get uppity with me, boy." The short man had obviously assumed the role of leader.

"I am not thy boy. My name is Zachary."

"I don't care what you call yourself. You ain't nothin' but a slave, and if I had my way, you would be back in chains."

Zachary unclenched his fists and took a deep breath. He'd faced this type of hatred before, and he would again. But as a Quaker, he could not respond in kind, no matter how much he wished to. The only bright spot was that his secret room was empty. No one else was in danger from the men being there.

Love thine enemies.

The words pressed against Zachary's heart. He wanted to ignore them, but he'd learned the folly of that a long time ago. As distasteful as it was—and that wasn't a strong enough word—Zachary went to the hearth and stirred the soup.

"Thee are wet and must be hungry. Would thee like a bowl of soup?"

The short man glared at him but the silent one nodded.

Zachary tasted the soup, added a bit of salt, tasted it again, and then filled a bowl. He wanted to spit in it, remembering an old mammy on the plantation who swore she'd done that more than once, but to do so would not be loving his enemy. He handed the bowl and a spoon to the man.

He should eat a bowl himself, but the rumbling in his middle had more to do with his struggle to remain civil than hunger. After checking the bandage, which seemed to have stopped the worst of the bleeding, he settled in a chair by the hearth. He closed his eyes, leaned his head against the chair's tall back, and prayed that Paul would arrive soon.

Before that loathsome man had him whipping his turned cheek back—along with a very non-Friendly fist.

His small house was cramped with all five slave catchers and Paul inside. Zachary was out of chairs to seat them and soup to offer them. He'd fed his enemies, but the Lord hadn't called him to bring anything up from the cellar or to fetch cheese from the springhouse.

"I will feel better with this man under my care." Paul rose from examining George, who had not regained consciousness. "Zachary, may we use thy wagon?"

"I will hitch the team."

"Excellent," Paul said.

The short man pointed to the other slave catchers. "You go with him. Keep an eye on him."

What did he think Zachary would do? Line his wagon with nails for George to lie on? He lit a lantern even though dawn was lighting the horizon and pushed out the door, the other two following. The black man untied the hounds from the porch and brought them, too.

Zachary woke Justice and Jubal from where they dozed under a tree, fat raindrops plopping around them. "Come on, boys. I am sorry to bother thee for the likes of them, but 'tis what the doctor ordered."

Paul could have—and normally would have—left an injured man in Zachary's care. No doubt he wanted these men as far away from Zachary and the secret room as Zachary did.

The other men had filed into the barn behind him and the horses, when one of the hounds pointed its nose at the ceiling under the secret room and bayed.

"You got someone up there?" the white man asked.

"Nothing but a family of raccoons I have not been able to evict." Zachary ignored the hounds, both of them baying now, and tried to harness two horses who weren't happy at the racket the dogs were making. "Can thee take them outside?"

"Tie them out and see what you can find up there," Daniel's former employee told the black man.

The dogs outside, the black man returned as Zachary got the bit in Jubal's mouth. "There is no opening to that space. The ceiling is to keep the pen warmer in the winter. I did not plan on storing anything above and have not cut a doorway. I am not even sure how the raccoons get inside." He was babbling and made himself stop.

"Here." The white man pulled the crowbar off its peg and handed it to the black man. "Use this."

"Thee would damage my barn when I have done nothing but help thy friend and feed thee?"

"Shut up," the man said.

Zachary's heart pounded, and it was with effort that he continued harnessing the horses. Had someone come to the secret room during the storm and taken refuge? Is that why the dogs still bayed outside? Was Zachary's work with the fugitives about to be discovered? He could almost feel the bite of chains on his wrists and ankles.

The black man used the side of the cow pen to climb high enough to wedge in the crowbar and loosen one board. Then he pushed it up until he could see inside the secret room. "Argh!" He let the board spring back into place and fell into the cow pen, the crowbar narrowly missing his head.

"What is it?" the silent man finally spoke.

"Rats, suh. Big ones." The whites of the man's eyes shone in the lantern's light as he scrambled to his feet. "A whole family of them. Ain't no wonder them dogs was ahowlin'."

There were no rats in that room. But whatever the man had seen—a fugitive or just the chest and buckets, evidence that the room was used—he was keeping it to himself and acting the part of someone scared out of his wits.

He worked alongside the slave catchers, was bound to them, and now he knew about the secret room. Would he keep it a secret?

Could Zachary trust him?

Although Daniel had told no one about paying off the slave catchers, word seemed to have spread throughout the community. On any given day, two or three extra men would appear and donate several hours of labor, asking nothing in return. And they all did so with good humor and a jolly outlook, quite unlike the dock workers Daniel had dealt with back in New Bern, or even the teamsters who'd moved his freight around the interior of North Carolina.

These Quakers weren't the dour, disapproving lot he'd always assumed them to be.

And why had he assumed that? He'd known and done business with Thomas for many years. The man was always pleasant and agreeable—even when Daniel had asked him to take on a young mother and child.

The lingering shame from that decision still plagued him at times. Like now.

Micah was helping the men finish the roof on the house under the broiling August midmorning sun, the cedar shakes adding their fresh fragrance to the air. Because so many were there that day, a bevy of women including Gwen were busy around a fire preparing the noon meal. Whatever it was, it smelled heavenly. But the delicious aromas hadn't slowed the progress on his house. Aside from those on the roof, another group of men were setting the windows in place. And during all this activity, Dinah stood watch over the young ones, a baby nestled in her arms.

But the best part by far was the little boy sharing Daniel's bench in the shade.

Daniel had chafed at the doctor's instructions to keep his weight off his foot after losing his grip on a timber the other day. The broken toes still throbbed when he moved, but if he remained seated and kept it elevated, it wasn't too bad.

"Grandfather, do thee know who the slave catchers are?"

What a question from a four-year-old. A boy his age shouldn't have to know about such things. "I suppose I do. Why do you ask?"

"I overheard Dinah and Bridget talking. One of 'em is hurt. Paul had to ride out to see him last night during the storm." The boy blinked up at him. "Storms scare me. Do they scare thee?"

Daniel latched onto the change of topic. "Some storms are scary, like the one that destroyed your cabin. Others are necessary because they bring the rain your daddy's crops need."

That seemed to satisfy Owen, but he scooted closer on the bench, so Daniel put his arm around him. Had he ever done so with Jonas? Or Constance? All that seemed a lifetime ago—and it was. This was his new life, and he wasn't about to make the same mistakes.

But if the boy was right, the slave catchers had returned—breaking their agreement.

How else could Daniel ensure the safety of the community he'd chosen to live in? He was already complicit in the escape of several slaves, having worked with Zachary, so he was guilty in the eyes of the law. Not that the Quakers would turn him in. The swarm of workers in front of him was a testimony to his acceptance. He belonged.

It was humbling and wonderful at the same time. It made him want to give back, to do more.

Perhaps he needed to speak with Thomas. That man was striding toward them, his arms outstretched toward Owen.

"Grandfather!" The boy launched off the bench and into the bearded man's arms.

For the first time, that exuberant display of affection for another man didn't bring a twinge of pain or regret to Daniel.

"I see thee are keeping Daniel company while he heals from his injury," Thomas said.

Owen nodded. "Momma said I could."

"Good lad." Thomas ruffled his hair. "But I need to speak with him now, so if thee will excuse us and join Dinah and thy sister, I would appreciate it."

"I will." The boy raced off as fast as his little legs would allow.

"A fine boy," Thomas said.

"His parents have much to be proud of."

Thomas tugged at his beard. "Ah, but pride goeth before the fall."

"Something I know too well with my own children." Daniel couldn't keep the bitterness from his tone.

"Thee may have made mistakes"—Thomas eased himself onto the other end of the bench—"but as adults, 'tis up to them which path they wish to choose. Each man and woman can make of themselves what they will. 'Tis the beauty of this country."

Daniel let those words sink in and heal a corner of his heart. "You wished to speak with me?"

"Indeed. 'Twould seem the slave catchers have returned."

"So I heard."

Thomas cocked his head, brows drawn down.

"From Owen, who overheard it from someone else."

Thomas sighed. "There are no secrets in a small town."

"What can I do about them? I tried to pay them off, but it did not last very long."

"So I heard." Thomas chuckled. "Small town. But do thee have any influence outside of the town that might help? A politician, perhaps?"

Daniel shook his head. "I have always stayed as far away from politics as I could. Some businessmen work hand-in-glove with politicians, but I found them generally to be a disagreeable and distasteful lot."

"There are good men who wish only to serve their country." Thomas leaned sideways toward Daniel. "Far too few, I fear."

"Without a change in the law, there is nothing more I can do to discourage them."

"Neither can we Friends." Thomas tugged on his beard. "It worries me greatly that they were at Zachary's again. He is legally a free man, but should they decide to kidnap him and get him across the river, there would be little we could do other than file a lawsuit. And who knows how long it would take to see justice?"

"'Tis an intolerable predicament."

"Thee are correct in that, my friend."

My friend. Daniel's heart swelled with gratitude at those two little words. When was the last time someone had called him friend? He'd very much like to hear it again.

But first, what could he do about the slave catcher problem?

Jonas.

Could he contact the son he'd disowned for the chance—slim at best—that Jonas could call off the human hounds?

Chapter 25

T HE WAIT UNTIL EVENING was the longest wait of Zachary's life, but he wouldn't approach the secret room until then. Wouldn't take the chance that one of the slave catchers had circled back to watch his place. He'd gone about his daily routine after a sleepless night, feet dragging and heart nearly as heavy.

Would the slave keep Zachary's secret? Or would he use it somehow to his own advantage? Use it to win favor with those who owned him?

Those were the questions plaguing him through the morning milking, during his deliveries, while picking off the garden, and while finishing the evening milking. He ate his supper of Gwen's delicious bread spread with butter, cucumbers from the garden, and a handful of blackberries he'd picked along the edge of the woods. But he tasted little of it.

Full dark came, clouds filtering the light from the moon and stars, and still Zachary waited another half hour. Then he blew out his lantern, slipped outside, and crept across the ground to the secret room. He climbed the ends of the overlapped logs that formed the corner of the walls and felt along the door until his fingers found the hasp. He eased open the door on hinges he kept well-oiled.

With no windows and no lantern, it was too dark to see much.

"Is anyone there?"

Nothing answered him but the thick kind of silence that hid the truth.

"This is my farm. I built this room. Thee have nothing to fear from me."

A rustle came from the far corner where not a trace of light penetrated.

"Fear not, I will not harm thee. I can bring thee food, water, whatever thee needs."

"Come, children." A female voice trembled. "We must trust him."

Children? How many were there?

He lifted the door as high as it would go and secured it with a rope and hook he'd fashioned for that purpose. As dark as it was, no one would see the opening from a distance, and it let in some of the feeble moonlight.

A woman came forward on her knees, as the roof did not allow her to stand. Clinging to her were two children, a girl in a ragged dress, maybe eight or nine years old, and a naked boy with his thumb in his mouth who couldn't be more than two. How had she made it this far with such young children?

Curiosity did him no good. Zachary didn't need her story. He was only a cog on her wheel to freedom.

"What do thee need most?"

"Food." At that word, the boy began to cry.

"Hush, Josiah." The little girl clapped her hand over his mouth. "Ain't no cryin' on this journey."

"Leave the door up unless thee hears someone other than me. I will call out before I will return with food and water."

"Thank you, suh."

Zachary let the title go. He never corrected them anymore. Almost all the fugitives he'd helped called him that. They did not follow the Friends' ways, and would not be there long enough to educate them. He sprinted to the springhouse and filled a pail with cold water, then stuffed a small wheel of cheese in his pocket. In the house, he put two loaves of Gwen's bread in a sack along with the cucumbers and tomatoes he'd picked that afternoon. Then he went into the cellar and cut three thick slices from a smoked ham and wrapped it in a square of linen.

"'Tis I, the farmer," Zachary called in a hoarse whisper when he reached the back wall of the barn. He hung the pail's handle over his forearm and took the end of the sack in his teeth while he scaled the wall. He lifted his chin once his head was in the opening, and the woman took the sack. Then he slid the pail inside.

The woman opened the sack, and the little girl gasped. "Can we eat the bread, Momma?"

"Thank you, suh." Tears glittered even in the dim light. "I doan know what else to say."

"Feed thy children." He pointed to the chest along the short wall. "Thee might find something to fit the boy in there. And maybe something for thyself and the girl. 'Tis for whoever has a need."

She broke one of the loaves and passed chunks to the children, who crammed it in their mouths. Manners meant little when one was starving.

"I must ask thee, did the man see thee when he pried up the board?"

She turned her chunk of bread over in her hands, as if unsure what to do with it. "We was huddled in the corner, but he seen us, certain."

Zachary sighed. "Then he knows thee are here, and he knows of this secret room. Thee are not safe."

"We safe, suh." Her clear eyes met his. "We safe."

"But he saw thee."

"He my brother."

"Brother?" What were the chances? Zachary's mind reeled. What were the chances? "And thee are sure he recognized thee?"

She smiled, a tired movement of her lips. "Samson ain't never been scared o' rats."

Of course not. But he'd been scared for his sister, so the fear had been real. Believable. The other slave catchers had been fooled.

"But if they question him—"

"He never tell them about me and the children." She shook her head so hard her kerchief slipped sideways. "Never."

Zachary chose to believe her. After all, he couldn't unmake the room. Neither could he tell Titus that it was no longer safe. And he would not turn away a fugitive in need—like those in front of him.

"Eat and rest for a few days. The children are too weary to go on." Both had wolfed down the bread. The small amount would have filled their shrunken bellies. They were curled together, if not asleep, not far from it. "I will speak to someone about an errand. Perhaps we can get thee farther north in a wagon."

"I have no money—"

"Nor would I ask for any. Rest easy. Thee are among Friends." She wouldn't understand the reference, but it didn't matter. Tomorrow, he'd speak with Daniel and see if there were any purchases he needed from Steubenville.

"As a matter of fact, I have a furniture order with a business there." Seated on the bench that'd been his perch for days, Daniel pointed to the house. Tad and one of the Quaker lads were applying the final coat of whitewash around the window casings. "Does it not look grand? I shall be ready to move in once the furniture arrives." He should give credit where it was due. "And that would not have happened without the generous labor of your community."

"They appreciate thy willingness to help with the slave catcher problem."

"Which is back, I am given to understand."

"Indeed."

"And"—he looked up at the tall man beside him and lowered his voice—"'tis why you need a trip to Steubenville. To move some of your... products." It was best not to say too much out loud, even in Mount Pleasant.

"My products will be ready to go to market in a day or two."

"Excellent. My furniture order should be ready by then as well. 'Tis a large order." He rubbed his chin. "Should not surprise me if it takes two or even three trips to bring it all." What did he need first? "Bring the bed, the small table, and as many of the chairs as you can fit. The table and sideboard can come later."

"I can do that." Zachary started to leave.

"One moment." Daniel pulled his purse out, ignoring the shake of the other man's head. He extracted a handful of coins and held them out. "Come and get them, man. I am still under the doctor's orders to stay off my foot." When Zachary got close he whispered. "If not for you, then spend it on what the others might need. 'Tis little enough I can do to help."

Except write to Jonas. He'd spent a sleepless night thinking on that very letter. What did one say when they wished a favor from the son they'd disowned? But he must try.

"Zachary?"

Halfway to his mule, the man turned.

"Stop by again before you leave if you can. I will have a letter to post."

Zachary nodded and continued on his way. He was a good man, risking so much to help people he didn't even know.

Daniel's respect for the tall dairy farmer grew with each encounter. And to think that, if Jonas had been successful, Zachary would be laboring in a field somewhere for someone else.

Tad was washing his brush out in a bucket, so Daniel waved him over. "I need to return to the tavern."

"You feelin' poorly? Should I get the doc?"

"Nothing of the sort. I have a letter to write."

"I will fetch the cart."

Daniel had rented a cart from Lawrence's livery, pulled by a pony almost as old as King. It worked to transport him while he couldn't walk and left the wagons free for the other work the men needed to do.

Once in his rented room at the cramped desk, he stared at the blank piece of paper. Even the salutation was difficult to write. A usual family greeting would hardly serve under the circumstances. Would Jonas even open it?

Would he open a letter from Jonas?

Yes, he would. Disowned from inheritance or not, Jonas was still his son. And Daniel still loved him. The disappointment—the disgust—at his choices of actions couldn't erase that.

He dipped the quill into the spattered inkpot.

Jonas,

> I hope this letter finds you well. As I write, I am laid up with an injured foot, but the doctor has assured me it should heal quickly. As you know by now, I have relocated to the Ohio Territory in a place called Mount Pleasant. And that it is, pleasant. Except for one recurring problem.

How best to word the next part? He tapped the feathered end of the quill against his cheek. Perhaps he should be bold and blunt. Jonas had never been one for finesse.

> The Quaker community I live in is being stalked by men who come in search of fugitive slaves. I believe you know something of this operation. The Quakers, being pacifists, are not law-breakers.

Well, maybe they were, but there was a law above human law. Daniel was as sure of that as he was that night followed day. God's law was what mattered. And the Bible said to love your neighbor. There was nothing of love in what the slave catchers were doing.

> My letter is to inquire of you whether there is something I can do, or perhaps something you can do, to ease this burden on my community. I came here to find peace after your mother died, God rest her soul, not to fight a battle I have no interest in. If you have any advice for me, please write me in care of the Mount Pleasant, Ohio Territory, postal office.
>
> Your father,
> Daniel Whiteford

He read it over again. It wasn't much of a letter. He blew on the ink to hasten the drying, then folded it and slid it into an envelope. He'd need to borrow some sealing wax from the tavern keeper.

Would he get a response from Jonas? He hoped so, and not just because it might contain something helpful.

Because he missed his son.

Maybe not the man he'd become, but he missed the boy he remembered. The boy who'd, once up on a time, looked so much like his nephew, Owen.

Zachary had never held his breath for so long. Maybe not literally, but it felt like it. As he pulled the horses to a halt beside the twisted oak, he heaved a sigh of relief. They'd made it without encountering anyone—not a single other traveler on a road that was normally quite busy.

It must have been God's doing, because one as young as the boy had been impossible to keep completely quiet. Yet there had been none to hear his hushed, childish babble. The children had remained under the hot tarp, bumping along in the wagon's bed with the sun beating down on them.

Zachary had no idea what their lives had been like before. Maybe this had been easy for them. The girl was old enough to have been put to work in the fields picking cotton, after all.

And the woman—whose name he'd never asked—rode beside him on the seat, posing as his wife. He'd struggled with that for two nights, but in the end, it seemed the easiest disguise of all. Slave catchers, other than the band who could identify Zachary, would be looking for a woman with two young children, not a married woman with her husband. They'd found a suitable dress in the chest, and she'd fashioned her hair so she no longer resembled a slave in a kerchief.

She was beautiful.

Another reason Zachary had been holding his breath.

He'd already gone over the directions to the next safe house with her several times. She'd repeated them back to him, word for word. And so had the girl last night when they'd made camp.

"Come, children. We are here." She climbed down and helped them out of the wagon.

Zachary dug into his pocket and handed over some coins.

She stepped back. "You done so much already."

"'Tisn't mine. A man in Mount Pleasant gave it to me and said to use them as needed. 'Twould be hard to explain if thee were found carrying a greater sum. Thee might be accused of stealing." He pointed to the sack of provisions the girl had over her shoulder. "But it can buy a little food when the sack runs out."

She accepted the coins, their fingers brushing briefly, their eyes meeting. "You be like some kind of angel on earth."

He didn't feel like an angel. Not at that moment. If the Lord had given him even a nudge to run north with her and the children, he would have Justice and Jubal at a gallop. But He hadn't. And not because Zachary hadn't prayed over it almost non-stop since he'd discovered them in the secret room. For all he knew, she had a husband somewhere. Although, the girl's skin was very light and the boy's as dark as Zachary's, hinting that they did not share the same father.

It was none of his business.

"Go in peace and safety."

"Thank you, suh," the woman said, the girl echoing her in her high voice, and the boy chuckled, no doubt happy to be out from under the tarp.

Zachary touched his hat brim and clicked to the team. The wagon jerked into motion, and Zachary didn't look back. He was alone again, and as much as he didn't like it, there was an odd sort of peace that came over him—the peace of knowing he'd done the *right* thing—not the *easy* thing.

When was the right thing ever easy?

Chapter 26

T HE FURNITURE CAME A long way from filling Daniel's new house, but he was tickled that Zachary had also found room to pack the office desk and chair he'd ordered. It was in the sitting room for now, taking up a little of the emptiness.

"Thee will live here now, Grandfather?" Owen twisted around in the center of the room, taking everything in.

"Soon." He gestured for Micah and Gwen to have a seat in the ladderback chairs arranged in a wide circle while Dinah sank to the floor with Sally Faye on her lap.

Owen turned back to Daniel. "'Tis so big."

"Enough, son." Micah's scold was gentle. "A man's house is his own business."

Owen hunched his shoulders, looking up at Daniel.

"'Tis all right. The lad is only curious," he said to Micah and Gwen. Then he bent down to Owen's level. "I will need a housekeeper to keep the place clean for me and cook my meals. And perhaps a stableman to tend to the outside, especially when I get my own horses. I will also need lots of visits from my grandson when I get too lonely in this big house."

"Can Sally Faye and Dinah come too?"

How could Daniel say no to those blue eyes? How often had he done so in the past when the eyes had been Jonas's or Constance's? He wasn't going to make those mistakes again. Perhaps with age—or maybe with heartache—there did come wisdom. "Of course they can."

"Yay!" Owen jumped and landed with a thump.

"Outside, son, with all thy energy," Gwen said. "Dinah, will thee take them out and mind they stay away from the street?"

"Yessum, Gwen." The girl herded the younger ones outside, and the room felt emptier.

"Thee mentioned a housekeeper," Micah said. "Cora Johnson might be a good choice." He looked at his wife. "What say thee, Gwen?"

Surprise lifted her brows. "Why did I not think of that? 'Twould be a help to her."

"Who is this Cora Johnson?"

"A recent widow here in Mount Pleasant," Micah said. "She and her husband lived in one of the cabins on the eastern edge of town. Edward was some years older and didn't leave her with much, I fear. They have a son, but he went to sea, and her daughter remains in North Carolina."

Gwen said, "There is some hope her daughter's family will join us in Mount Pleasant when they can, but it may not be for a few years. And she has not had a letter from her son in a long time. She fears the worst, of course, but tries to remain hopeful."

Many a good man went to sea never to be seen again. It was a rough life and not without its dangers. Disease, injury, pirates, and England had been flexing her muscles on the seas in recent years, capturing and conscripting sailors from any vessel they overtook. It wouldn't surprise Daniel if the United States were to come under attack from England again. But that was a worry for another day.

"Is she a good cook?" Daniel tapped his belly, much flatter than when he'd left North Carolina.

Micah chuckled. "I remember her pickled beets being the favorite of every picnic."

"Thee always did prefer them over mine." Gwen scowled at her husband but smiled at Daniel. "Thee will be pleased with her cooking.

And Micah tells the truth. None makes a better pickled beet."

"Would you introduce me to her? Perhaps after meeting on Sunday?"

"Even better, join us for dinner Sunday evening at the Baldwins'. I will invite Cora as well. We should ask Zachary to come. That one keeps far too much to himself these days." She gave Daniel a pert grin. "I will tempt thee with a blackberry pie. The children and I plan to pick at the farm tomorrow."

"Indeed," Micah said, "which is why I shall be a little tardy in the morning. I must drive them out there first."

"What is tardy when there is a blackberry pie involved?" Daniel laughed, but the impact of his words washed over him.

The idea of another delay, even if not more than an hour, didn't ruffle him. Not even a little. His association with the Quakers—the Friends—was changing him.

And he rather liked it.

A dinner party with good friends should be a happy occasion, a light-hearted affair. So why did Zachary dread the whole ordeal?

Perhaps Gwen was right. She'd chided him for becoming a hermit in their midst. He was finding it more difficult to mingle with others. Was it because of the secret he kept? Not that he kept it all that well. Paul, Mark Allen, Micah, and Daniel knew of his work with the fugitives. But he'd like to keep the circle as small as possible. And keeping to himself seemed the best way.

But he couldn't turn down the invitation without causing more questions than he wanted to answer. So he finished washing the cow smell off his hands and arms, then dressed back in his Sunday best. Friends might dress plain, but they still took care to wear their best plain clothing on a Sunday.

He'd hitched the team before washing up. Annabelle had a bruise on her foot, so he wouldn't ride her until it healed. He climbed up and unwrapped the reins, then disengaged the brake.

"Hup, Justice. Hup, Jubal." The matching blacks leaned into their harnesses and set off in a steady trot. The breeze created was welcome in the August heat. Even with the sun sinking toward the west, it was still hot. And muggy. He wouldn't be surprised if it rained that night. And they could use it. His corn was looking spiky in the field.

He passed Mark Allen and Faye's budding orchard. Row upon row of apple trees too young to produce yet, but soon. Micah and Gwen's farm was next, where several piles of bricks waited beside the barn. Talk was that construction on their new house would follow as soon as Daniel's storage building was finished, and that might be by week's end. The Friends who had labored alongside Daniel's hired man, Isaac, had learned the art of bricklaying well. The new house would go up in no time.

Once Zachary reached the town, he slowed the team to a walk. It being a Sunday, nearly everyone was relaxing, sitting outside under a shade tree. He called greetings and exchanged nods with many. Several youngsters jogged alongside the wagon, sharing stories, happy and carefree. It was a good life in Mount Pleasant. A good community of Friends.

Gwen was right. He needed to get out more. And being alone had grown wearisome. Maybe he was ready. Maybe it was time to engage with his community again.

He parked the wagon and unhitched the team, since it would be a lengthy dinner. Micah appeared, and they led the horses to Thomas's stable and tied them in the shade in front of it.

"I am glad thee came. Gwen has worried about thee."

"She needn't."

"But thee know Gwen. She worries for those she cares about. And thee are special to her."

"She is special to me as well." From the frightened girl he'd encountered in the hold of a ship to a confident young mother had been a journey he was proud to have played a small part in. And he'd been well rewarded for his efforts when she saved him from Jonas Whiteford's attempt to kidnap him and resell him into slavery.

"Were it anyone but thee saying that"—Micah leaned close as they walked to the house—"I would worry."

Zachary's laugh was rusty from disuse, but it felt good.

The dinner was as all such dinners. After the silent prayer, food was passed, stories were told, and news was shared. Through it all, there was more laughter, even from Daniel. Zachary couldn't remember having ever heard the serious man laugh before.

The women had cleared away the dishes, and darkness had fallen. The men were discussing the latest news from a paper Thomas had picked up on a trip to Roberts Landing that week when someone knocked on the door.

"I wonder who that could be this late in the evening." Thomas stood and answered the door, then exclaimed, "Titus!"

Zachary bound to his feet and rushed to see. "Titus?"

Dark rings hollowed the boy's eyes, his floppy hat was missing, and a nasty scar slashed jaggedly across his cheek. He swayed on his feet. But it was Titus, all right.

"Come in, come in." Thomas waved him forward.

"I got others with me." Even his voice was weary.

"Bring them in, by all means." Betsy had joined them, wiping her hands on a towel. "Do not leave them waiting outside."

A young girl came first, followed by two older women.

The young girl resembled Titus so much that Zachary couldn't take his eyes off her. "Is this thy sister?"

"'Tis." Despite his fatigue, Titus straightened, chest out. "My sister—"

"Miriam? Titus?" Dinah handed Sally Faye to Gwen without taking her eyes off the two.

"Dinah?" Titus and the girl spoke as one. A hush fell over the room as the three came together, tears falling, arms wrapped around each other.

Dinah was Titus's other sister?

How had Zachary not connected that? He remembered now, feeling foolish for having forgotten. When they'd first met, Titus had mentioned two sisters—Miriam and Dinah.

She looked nothing like the other two. While Titus and Miriam were dark and slight, Dinah had fairer skin and longer legs. She was as tall as her sister, who was obviously quite a bit older.

"Come." Betsy motioned from just inside the door. "Please, come inside."

In all the surprise, the two elderly women had been left on the porch.

"We need more introductions," Betsy said.

Titus tore himself away from his sisters, mopping his cheeks with a sleeve. "These be Sapphira and Evie."

Evie? Could it be? Zachary whirled and faced them. The old woman was staring at him, moisture gathered in her eyes.

She pushed around Sapphira and reached up to cup his face.

"I doan know which one you be, but you be my husband's boy. You got the look of him."

"Momma?" Zachary squeezed the name out of a throat that didn't want to work. "Zachary, I am Zachary."

"My baby." The frail hands trembled on his cheeks as she pulled his head down with surprising strength and kissed first one cheek and then the other. "My baby." Then she raised her eyes to his. "Do you know where your brothers be?"

He shook his head, and she clutched his waistcoat before collapsing against him.

"Someone fetch the doctor!" The cry tore from Zachary's lips.

The hand in his was wrinkled, skin thin to the point of papery, nails thickened and yellowed. But Zachary had never seen anything so beautiful.

Paul had insisted that Momma not be moved last night, explaining that she'd succumbed to exhaustion and shock, according to him. She was still asleep in a bed at Thomas and Betsy's. Zachary had spent the night in the chair, dozing sometimes, but mostly watching Momma sleep.

Exhaustion and shock were part of what happened, but also grief. Zachary had seen it in her eyes. Not that she hadn't been happy to see him, she had. Perhaps the sight of him had raised hope that her other sons were also there.

How had she survived the journey? She had to be somewhere in her late seventies. Details were still cloudy, but he would speak to Titus when he could. Until then, he'd hold her hand and pray that God didn't take her away too soon now that he'd found her.

Or rather, she'd found him.

Or more correctly, that God had brought them together.

Micah and Gwen had taken the children to Zachary's place, where

Micah would take care of the cows for the next few days.

Daniel had taken Dinah and Miriam to his house. Since he still legal-ly owned Dinah, he was the best one to protect Miriam by claiming to own her as well.

Cora and Sapphira had gone with them, saying they'd see the girls settled upstairs and share the housekeeper's rooms. Which left Zachary at the Baldwins' with Momma and Titus. The boy slept on the floor at the foot of the bed on a pallet of blankets Betsy had provided.

So much for keeping secrets.

And yet, it was a testament to the conviction of the Friends that everyone had pitched in to help. Even Daniel, who was not a Friend. Not yet, anyway, though Zachary would not be surprised on the day when he came forward at meeting and officially joined the Soci-ety of Friends. He was a man Zachary had misjudged badly. Lesson learned—do not judge people based on their family relations or even their actions without full understanding.

Even a white man who owned a slave.

The fingers nestled inside of his twitched, and then Momma's eyes opened. They were glassy with age, her cheeks webbed, and her white hair thin, but hers was the face that'd flashed a thousand smiles his way when he was a boy. Hers were the lips that'd kissed his hurts. Hers were the hands that'd held him close.

"Good morning, Momma." He kept his voice low so as not to disturb Titus.

She smiled, the wrinkles deepening. "My baby."

"Momma, I am thirty-eight years old."

"And still my baby."

He squeezed her hand. "I wish I knew where the others are."

"Oh, hush. 'Tis enough that my old eyes can see you."

"Whatever made thee run, Momma?"

Her eyes widened. "You say thee?"

He shrugged. "'Twas a Quaker man who bought me at the auction. He freed me many years ago. Even more, he taught me to trust in God and live the faith thee always tried to get through to me."

"Glory be." She sat up. "You be a Quaker and free? Not a runaway?"

"I am a free man."

Tears glistened from the morning sun coming through the window. "Your daddy would be so *proud*." She gripped both his hands and squeezed. "His son a *free* man."

Zachary swallowed the flood of emotion that swamped him, taking several minutes until he could speak again. "What made thee run, Momma?"

"I doan know what else to do. You see, my massah done up and died right there in his bed. He doan have no family, so Sapphira and me, we bury him in the little cemetery next to his wife, her already dead many years. And then Sapphira and me, we doan know what to do."

"That be when I find 'em." Titus sat up and rubbed his eyes. "Me and Miriam." His jaw cracked in a huge yawn. "And we brung 'em here."

"But I never expected to find you, my baby. Nor Massah Whiteford neither."

"Thee know Daniel?"

"Know him?" Momma shook her head. "But I seen him from time to time. 'Twas his sister-in-law who owned me for many years. 'Twas him who sold me and Sapphira off after her death."

Anger spiked through Zachary. "Daniel *sold* thee?" Maybe he hadn't misjudged the man after all.

"Mmm-hmm. As good as. His man come and say we all goin' to the auction." Then she squinted and seemed to look through him for a moment. "There were someone else I recognized last night, a woman with dark curly hair."

"Gwen?" How could Momma know her?

Momma gasped. "She with the Quakers here? She with you?"

"How do thee know Gwen?"

She shook a finger at Zachary. "So Massah Whiteford, he come for his grandson, did he? I hope Gwen doan give that boy up. Massah give him to her. He belong to her."

Zachary's head spun. How could Momma know so much about the people here in Mount Pleasant?

Clearly, there was more to the story than he knew, but he intended to find out.

Chapter 27

C ORA JOHNSON WAS A force to be reckoned with, and Daniel wasn't sure about hiring her. Her red hair might be streaked with gray, but she had the energy of a woman half her age. She'd come to the house with Dinah and Miriam, and in very short order, had taken charge. The girls were installed in the two rooms under the eaves that he'd thought would be for storage, but Cora—as with all the Quakers, she preferred the use of her given name instead of Mrs. Johnson—proclaimed them rooms for the hired maids.

Daniel hadn't known he'd need a maid, much less two. Couldn't a housekeeper both clean and cook?

He leaned back in his chair at the desk. Margaret had always managed the household. Apparently, he'd taken that for granted. He should have paid more attention. They'd had a housekeeper, and Gwen for a maid until she'd left with Owen. Then there'd been Cook and Arthur and Silas the butler. Oh, and Mark Allen until he'd left. Daniel hadn't replaced him or Gwen, since Constance and Jonas had moved out of the house around the same time.

But he was one man living alone. How much staff could he need? Surely a housekeeper and a stableman would be more than sufficient. Wouldn't they?

On one thing, Cora would not have her way.

Dinah wouldn't be staying. Owen was very attached to the girl, and Gwen needed her help. He'd send her back to them as soon as it was convenient.

But what about Miriam, a runaway under his roof? If he were caught with her here, everything he'd worked for could be ruined. Including his chance to be a grandfather to Owen.

He could hardly build a relationship with the boy while he was sitting in jail.

"Daniel?" Cora tapped on the open door to his house office.

"Yes?" Would he ever get used to the help calling him by his given name? It seemed so... out of order.

She folded her hands in front of the white apron she wore over her dove-gray dress which didn't hide her trim figure. "If thee were sincere about offering me the position as housekeeper, then I would like to accept. Everything here is most agreeable to me." She smiled, the expression a combination of tender and stern and made him feel not entirely comfortable.

But what choice did he have? He hadn't the name of anyone else to serve as his housekeeper. The frontier was generally short of women, must less single women.

"Of course, well, I shall have to have the kitchen stocked with"—he waved a hand—"whatever it needs."

"I am happy to make thee a list. 'Twill require pots and pans, dishes, glassware, and utensils, as well as the necessary linens, of course."

"Of course. A list would be most appreciated." He wouldn't have a clue what to purchase on his own. "I will hire Zachary to make a trip to Steubenville as soon as 'tis—"

"I will accompany him." She gave a serene nod. "To be sure the purchases meet the needs here."

"Of course." Was that all he could say in the face of this woman who seemed to know more about running his house than he did? How did she manage to be both formidable and sweet at the same time?

She made him feel... itchy.

"Very well. Let me know when Zachary is ready to go, and I shall be ready. Sapphira and I will bring what things I have to use in the meantime. Then I have arranged for someone to take Sapphira to Zachary's farm to be with his mother. She will be happier there with someone she knows."

"Of course." Stifling a cringe at his limited vocabulary around her, he stood to walk her to the door.

"I can find my own way out. After all, 'twill be my home now." Another smile. "I believe we shall get along fine." And with a tilt of her head, she was gone.

Daniel sank back into his chair and pulled in a long breath. Had he hired her? Or had she made herself at home? He wasn't exactly sure.

The elders called the meeting three evenings after Titus had brought Momma and the others in, because word of fugitives arriving in the midst of a Sunday gathering had been too much to contain.

Zachary rubbed his gritty eyes after the sleepless night beside Momma. He'd taken her home before coming to the meeting house. He shifted on the hard bench and faced the front when Thomas addressed those assembled, which included Daniel, as he was housing one of the fugitives.

"We left our homes four years ago to escape the issue of slavery, having found it too difficult to live amongst. However"—Thomas raised a hand to quell the growing murmurs—"the issue has reached us here in Mount Pleasant and we must decide what we are going to do about it. Zachary has been shouldering the burden by himself for too long. 'Tis for all of us to face. Together."

"Agreed," Paul said. While not an elder, they'd invited him because he was already involved, tending to those who arrived in poor health. "We cannot turn our backs on these people who are bravely fighting for their freedom. My biggest regret is that we cannot offer them sanctuary here in our community."

"'Twould be easy to open our doors and our hearts to them, but too dangerous," an elder said. "And I speak not of danger to us, the Friends, but danger to them, always fearful of being caught and returned to an abominable fate or even death."

"Indeed." Another spoke. "They will do better to make it to Canada where there is no law mandating they must be returned."

Another stood. "What we need to do is work to change the law!"

"Which will take time." All eyes turned to Zachary as he stood. "And time is something these people do not have. We must help them along their journey now. We must be content to be cogs in the wheel. They need food, clothing, and safe places to sleep." He nodded toward Paul. "And often medical attention."

"Is that truly the best we can do?" The question came from Daniel.

"I fear so." Thomas shook his head. "'Twould seem none of us has a politician in his back pocket."

A halfhearted chuckle went around the room.

"What we need are contacts." Everyone's attention came back to Zachary. "We need work with people farther north so that our job will be only to get the fugitives to the next safe house. From there, the next community will have charge of getting them to the next safe house even farther north, and so on. We need..." His words came slowly, the idea coming together as he spoke. "We need a network like a spider's web of connecting communities of Friends who will work together to move the fugitives all the way to the Canadian border."

Silence followed as the others digested his idea.

"Who would head this up?" Paul asked.

"No one." Zachary was sure on this point, as if the words came from beyond himself and he was just the messenger. "Each community would know of their contacts on both their southern and northern borders, but nothing beyond that. In that way, if caught, they could not expose the entire system. The trail could be rerouted and would never completely fail due to a discovery."

"'Tis a good plan," Daniel said. "But can we not shelter some here?" He looked at Zachary. "Like your mother and the other old woman who arrived last night? It hardly seems humane to force them on."

Force them on. Zachary had been doing his best not to think about that. And not to connect Momma to Daniel. The simmering anger at what he had learned that morning hadn't eased. Daniel—who'd had Momma *sold*—was now wanting to help other fugitives. Had, in fact, helped other fugitives.

"We must get them to where they will be safe," Thomas said. "That must be our goal. So we all agree?"

Everyone nodded—including Zachary. As much as his heart would be torn from his chest, he would see Momma safely to Canada. Or, if the Lord willed, he would go with her. But so far, he felt a strong push in his spirit against that idea. His mission here in Mount Pleasant wasn't yet accomplished. He knew that. He didn't know how he knew it, but he did.

The meeting dragged on for another half hour with different men assigned to seek out other communities and start the process of creating the web of Friends.

When they adjourned, Zachary approached Daniel. "We need to talk."

The other man's brows rose at his tone. "Of course."

"Not here."

"My house, then?"

Zachary followed him out the door and across the street to the new brick structure.

Once inside, Daniel offered him a drink.

"Thank thee, no. 'Tis not a social call."

"So I gathered." Daniel sighed. "What have I done to offend you this time?"

"Thee sold my mother."

Daniel's mouth dropped open, and he seemed to struggle for words.

"She belonged to thy sister-in-law, and thee had her and Sapphira sold when that woman died."

"I had no idea"—Daniel waved Zachary toward a chair while he dropped into the one across from it—"that one of Matilda's slaves was your mother."

"She was." Zachary rested his elbows on his knees and his forehead on the heels of his hands. "And thee had her sold."

"I am..." Daniel's voice broke. "I am so sorry. When I found out I had inherited Matilda's slaves, I was appalled. Angry. I never wanted to own a slave. I had fought against my father on the issue. Argued with my wife over it. Broke a relationship with my sister over it. Lost a son to it." The last words were barely a whisper.

Zachary looked up.

Daniel's face was covered with one hand's splayed fingers.

The pain on his face was apparent even through those fingers. "I am sorry. Here I came to accuse thee again, something I seem to do all too often. But slavery has cost thee as well."

"It has." Daniel lowered his hand. "But I am sorry about thy mother. It hurts to know that even for a short time, I owned her. And now she must leave you again. Her master will be looking for her, of course."

"He will not." Zachary shrugged at the confused look Daniel gave him. "He died without an heir, it seems." He explained what happened and how the women had buried the man before leaving.

"If we lived in a just world, your mother would be free now."

Zachary could only nod, the pain of the coming separation already crushing him.

"Wait one moment." Daniel popped up from his chair and hurried out the door into the hallway. He came back clutching a handful of paperwork, shaking it at Zachary. "I may have the answer." He dropped into the chair and rifled through the papers until he lifted four of them.

Zachary left Daniel's house and raced for home. Justice and Jubal took the turn into the farm's lane at a gallop, Zachary urging them on, the wagon lifting onto two wheels for a breath-stealing moment. When all four wheels were on the ground again, he slowed the horses. Bringing them to a stop in front of the house, he set the brake, and jumped from the wagon to the porch.

"Momma!" He jerked the front door open.

Momma and Sapphira had their arms around each other against the back wall of the single room, fear filling both dark faces.

"'Tis good news, Momma. Good news for both of thee." He let out a full breath and laughed.

"What happened?" Momma stepped away from Sapphira and came toward him, eyeing him as if he had gone mad.

"Thee can stay, Momma. Thee can stay here, with me." He motioned Sapphira to join them. "Both of thee. Thee have no need to run any farther. Thee can be safe here."

"How?" Sapphira's question was full of doubt.

"Daniel has thy papers. When the man purchased thee, he forgot to take thy papers. As he paid in cash, no one at the auction house knew where to send them, so they returned them to Daniel." He wrapped

Momma in a hug. "Thee are free to stay here."

Sapphira crossed her arms and scowled. "Sounds to me like we belong to Massah Whiteford."

Zachary reached into his coat, keeping one arm around Momma, and pulled out the papers. "Thee do not. He signed these over to me. Legally, thee now belong to me. But only on paper. Thee are free."

Momma looked up at him, her cloudy eyes misting over. "We free?"

"Free?" Sapphira's whisper echoed her.

"As free as we can make thee." He rattled the papers. "These will keep the slave catchers at bay, but in all other ways, thee are free."

"Free." Momma sagged under his arm, and he helped her to a chair.

"I want thee to stay with me, Momma." He knelt beside her chair. "But thee are free to go on north if that is thy heart's wish. I will help thee all I can."

"Go? When I just found my baby?" She cupped his face with hands that trembled. "Why I wanna do that?"

A joy and a peace broke over Zachary that nearly toppled him over. Momma wanted to stay. Then he raised his face to Sapphira. "I hope thee will stay as well, unless there is family thee are trying to find. And if so, I will help thee find them."

"I doan got no one but Evie here."

"Then stay." Zachary stood and held out his hand to her. "Stay and be part of our family."

"I wish you would." Momma faced her friend. "I doan know how I would get along without you after all these years we been together."

Sapphira looked around the small house. "We three gonna be cozy in here."

"I have time to add on before the snow falls." Zachary scanned the single-room house. "'Twas always my plan to put two rooms on the north side. Until then, I will sleep in the loft and thee can have the bed."

"It be big enough for the two of us all right." Momma chuckled. "You sure got your daddy's size."

A lump lodged in Zachary's throat. "I miss him. And I missed thee."

"How come you to be a Quaker?" Momma asked.

For once, that question didn't bother him at all. He sat and told them the story about Eli and how he'd brought him north, telling him all about the Lord.

When he was finished, Momma gripped his hands. "I always believed in Jesus, you know that."

"I remember, Momma. Thee would sing me songs about Him."

"Oh, chile, I sang and I sang and I prayed over you, just as I did all your brothers."

"I heard you. I never forgot."

"But you was so full of anger." She shook her head. "You worried me as much as my oldest did."

"I never wanted to cause thee worry or hardship, Momma."

"There ain't no momma who doan worry none about her children." She glanced around the house. "Ain't no sign of a wife or chile here." It wasn't a question, and yet it was.

"Not for lack of wanting them, I assure thee. But black Quakers are few and far between. We are something of an oddity, I fear."

"Do you have to marry a Quaker if you be a Quaker?" Puzzlement crinkled Momma's brow. "Is that how it works?"

"Not have to, but want to. I believe"—he pressed his fist to his chest—"that the Light of Christ lives in me. I believe that the Quakers understand that and believe the God of the Bible loves all people, no matter what color their skin. And I know it to be true. So I cannot walk away from that." He gripped his hands between his knees. "Not even for a wife and children."

Momma's worn hands closed over his. "Then you got all the family you need, son."

Chapter 28

DANIEL ATE THE EGG-AND-CHEESE breakfast prepared by Dinah and Miriam. They'd used the kitchenware Cora had brought from her cabin to cook a simple meal. The dining room held only the table and four chairs, but it was a start. He'd get some paintings for the walls and a sideboard, maybe even a chandelier to hang above the table. On second thought, that would be too pretentious in a community of Quakers.

There he went again, thinking like a Quaker. But they were right about so many things. If he had paid more attention to the things that mattered in his younger years, he would be in a very different place today. Or would he? He might have joined the Quakers when he was a young father—and still wound up in the exact same place.

Was this where God had always wanted him?

He'd never wondered about what God wanted for his life before. He'd just plunged on, determined to make the most of himself—his way.

He'd had a good life. He'd been prosperous, respected, and admired.

One could say that he hadn't needed God. But those thoughts brought a heaviness to his spirit now. Who didn't need God? The foolish. Those who thought they could live their lives entirely to please themselves.

The younger Daniel Whiteford.

He wasn't that man anymore.

"Mr. Whiteford?" A timid voice pulled him out of his weighty thoughts.

"Yes, Dinah?"

The girl came into the dining room, Miriam beside her.

"We was wonderin', can we see Titus?"

"Of course you can. He is at the Baldwins'."

"It be safe, us goin' outside?" Miriam's voice was huskier, and filled with uncertainty.

As it should be. The slave catchers were still out there, somewhere. Daniel should have thought of that. Should have reunited the siblings days ago.

"Perhaps 'twould be better if I bring him here. You can all stay in the rooms upstairs."

The girls grinned, looking at each other. Of course they'd all want to be together. They were a family, after all.

Daniel rose. "I will do it before work." He took up his cane and hobbled to the door. "Keep yourselves out of sight while I am gone." He'd given them the same instructions since they'd been there. Had it only been four days?

Micah was pulling his wagon up the house when Daniel reached the porch. "Good morning, Daniel."

"Good morning." He navigated the steps and climbed onto the wagon. Once settled on the seat, he turned to the younger man. "I believe tomorrow I will walk. 'Tisn't too far, and my foot is much better."

"What does Paul say?"

Daniel snorted. "He would have me wrapped in cotton wool and stored on a shelf."

"He *is* the doctor."

"That he is. I need to stop by the Baldwins' this morning."

Micah clicked to the horses, and they moved away from the house. It wasn't far to the Baldwins', and when they drove up, Thomas was sitting on the porch with a steaming cup in his hands.

After greetings, Daniel said, "The girls would like Titus to visit, but

I think 'twould be good for him to move in with them. I have plenty of room, and they are family. They need to be together."

"I believe thee are correct." Thomas held up a finger. "But let me caution thee to put up a store of food. That boy can eat his weight in a day." He chuckled.

"As a growing boy should, I suppose. Send him over whenever 'tis convenient."

"I will. Have a good day, my friend."

My friend.

Those words hit Daniel right in the chest. Would he ever grow tired of hearing them? Or ever take them for granted? He hoped not.

"Let us proceed to the work site, Micah. There is much to do."

"No reason we should not finish today." The younger man got the horses moving. "And I must tell thee, I am looking forward to being done."

"So you can start on your house, I assume."

"Indeed. I would like to have something built before the babe arrives. 'Tis more than a little cramped with Thomas and Betsy already." He slowed the horses while another wagon entered the street. "'Twas nice of thee to take Titus off their hands. Not that they would ever complain, but one less mouth to feed will ease things for them." He shot Daniel a pointed look. "Thee have become a good friend."

And there was that word again, bringing with it a fresh spike of... was it joy?

Daniel worked up the courage to ask, "What would you think if I were to become a member of the Friends here?"

"That would be tremendous!" Micah's answer was swift and sincere. "We would be honored to welcome thee into the meeting, providing thee accepts that the Light of Christ lives in thee."

"I know not enough to say that for sure yet, but I believe I am getting close."

"Then I and my family will pray for thee to find the final steps toward knowing."

"Thank you... my friend." Saying the words was almost as powerful as hearing them.

Zachary poured his heart and soul into building the addition to the house. While he'd constructed the main house with milled boards, the addition would be a log structure. He could get that done before the snow fell. The wait time for milled boards was too long, and he was impatient to have Momma and Sapphira in their own room with curtains on the window, rugs on the floor, and a mattress stuffed with sweet grasses dried in the sun.

They would not sleep like slaves under the eaves with a wool blanket and a pokey straw-filled mattress.

"Hup, Jubal." The black horse leaned into his harness and dragged the log from the woods toward the house. Once there, Zachary stopped beside the growing pile of logs waiting to be shaped with an adz and notched to fit. He was hooking the log when two wagons and a few riders on horseback turned into his lane.

"Zachary!" Mark Allen hollered from the back of his flea-bitten gray horse. "We finished Daniel's warehouse on Saturday. Today we will help thee put up the walls."

He propped his hands on his hips. "But Micah needs help with his house, and he needs it done before the babe comes."

"True, but he is putting up bricks." Mark Allen stopped the horse beside him and gestured to the men gathering around. "We are the ones who know not how to erect brick walls. But logs? This we know." The men grabbed tools from the wagons, broke off into groups, and started to work.

Momma and Sapphira came onto the porch, Momma with her fingers pressed over her lips.

"Did thee hear, Momma? Thy room will be finished in no time."

She raised both hands. "Praise the Lord. Me and Sapphira will raid the garden and have lunch ready by high noon."

Zachary chuckled as the two women grabbed the gathering baskets he kept on the porch, heads bent together, and hurried off. The men were in for a meal they wouldn't soon forget. In the few days Momma had been cooking for him, he was pretty sure he'd put on weight.

Titus jumped from the bed of one wagon and sauntered over.

Zachary's heart squeezed at the cocky grin and squeezed a little tighter at the sight of the mostly healed scar that still puckered the boy's face. "'Tis good to see thee, but 'tis a risk, thee being here in broad daylight."

The boy shrugged. "Been cooped up with my sisters for days. A man needs some sunshine now and again."

"I have missed thee."

Titus ducked his head and rolled his shoulders. "Me too."

"Keep thy eyes open and use the secret room if needed."

"I will. Did you have many travelers while I was gone?" There was a confident tilt to his grin.

"Indeed. They kept me informed of thy whereabouts, which I greatly appreciated." Zachary should be helping the men, but he didn't want to rush the time with Titus.

The boy looked up at him. "Those will be the last ones I send."

Pain blossomed in Zachary's chest. "Because thee are taking thy sisters north to Canada?"

Titus nodded, fishing a piece of paper from his pocket. "Daniel asked me to bring you this. He needs supplies in Steubenville. Says Cora Johnson wants to go with you and make sure you get just what he needs for the house."

Zachary took the paper, scanned the list, and then stuffed it in his pocket. "I can do this once the rooms are framed in."

"'Twill be soon, with all these men workin'."

"I suppose so." Zachary sensed what was coming next and almost walked away, not wanting to hear it.

"I was thinkin', if it be okay with you, that me and the girls could stow away in your wagon as far as Steubenville."

If it would be okay?

Emotions raged inside Zachary until he managed to harness them. He would miss this boy—this young man. But he was happy for him to be reunited with Dinah and Miriam. Thrilled that they would, the Lord willing, reach Canada and build lives for themselves. Together. As a family. Growing and maturing in freedom.

The Lord wasn't leaving Zachary alone. From the garden came singing, the wavering voices of two elderly women who would stay with him. Be his family for the years they had left.

"Has Daniel agreed to let Dinah go?"

"He did. She fussed a bit between going and staying with Gwen's family, but in the end, me and Miriam talked her into it."

"'Tis good for family to stay together."

"Like you and your momma." Titus cocked his head. "I doan know why I stopped at that house on our way back. Ain't never stopped there before. But I seen those two old women and nobody around, and I felt..." He shrugged. "I doan know—a push. And I walked up to them bold as brass. I never knew she be your momma."

"The Lord knew." Zachary put his arm around Titus's shoulders, shoulders that had filled out since they'd first met. Shoulders that were higher, for the boy had grown. "And that push? That was Him directing thee where He wanted thee to go. When thee reaches Canada, find a community of Quakers, Titus. Find them and learn more about the Lord."

"I will."

"And when thee can, send me a letter and let me know thee are safe."

Titus nodded, then cleared his throat. "Best get to work before they have this done and we ain't helped a lick." He stalked off and grabbed an adz from the back of a wagon, wiping his sleeve across his eyes.

Zachary watched for a few minutes, his heart full and hurting at the same time. Full of love for the community he lived in, for Momma and Sapphira singing in the garden, for the young man whose leaving was breaking his heart. But most of all, for the Lord who had orchestrated all of it.

In His time.

"You are sure you have everything you need?" Daniel asked Dinah. "The papers?"

"Yessuh, I got 'em right here." She patted the new pocket tied around her waist, sewn by Gwen and given to her at their tearful parting the evening before.

"And remember," Daniel said, "once you arrive in Canada, you will not need them anymore. You can burn them after that."

Miriam was only sixteen, but Daniel doubted anyone would question her being the adult of the trio. She certainly looked much older, no doubt from the hardships she'd faced while a slave. And as resourceful as Titus was, he'd be employed somewhere and providing for them as soon as they crossed the border, of that Daniel had no fear. But even so...

He pressed a few coins into Dinah's palm. "I would give you more, but 'twould only raise suspicion, I fear, if you were found with a greater amount." He gave the other two as much. "These coins you might have earned on your travels by doing odd jobs."

"There should be plenty of wild food to gather and eat along the way." Titus pocketed his coins. "But we got to get across the river to Canada. This should cover the ferry fee for the four of us."

"I had forgotten about your other sister already up north." Daniel withdrew more coins from his purse. "Take this."

"Thank you, suh." Miriam held up a palm as if to stop him. "But you done so much already."

He took her hand and put the coins in it. "Take it, please. I wish I could do more." These young people had something he didn't. He was free, true, but they were *family*. He would gladly trade places with them if he could have Margaret back, if he could have a second chance to raise Jonas and Constance. If he could set out with them on a journey that would see them all together and enjoying each other. But he couldn't, so the next best thing was helping others.

Wagon wheels crunched on the new gravel he'd had hauled in for the circle drive in front of the house. "It sounds like your ride is here."

Dinah stepped forward and hugged him, her skinny arms around his chest, bringing surprise and delight as he awkwardly patted her back.

"Thank you. Thank you for everythin'." She looked up at him, tears in her eyes.

"You are most welcome, my dear child. Go now, and build your new life."

She followed her brother and sister out the door.

Daniel stepped onto the porch and watched as Cora climbed onto the high seat and sat as straight as a fire poker next to Zachary, her fiery hair contained within a linen cap and a straw hat pinned over that.

The three siblings were in the bed of the wagon and pulling a tarp over the top of them.

Zachary moved several crates to further conceal them. Then he carried two crates and one large canvas bag onto the porch. "These are Cora's. I fetched them from her cabin. Would thee like me to take them into the house?"

"I can manage." He wasn't an invalid, after all. And how heavy could they be?

"And then there is this." Zachary lifted a crude cage from the wagon and brought it to the porch. Inside, a gray feline with sinister yellow eyes hissed at him.

"What am I do with that?"

"Her name is Sissy," Cora called from the wagon. "'Tis her job is to keep the mice away. She is a good house cat."

"There are no mice in my house." Daniel drew himself up and thumped his cane on the porch floor. The nerve of her suggesting such a thing.

"And Sissy will ensure none move in." Cora's nod was one of utmost assurance.

"What do I do with it until you return?" He'd never had a cat and certainly did not wish for one that hissed at him.

"She will take care of herself. Just let her out when she goes to the door, and fill her water bowl. 'Tis in the cage with her."

"Madam, you expect me to let this... this creature loose in my house?"

"She cannot do her job locked in that cage, now can she?" The tilt of her head was both a chide and a challenge.

How was Daniel supposed to answer that?

Chuckling, Zachary had returned to his seat on the wagon and lifted the reins. "We shall return tomorrow evening or the next morning with thy order. We shall see thee then if Sissy has not dispatched of thee along with the mice." He touched the brim of his hat and slapped the reins on the horses' rumps.

"There are no mice here!" Daniel called after them.

The cat hissed again.

Maybe he should go north with Dinah and her family.

Chapter 29

W HEN THE GNARLY OAK outside of Steubenville came into view, Zachary's insides twisted to match it. It hadn't been a smooth trip. They'd met several travelers along the way. Cora had done most of the talking, and the woman could *talk*. Even had anyone suspected they carried fugitives in the wagon, by the time they cut into Cora's ramblings, they were happy to make their excuses and ride on.

Zachary parked the wagon near the rock and climbed down. "We have arrived."

Titus poked his head up first and looked around. "This be the right spot. Come on, girls." He scrambled over the side.

Zachary helped both girls out of the wagon, then reached in for the three sacks of provisions, one for each. That way, should they be separated, no one would be left without food. Titus had explained that, and Zachary had tucked it away for use in the future. Because even with Titus no longer going south, as Mount Pleasant built its web of safe houses, there would be more fugitives needing his assistance.

"We best not linger. Ain't safe out here in the daylight." Titus stuck out his hand.

Zachary grasped it, squeezed, and then forced himself to let go. "Go in peace. Go with God. And be well, my friend."

Titus nodded, rubbing the tip of his nose with the back of one hand, and then motioned for the girls to follow.

Neither said a word, but both raised a hand in farewell. And then they slipped into the thick underbrush and disappeared.

Never to return.

"'Tis difficult to say goodbye to such delightful young souls as those," Cora said, still on her side of the wagon's seat.

"Indeed." It was all Zachary could force around the lump in his throat until he climbed back onto the wagon. "Hup, Justice. Hup, Jubal." The wagon lurched into motion, each revolution of its wheels taking him farther and farther from Titus, the boy who was probably as close to a son as he'd ever have.

But home at the farm was Momma. For the first time, Zachary had more than an empty house awaiting him when he returned.

Zachary and Cora had stayed the night in a boarding house in Steubenville, before setting out for Mount Pleasant that morning, but Zachary hadn't slept much. He'd tossed and turned and worried about Titus and the girls until he'd finally sat up and prayed. First, he'd thanked God for bringing Momma to him and for using Titus to do it. After asking God to grant Titus and the girls a safe passage to Canada, he thanked God for everything he could think of in the wee hours of the morning, like the farm, his horses, the cows, and Annabelle. Even his health. He had so much to be grateful for.

He had no business grumbling about what he didn't have instead of rejoicing for all he did. Finally, when he'd run out of things to be thankful for, peace had filled him and allowed him to sleep.

His jaw cracked on a long yawn.

"Would thee like me to take over the reins while thee rests?" Cora asked.

Zachary nearly jumped at her voice. For someone who'd jabbered to everyone they passed on the way to Steubenville, she'd been quiet on the return journey. Had her chattering been a ruse to distract people from their precious cargo? He shot her an appraising look.

She raised her eyebrows in return.

"Thank thee, no. We are nearly there." He yawned again. "'Tis just over that next rise."

"I see." She looked around. "Edward and I never went to Steubenville. 'Tis pretty country he brought me to. I wish we had explored more of it. He fell ill so soon after we finished the cabin."

"He was a good man."

"He was." She folded her hands in her lap. "But we must go on living, must we not? Whether our loved ones have left the earth—or just the area."

"Indeed, we must."

"I am so happy that thy mother has come to thee in her old age. What a comfort it must be for her. And thee as well, of course."

"I wish I knew where my brothers were, for her sake. 'Tis hard for her, the not knowing."

"I understand."

"Oh, pardon me. I had forgotten..." He wished the words back rather than add to her sorrow.

"'Tis fine. I do not expect I will ever know what happened to my son this side of heaven, but I rest assured that I will know then. My hope lies in what is ahead and not in what lies behind. As it should."

And as it should for Zachary as well.

"Thank thee, Cora. Those were words I needed to hear today."

"I rather thought so." She patted his arm. "Thee have a kind heart, Zachary, and many will be blessed by it in the years to come. Make no mistake, slavery is not going to go away without a fight. There will be many more like Titus who will need thee ahead."

"I wish it were not so. I wish the laws would change—that people's hearts would change." He stared at his dark hands gripping the reins. "I wish they could see people like me for what we are."

"God's children."

He nodded.

"They will, eventually. I have that hope." She chuckled and covered her mouth with one hand before facing him. "Imagine when some of those slave holders get to heaven and find people of all shades walking the streets of gold. They are in for a rude awakening."

Zachary laughed, a full-on belly-jiggling laugh. And it felt good. It felt very good.

If Daniel wasn't careful, he'd fall off the wagon's seat. He forced himself to sit back until he connected with the backrest. He had the irrational urge to swing his feet like a nine-year-old boy fidgeting on a church pew on Sunday morning. Roberts Landing had never seemed so far from Mount Pleasant as it did on this all-important trip.

"Almost there." Micah cast him a glance. "Thee has waited a long time for this. I do not blame thee for being anxious."

A long time indeed.

The poplar leaves wore a tinge of gold. The grass that waved in the open meadows was more brown than green. And just the last afternoon, a flock of geese had honked their way over the roof of his house. He'd pulled up roots from Greenesville in March, and here it was, mid-September already. The time had dragged and yet flown by. So much had happened. So much had changed. And so much more was yet to be done.

But today, he would see the first of his inventory. It would have made more sense, he supposed, to have set up a business right on the river. But then he wouldn't have been close to Owen. It was much better to have his business and his grandson close together, even if it meant his business would be less successful.

Of course, that depended on one's view of success.

"I had many grand plans when I left Greenesville," Daniel said. "Some of them have come to fruition, others have not. But so many things have happened that I could have never dreamed of." He turned toward the younger man. "Like you and your family accepting me as you have."

Micah's lips twitched. "Thee took a little getting used to."

Daniel laughed. "I am sure that is an understatement."

"We all thought you was trouble," came a voice from the wagon's bed, "and no doubt about it."

"Bran." Micah turned and scowled at the boy.

But Daniel grinned at the boy. "I thought that same of you, young man."

"We almost there?" Bran asked. "I could eat a horse."

"Thee must be growing, since thee ate enough breakfast to fill Sassy and Hap." Micah pointed to his team of red roans.

Bran patted his flat stomach. "Cora makes the best pancakes I ever had, but don't be tellin' Bridget I said that."

"Your secret is safe with me." Daniel had never eaten any of Bridget's pancakes, but he couldn't imagine anything better than what Cora had put before them that morning. He'd eaten five of them himself, along with three sausage patties. His new, trimmer waistline wasn't going to last with her in the house.

He still wasn't sure what to make of the woman, sweet one minute and bossing him around the next, but she could cook and clean and keep the house to suit him. If only she would get rid of that cat. He rubbed the back of his hand where scratch marks were healing from his unwise attempt to befriend the beast earlier in the week.

"I see rooftops." Bran stood in the wagon's bed.

Daniel inched forward on the seat again, hanging on to the edge. The plodding team climbed to the top of a small incline, and then Roberts Landing was in full view, including the livery stable with the paddock behind it filled with horses.

Some of them were his. He rubbed his hands together. He'd always loved fine horses, always had more than he needed simply because he enjoyed them. And now that his stable had been built behind the house, he was ready to stock it. No more rented horses for him.

Micah brought the wagon to a halt next to the paddock. "Do thee know which ones they are?"

"Two pairs of drafts, so I am assuming all four of the heavy horses." Daniel pointed to the caramel-brown animals with white faces and legs that stood dozing on the far side. "And two riding horses, a chestnut and a dappled gray." It wasn't hard to pick them out, either. Their thoroughbred lines were unmistakable among the smaller horses.

"Ain't they grand?" Bran's voice held a note of awe, something Daniel hadn't heard from him before. He obviously knew good horseflesh when he saw it. Daniel felt better about letting him drive one team and wagon back to Mount Pleasant.

It took longer than Daniel had hoped to get everything signed for and loaded and a meal of cold meats, bread, and cheese eaten. But once done, he had his two new wagons plus Micah's loaded with inventory, the two teams hitched, and both riding horses tied behind the one he'd drive. It had been years—more than he cared to count—since he'd driven a wagon, so he would follow Micah and let Bran bring up the rear. He couldn't get into much trouble if he just stayed in the middle.

"Mr. Whiteford?" An aproned clerk came out of the store brandishing an envelope. "I nearly forgot, sir. A letter arrived for you on the same barge as your goods." He handed it up to Daniel on the wagon.

Daniel took it and turned it over to the front. From Jonas.

Was his excitement over his new business—his new life—about to be squashed by the realities of his poor performance as a father all those years? Or did Jonas write with good news? Would he help control the route of the slave catchers around Mount Pleasant?

Daniel tucked the letter in his inside coat pocket. Whatever it said would have to wait. He had his hands full driving a new team. And they needed to get on the road if they were to make it back before full dark.

"Ready, Daniel?" Micah called back.

Was he? Yes. He'd have to be. He lifted the reins, threading them through his fingers, which were encased in a new pair of fine leather gloves.

"Ready." He disengaged the brake.

Micah's wagon moved out, and even before Daniel shook the reins, his team followed. The rattle behind him said Bran was handling that last wagon.

Daniel's business was about to open.

They'd been on the road home for two hours when Micah drew his team to a stop, so Daniel did the same. The younger man pointed to their right where a thicket of brambles and saplings grew fifty feet from the road. Above it circled half a dozen buzzards.

Daniel hadn't noticed them on the way through early that morning.

Micah set the brake on his wagon and walked back to Daniel. "I thought I heard something. Whatever they circle might still be alive. I will check it out."

"Be careful. It might be wounded." One of them should have thought to bring a rifle. The Quakers didn't carry them for protection, but Daniel could have. After all, a wounded badger, bear, or coyote was nothing to mess with.

"I shall." Micah walked through grass that rose above his knees. He approached the area cautiously, picking up a long stick and parting the grass. Then he whirled and pointed at Bran. "Bring thy wagon here." Urgency filled his voice.

What was it?

Daniel set the brake and wrapped the reins around the handle, then hopped down and followed Bran's wagon. "What is it?"

"'Tis a lad." Micah waved him over. "He is in bad shape."

Bad shape?

The words hardly prepared Daniel for the sight that met him.

The young man was hardly recognizable as human. Wearing the tattered remnants of a pair of breaches—and nothing else—the dark skin of his back was a mass of criss-crossed lines, some scars, some fresh wounds still oozing blood. The ridges of his backbone rose to alarming points in the tortured skin as he lay curled into a ball, hands over his head, eyes closed.

"Lord, have mercy." Daniel barely recognized his own voice.

"He has, and He sent us." Micah knelt beside the lad. "Can thee hear me?" He touched a spot on the dark shoulder that wasn't bleeding.

The boy jerked and rolled, crying out and slapping at Micah's hand. "Go 'way!" His voice was dull, his eyes barely opened, his lips dry and cracked.

"Hand me your water bottle, Bran." Daniel reached up for it, then knelt on the youth's other side and cradled his head, pouring sips of water between the dry lips until the boy revived enough to grab the bottle and drink.

Eyes wide now and filled with terror, he clutched the bottle as if it were a weapon and scooted back.

"We mean thee no harm," Micah said. "We are Friends—Quakers. Thee are safe with us."

"Ain't safe..." The youth tipped back onto the ground, as if scooting the short distance had robbed him of the last of his strength. "Ain't safe nowhere." His head lolled to the side as he passed out.

"We must get him to Paul without delay." Micah looked in Bran's wagon. "All the wagon beds are full, but we can lay him on the floorboards in front of the seat. He would not be seen from any distance."

"We will put him in my wagon." Daniel got to his feet and dusted off his hands. "If we are approached by anyone, they will be more likely to look in the front or rear wagon, would they not?"

Micah rubbed the back of his neck. "I could not say for sure, but maybe."

"They for sure would if you and me was the ones to make a fuss," Bran said to Micah.

"And I the one who appears to be in charge," Daniel said. After all, he *was* the one in charge. And he was going to help this poor boy. "Should we take him to Zachary?"

"Too far." Micah raised troubled eyes. "We lost one not long ago who was in bad shape like this. He needs Paul as fast as we can get him there."

"Can you carry him to my wagon?"

Micah nodded and lifted the lad. "He weighs almost nothing."

"Bran." Daniel looked up at the boy who had remained on the wagon. "Are you comfortable with this team?"

"They be good horses. Give me no problems."

"Can you whip them up and make a run for town?"

Bran scrunched his face. "Might break some of what be packed in all them boxes."

"A boy's life is in danger. Do what you can without putting yourself in danger, you understand?"

Bran nodded, eyes solemn.

"Find Paul and get him to my house. We shall take the lad there, since 'tis the closest." He raised a finger. "But remember, only as fast as you can safely go. Take no risks."

"I won't. I will take good care of your horses."

"I know you will, lad. I was speaking of danger to yourself." Daniel stepped out of the way so Bran could drive off, and then he followed Micah to his wagon. "I sent Bran ahead to find Paul. We will take this one to my house." He climbed onto the seat, careful not to step on the lad stretched on the floorboards. Stretched out as if he'd already died.

Not if Daniel could help it.

Chapter 30

B Y THE TIME DANIEL retired that evening, he could barely lift his arms to undo the buttons of his coat. When had he ever been so tired? And sore. Making the trip to Roberts Landing and back in a single day, driving half the way. He flexed shoulder muscles that protested the movement as he shrugged out of his coat.

An envelope slipped to the floor.

Jonas.

In all the rush and worry, he'd completely forgotten the letter. But now the injured lad was safe in the room under the eaves.

Paul had assured Daniel that with plenty of rest and good food, he'd recover from his mistreatment.

Mistreatment—bah!—cruel, sadistic abuse and nothing less.

Cora was stationed beside the boy's bed, promising not to leave his side until he awakened and drank the broth she'd already concocted.

Daniel picked up the envelope. Should it wait until morning? Would the news be more palatable after a good night's sleep and a strong cup of coffee? Or would he toss and turn and wonder what was scribbled on its pages?

He placed the letter on the bed and finished undressing. Once in his nightshirt, he moved his lamp from the desk to the table beside the bed and climbed in. Then he picked up the envelope again.

It was of the finest paper, thick and smooth, if slightly soiled and wrinkled from its journey. He broke the seal with his thumbnail and withdrew the single folded sheet. Unfolding it, he stared at his son's handwriting.

Would the pain ever lessen? Or the feelings of disappointment, guilt, and loss?

He rubbed his eyes and focused on the fine script, which had been hammered into his son's rebellious hand by a series of stern tutors from an early age.

It began with one word—father. No other greeting. No date. Just those letters in stark black at the top.

Father,

I'm sure you can imagine how surprised, even shocked, I was to receive your letter after all this time. How touched I was to be remembered at all, after you sold off the family business and our family home, leaving me nothing. Leaving Constance nothing. You asked not after her, but should you be interested, she is living a quiet life now, in a separate building on Landon's estate. It seems her husband dislikes even the sight of her these days. Perhaps she will one day regret having given away her only child.

Oh, but you are near him now, are you not? I assume that is what prompted you to write me with such an impossible request. I have no authority over who does or does not do the work of returning property to its rightful owners. But unlike you, I admire them for enforcing the laws of this country. So, no, Father, I cannot render you any such aid as you requested. Nor would I. I am, after all, a law-abiding citizen, and I intend to remain so.

Jonas Whiteford.

Law-abiding citizen? With his small fleet of slave ships that routinely flaunted the law?

The paper shook between his hands until he let it drop to the bedding. And then he flicked it off the bed. He could throw it in the fire in the morning.

Why had he allowed himself to hope?

Because of people like the one under his roof at that very moment, hanging between life and death. Life, if Daniel could keep him out of the hands of people like... like Jonas. Very possibly death if he couldn't.

He stared at the ceiling. "Why, Lord? Why make it so difficult to do the right thing?"

He didn't exactly expect an answer, but he'd hoped for something—anything—to help him make sense of it all. What was the purpose of his life? It hadn't been raising his children, at which he'd failed miserably. It hadn't been providing for his wife. She'd been taken by death far too young. And deep down, he knew his life's purpose it had nothing to do with his businesses, the one he'd sold or the one he was just getting started. No, it had to be more than that.

He wanted to he wanted to find answers, and he was sure the Quakers could help him—would help him—learn how to find them. Daniel was already convinced from Whom the answers would come.

Zachary tightened the girth on Annabelle's saddle, glad the mule was sound once again and ready to ride. He put a foot in the stirrup and swung aboard.

Oh.

He adjusted in the saddle as Annabelle swung her long face around to look at him.

"I know. I feel it. Momma is feeding me too well. I shall have to curb my enthusiasm for her offerings or I shall be too heavy to ride thee before long."

Annabelle shook her head, ears flapping, and blew out a sharp snort. Sassy girl.

He headed for town. Momma needed more salt to preserve what she called the pitiful amount of produce his garden offered. It'd been plenty to feed just him, but the Lord had brought a lot more mouths of late.

Next year, Lord willing, she assured him they'd have a proper kitchen garden with everything she considered necessary to see them through the winter. He'd tried to tell her that he could afford to purchase provisions and didn't need to put up a year's worth, but she would have none of that, and Sapphira had backed her up. He was outnumbered and outflanked.

And couldn't be happier.

It was a practically perfect day, the sun bright and cheery, the breeze cool and refreshing, and last evening's rain shower had settled the dust without muddying the road. Birds chirped in the trees. Annabelle clip-clopped along at her swinging pace, the motion relaxing.

Until a group of men with dogs came out of the treeline and spread across the road—facing Zachary.

Four men with three hounds that were huge and black with tan markings. One of them curled its lip and exposed its teeth, clear even from a distance.

And the fair-haired man in the middle cradled a musket in his arms. The first slave catcher he'd ever seen with a gun. That changed everything.

Zachary's papers were in the house.

Fear pebbled the skin on the back of his neck, across his shoulders, and down his arms. He stopped Annabelle, who had her ears pinned, even though the men were still dozens of rods away. This area of the road was bordered by woods on both sides. Thick woods that would be difficult for Annabelle to run through. Going back would lead these men to the farm. To Momma and Sapphira. Trying to go around them would probably get him shot.

On his left, past the woods, was the creek. If he could get that far, Annabelle could leap across the narrower part where it ran deep.

Crossing would slow down the men on foot.

If he could get that far.

He tightened the reins, and Annabelle shuffled her feet in anticipation.

"He gonna run!" yelled one of the men.

Zachary thumped his heels to the mule's sides and pulled her head around to the left. She sprang forward like one of Daniel's thoroughbreds. Out of the corner of his eye, Zachary caught the motion of the dogs racing toward them.

They'd loosed the hounds.

Annabelle crashed into the treeline, and it took all his attention to keep from being swept out of the saddle. He ducked and dodged and blocked limbs with his arms. The baying behind them grew closer, and Annabelle found another burst of speed when they came to a clearing. She raced across it, making it to the middle before the dogs broke into the open.

Beneath him, muscles bunched as the mule launched them into the trees again. This was older growth with open areas under the high canopy of leaves. Zachary still had to dodge and duck, but not as much. And straight ahead was the creek, its water burbling over a rocky stretch with high banks.

"Come on, girl. I need thee to jump like a fox hunter."

The big ears swiveled at the sound of his voice, or maybe at the sound of the hounds closing the gap, able to run faster through the trees than the mule could. The land slanted downward to the creek. Zachary urged Annabelle on with his hands and heels. Closing fast, the largest hound snarled behind them as they reached the creek's bank.

"Lord, give this old mule wings." He jabbed his heels into the animal's flanks and leaned over her neck as they left the ground. It was a long, surreal moment, suspended between earth and sky. And then Annabelle's hooves clattered to the shale on the other side, slipping and scrambling to gain her footing.

Zachary clung to her wisp of a mane, legs clamped behind her shoulders. When he glanced back, the dogs were running along the far bank of the creek. Away from the farm.

They'd find a place to cross soon enough.

Zachary wheeled Annabelle to the right and urged her back into a gallop. Micah's place was not far. If he could make it there, and if the builders had arrived, he'd have men who would vouch for him. Men who would help him redirect the slave catchers away from the farm.

Away from Momma and Sapphira.

Daniel carried the tray with bread and broth up the narrow staircase to the room under the eaves. The door was open, but he stopped just outside.

"Are you awake?" It seemed rude to enter without some sort of greeting, even if it was his house.

"I am, suh." Alexander eased himself to a sitting position on the pallet until he rested his back against the wall with a wince. He eyed him warily.

There wasn't a proper bed up here yet. Daniel would need to see to that soon. But at least the lad was safe. "Cora sent me up with your breakfast."

The young man frowned, head tilted. "I thought you the massah here."

"I used to think so, too, but then Cora came." He held out the tray.

Alexander took it, eyes gleaming with appreciation. "Why you help me?"

"'Twas the right thing to do."

"That's what them Quakers say, but you doan talk Quaker."

"Ah, as to that." If there'd been a chair in the room, he'd have sat. Instead, he leaned against the doorframe. "I have not officially joined the Society of Friends here—the Quakers as you call them—but I will do so soon." He motioned for the lad to begin eating. "You see, they have become like family to me. They are good people who believe in God and believe that He directs our lives, if we allow Him. I'm finally ready to admit that they are correct." It felt good to admit that to someone.

Alexander took a bite of the bread and asked around a cheekful, "You believe that?"

"I do." Conviction surged through him. "I believe He led us to you three days ago. I believe if He had not, you would be dead."

The young man set the bread back on the tray. "My momma believed, but she died."

"If she believed, then she is in heaven now, a much better place—so the Quakers assure me—than this sinful earth."

He stared at the food Daniel's talking was keeping him from.

"But you should eat. The doctor said you need food, lots of it, and rest. Ask Cora for anything else you need. That woman is a marvel of resourcefulness."

He backed out of the room and almost stepped on the woman.

Cora looked him up and down and smiled, the kind of smile that made a man itchy without him knowing why. But it hinted that she knew something he didn't, and she liked what she knew.

Daniel beat a hasty retreat to the stable.

He had yet to hire a stableman, but he could saddle a horse for himself. He chose the dapple-gray gelding he'd named Bullet. Once it was saddled, he mounted and turned the animal toward Micah's place. What he needed was a little time with his grandson to clear his head.

But the image of Cora's smile followed him down the road.

The brick structure was two stories tall and had chimneys at both ends. While nowhere near as grand as Daniel's house, it was more than respectable. Daniel had made sure there were enough bricks to complete it. He'd made his wishes known to Isaac—in private—that the house was not to be scrimped on. If Isaac needed anything extra, he was to come to Daniel without saying a word to Micah or Gwen. Not that he wanted to undermine them or their wishes, but he wanted to avoid any argument about whether or not he should contribute more toward the house.

After all, his grandson lived there.

Micah had moved his family in as soon as one side was complete enough to keep them out of the weather.

As Daniel approached, Gwen came into view. She was cooking, or perhaps boiling laundry, over a fire outside. Owen's fair head was easy to spot where he sat next to his sister on a blanket. With Dinah gone, the boy was having to pitch in and help.

Daniel should hire a nanny to replace—

He stopped Bullet and studied the scene before him. Owen and Sally Faye, Gwen with her apron stretched across her rounded middle. Quaker men working on the house. No. They didn't need his interference. Helping his mother wouldn't hurt Owen one bit. In fact, it might even build character. The easy way—having whatever money could provide—had done nothing for Jonas or Constance. Daniel wasn't going to make that mistake again.

At least, not once the house was completed.

"Someone is riding in fast." A man on the roof pointed behind the house. "Must be something wrong."

Then the baying of hounds reached him, and Daniel pulled his rifle from its scabbard and sent the gray horse into a gallop.

Chapter 31

W HEN MICAH'S NEW ROOFLINE came into view, Zachary turned
Annabelle toward the creek. The mule was laboring with each
stride now. The creek was shallow here with low banks, so they could
ride across rather than jump. Her front hooves had just hit the water
when the baying of hounds reached him from behind. The dogs must
have crossed somewhere farther upstream and found their scent again.

The flagging mule waded through the hock-deep water. They would
reach Micah's house before the hounds did.

The sight of a man on the roof, pointing in Zachary's direction
brought a surge of relief through him. He'd made it. And there was
help.

Another man on a dapple-gray horse rounded the corner of the
house, rifle in his hands.

Daniel?

Annabelle stumbled scrambling out of the creek, going to her knees
and nearly unseating Zachary. He found his balance again as she
righted herself. Glancing back, the black-and-tan faces of the hounds,

ears flapping with each stride, bobbed above the tall grass on the other side of the creek.

"Come on, girl." Zachary urged the mule into a lumbering canter. "Just a little farther."

Daniel stopped his horse and turned it sideways, raising his rifle and taking aim at the hounds. Several other men ran toward them, each brandishing a rake, shovel, or pitchfork.

"Do not shoot," Micah yelled from the front of the group. "'Twould only cause more problems." He faced Zachary and gestured at the house. "Get thee inside, mule and all, and let us deal with this."

There was no need to explain anything. They all knew that only the slave catchers would be chasing him with hounds.

Zachary wanted to turn and face the dogs, and the slave catchers who were no doubt not far behind. But that was his pride getting in the way. Better to let Micah and the others handle it.

What was it Titus always said? *Go unnoticed.* Better to keep out of sight and give Annabelle his attention.

The poor animal stumbled again as they rounded the corner of the building.

"Take her inside." Gwen pointed to the open doorway, its door not yet hung.

"But thy floors—'

"Have yet to be set." She shooed him on. "Go."

He flattened himself against Annabelle's neck and rode into the unfinished house onto the dirt floor. Then he slipped off the mule and loosened the saddle's girth from her heaving sides. "Breathe easy, girl." He rubbed her lathered neck. "Thee were a valiant steed today."

Gwen came in behind him with the puppy on a rope and the children wide-eyed and silent.

The hounds' baying had dissolved into confused barks and whining.

Zachary positioned himself at a window opening, but back far enough that there was no danger of being seen from outside.

His friends were spread in a line, blocking the hounds. One got too close to Daniel's horse, and the animal whirled and kicked. Daniel managed to keep his seat, while the dog rolled away. It got back on its feet and rejoined the other two.

Shouts came from the far side of the creek.

If the men would not be turned away, Zachary would walk out and turn himself over to them. Better that than to have them charge the house and find Gwen and the children. Or go farther down the road and find Momma and Sapphira.

He would do what he must to protect those he loved.

The rifle gripped in one hand, Daniel kept a tight rein on the thoroughbred, who was still eyeing the dogs and pawing with a front hoof.

But Daniel's attention was on the men coming forward. One of them was hatless, his fair hair waving as he ran. The similarities were there, but it was hard to imagine.

Could it be?

Daniel's eyesight had weakened over the years, but he strained to make out the man's features. Would Jonas have followed him here? If he'd set out a day to two after he'd sent the letter, it was possible. But why?

All four men reached the middle of the creek before Micah called out, "Come no closer. Call off thy dogs and return the way thee have come. Thee are not welcome on my property."

The blond man took a few steps closer, water lapping to his knees. "We got every right to search for runaway slaves."

Daniel's heart dropped. He couldn't make out the features, but he knew the voice. Without thinking, he urged Bullet forward.

"Jonas?"

A murmur broke out among the men surrounding Daniel, but he ignored them, although Micah jogged to Bullet's side and walked toward the creek with him.

"Why are you here?"

His son stopped and crossed his arms. "Father, I did not expect to see you out here on the frontier." Sarcasm dripped from his voice.

"You knew where I was, and your letter made your thoughts perfectly clear. So I ask you again, why are you here?"

"You were kind enough to lead me to someone I have long wanted to take back where he belongs." Jonas spread his arms. "And the law is on my side."

"Zachary Brown is a free man." Daniel worked to keep his voice steady against the anger rising within him. "You know this. Everyone standing here—everyone in Mount Pleasant—knows this. So I ask you again, why are you here?"

"Unfinished business." Jonas pointed at Micah. "This one stopped me once before, but now the laws have changed. If that black man does not have his papers on his person, I am well within my lawful rights to take him in."

"What do you care about the law?" Daniel stood in the stirrups. "You, my son, are little more than a pirate!" He shouted the last words.

"Oh, Father." Jonas clasped one hand to his heart. "You wound me."

"I never laid a hand on you, and perhaps that was my gravest error."

Jonas went rigid. "Stand aside, Father, and let that slave show his papers—as the law demands—or come with us."

"He is a free man," Micah said from beside Daniel. "Thee will not touch him."

"And *thee*, Quaker boy, are a pacifist, so *thee* will not stop me."

"But I will." Daniel's words were thick and low. He didn't want to say them out loud. Didn't want Micah and the others to hear, but they must be said. "Before I left New Bern, I gave my lawyer the evidence necessary to stop you from ever contesting my will. Evidence that could put you in jail for a long, long time."

Jonas's fair skin paled. "I know not what you speak of."

"The cargo lists of several of your ships, with dates, and three signed testimonies from sailors you fired. My lawyer assured me it was more than enough to put you away." Each word left Daniel with a stab of pain. After all, he was blackmailing his own son to protect a man he hadn't known even six months. A man who had falsely accused Daniel more than once. But a man with more integrity than Jonas could ever dream of. And as much as it hurt, it was the right thing to do.

He'd never planned to use those documents against his son. He'd kept them only because... because deep down, he knew Jonas's character and feared he might try to wrestle Owen's inheritance away from him. He'd kept the evidence so that—only if necessary—his lawyer could use it to blackmail Jonas into letting the boy inherit without interference.

But it had come to this. Jonas had pushed it this far. All for what? Revenge over wounded pride?

Years ago, Daniel might have done something similar. Not about slavery—he'd always been fully against that institution—but in some other area he might have let his pride push him to do something unscrupulous. Looking at the hard lines of his son's pale face, it saddened him that he had to admit it, even to himself. But for the love of Margaret and now this community of the Quakers, he might be that man standing in the river having to decide between backing down and self-destruction.

Which would Daniel have chosen? Which would Jonas choose?

A fly buzzed around Daniel's ears. Rifle in one hand and reins in the other, he could only ignore it. And wait.

One of the slave catchers whistled, and the dogs splashed back into the creek, giving Bullet a wide berth.

The Quakers waited on the bank, most of them resting their farm tools on the ground now, leaning on the long handles. Waiting. They were, for the most part, a patient lot. But Micah stood at Daniel's stirrup, his whole posture saying he was ready to throw himself on Jonas. Maybe even wanted to.

And then the truth hit Daniel.

Gwen. Jonas had been after Gwen for months before Daniel had sent her and the babe away. He'd known of it, had even directed Silas to keep his eye on the situation for him. And Cook, of course, had kept things from getting out of hand. But no doubt Micah knew of it. He was the picture of a man protecting his wife.

Pacifist or not.

It was time to end this. "What will it be, son? Will you leave and take your minions with you—never to return—or do I contact my lawyer and start the process? Oh." He jerked his head toward the men waiting behind him. "They all know of this now, and know who my lawyer is, since we have been in contact with him regarding my new business. So should you try and stop a letter from me reaching him, these good men will see that one gets through."

"Why are you doing this, *Father*?"

Daniel winced at the venom Jonas put into the last word. "Because, son, these are peaceful people. Zachary is a free man. And 'tis the right thing to do."

Jonas charged forward, stopping only when Micah moved to the front of Daniel's horse. "Who made you judge and jury over what is right?"

"I am sorry, son. I truly am, for all the ways I failed you when you were a boy." Daniel bent his head and studied the hand holding the reins. "I was not the father I should have been for you." He raised his eyes then and met Jonas's blazing blue pair. "But you are an adult and must make your own choices. So choose. Will you leave and take these men with you, or will you face prison?"

Jonas pointed a finger at him. "You are no longer my father."

With a sigh that came from the depths of his soul, Daniel said, "I will always love you, son, and I will never stop praying for you to change your ways."

Jonas's mouth opened, then snapped shut. He turned and waded back toward the men and dogs waiting on the far side of the creek, muttering something Daniel couldn't make out. When he reached the far bank, he turned. "I have called off my dogs. Be sure you call off yours."

Daniel didn't move until the men and dogs were out of sight, although his sight grew watery at the end.

"Come." Micah took Bullet's bridle and turned the horse around in the creek. "Come and see the progress on the house, and spend time with Owen." Micah looked up at him. "With thy family here."

Family. Here. With Micah and Gwen and the children. And the Quakers.

With time and their acceptance, and with the Lord's help, Daniel would heal.

Zachary approached Daniel, where he leaned against the brick wall and gazed toward the creek. There were lines on his face that hadn't been there before.

"I am sorry for thee."

Daniel gave a soft snort and faced him. "'Tis my own fault, I suppose."

"Nay, I think not."

"I am his father. I raised him. Or more to the point, I failed to raise him. I hired tutors and expected them to turn Jonas into a respectable young man."

"As, I suspect, thy father did with thee."

"Indeed." Daniel glanced toward the creek again. "'Twas a very different way of life than what I see here. Father kept slaves, you know. 'Twas knowing them, being close with them, that taught me the vileness of slavery."

"Was thy father a harsh master?"

Daniel grimaced. "By harsh, you are asking if he beat his slaves. He did not. Not personally. But neither did he restrain his overseer from beating them. Or using the women. I do not believe my father ever approached a slave in that way, but too many of the children born to them were light-skinned. And the overseer was—"

"I understand." No need to make the man spill out what they both knew. He'd heard of a kind overseer, once, but hadn't believed it. Experience had taught him that a man with complete control over another would become a tyrant.

"What will thee do now?"

"Do?" Daniel's brows rose. "What I came to do. Get the business up and running. Become a larger part of my grandson's life." He shrugged. "Not that he needs me. He has everything he needs here with Micah and Gwen."

"But thee need him."

"Indeed." The lines pulled at his face again.

"I believe thee are needed here, Daniel." Zachary chose his words carefully. "I need thee."

"You?"

Zachary pointed at the creek. "Today proved that, did it not?"

"The others would have held them off if I had not been here."

"They would have. But Jonas would have come back, time and again, until he was successful at catching me out." Zachary faced him squarely. "But I need thee in another way. I need thee to help me move the fugitives farther north. By myself, I can only do so much, but as one of thy occasional employees, I have a reason to go to Steubenville with a wagon."

"And haul fugitives that far."

"From there, they can make it to another safe house."

Daniel nodded. "You let me know when you need to make a trip, and I will supply a reason."

Zachary offered his hand. "Thank thee."

Daniel grasped the hand with a surprisingly strong grip. "Nay, Zachary. Thank you—for giving me the opportunity to help. To do something... worthwhile in this community."

"Have thee thought more about joining our Society of Friends?"

"I have."

"Are thee ready to speak with the elders?"

"I am."

"I would be happy to accompany thee when thee do." He grinned. "After all, 'twould seem we are to be partners."

Daniel blinked, then nodded. "Partners in seeing people reach freedom."

Zachary couldn't think of a better kind.

Chapter 32

A NNABELLE GRUNTED AS ZACHARY tightened the girth. "Sorry, old girl. We're going home now. Momma will have to wait until tomorrow for her salt."

"Still talking to thy animals, I see." Gwen came into the barn.

"'Tis a habit I have no desire to break." He grinned over his shoulder at her. "And if memory serves me rightly, 'twas I who caught thee in a discussion with a certain white goat."

She leaned against a barn beam. "I cried when Tiny died last winter." But she smiled up at Zachary. "Thee and I go back a long way together."

"That we do."

"I worry for thee." Her tone turned serious.

"Worry not. I am in good hands." He glanced at the beams overhead.

"I know, but thee spend too much time alone. I wish thee had a wife and children of thy own. A family to go home to."

"Momma and Sapphira wait for me."

"'Tis special, but 'tis not the same."

He sighed. "Once I wished for a wife and family more than anything, but God had something else in mind."

"Oh?" She straightened and came forward, running her hand over Annabelle's rump, eyes on him as she waited.

"Since this spring, I have been assisting people to move north." How much should he tell her? Everything. There was no one else on earth he trusted more than the young woman in front of him. "Working with a fugitive who went back and forth, leading people here, I was able to assist quite a few."

"The boy in the floppy hat? Was that Titus?"

"Thee knew of him?"

"I saw him more than once before that night at Thomas and Betsy's, but only from a distance. I wondered if he were a fugitive. Oh." She pressed her fingers to her lips. "I should have tried to help him."

"Nay, Gwen. Thee should not. Thee have a family to protect."

"But they need—"

"'Tis my calling to help them. If thee speaks to any who need help, send them to me. Do nothing else."

"But I could give them food or—"

He took her hand and held it, meeting her eyes. "Thee must not. Please, Gwen, promise me thee will not. Send them to me. I will take care of it. I would not have thee put thyself or thy children in danger."

"But are thee not in danger?"

He released her hand and rubbed the back of his neck. "'Tis because I have no family of my own that I can do this work. Do thee not see? God has gifted me with singleness that I might be free to do His will in this way."

"Thee truly believes this?" Her brow wrinkled as she searched his face.

"As firmly as I believe thee are in front of me now."

"Then, if thee has heard from the Lord on this issue, thee will hear no more about it from me." But her eyes clouded and her chin drooped.

"Do not be sad for me, my friend. What God gives, He gives abundantly. Did He not give me back my mother? Did He not have Daniel here to confront and rebuke his son?"

"Sometimes I forget what strong faith thee has."

Strong? Zachary didn't feel like it was strong. Many days, he felt as if he were barely hanging on. But in his course of action, he was sure. He was doing what he was supposed to do. In the process, he was touching the lives of people like Titus and Darius. And maybe more importantly—they were touching his.

Daniel arose three days later and ambled into the kitchen, rubbing the sleep from his eyes and inhaling the delicious scents of something baking.

Alexander, wearing a clean shirt and breeches, sat at the table while Cora slid a plate of pancakes in front of him. He jumped to his feet at the sight of Daniel, nearly tipping over until Cora steadied him.

"No need to fuss," Cora said in a soothing tone. "Sit back down and enjoy thy breakfast."

It was clear the boy was afraid. Slaves were taught to stand when their master—or any white man—was around. Sitting in their presence was considered insubordination and could be met with severe punishment. He had every right to be afraid. But not of Daniel.

Daniel took the chair across the table from him, but looked at Cora. "I hope you saved a plate of those for me. They smell delightful."

"I would have brought them to the dining room for thee."

"I would prefer to eat them here this morning, if you will join Alexander and me?" He made it a question, unsure how she'd react to something that many could consider scandalous. Margaret would have. A master eating with the servants? With an escaped slave?

With fellow human beings.

"Sit, Alexander, please," he said. "I shall get a crook in my neck if I must look up at you."

The boy perched on the edge of his chair, as a bird poised for flight.

"Eat while they are warm." Daniel leaned closer to the table as if sharing a secret. "They are the best pancakes this side of the Ohio River, and I can attest to that." He leaned back, not missing the satisfied smile Cora sent his way. Was it due to his praise of her cooking? Or because he was trying to put the lad at ease? Whichever, he enjoyed seeing it.

Alexander picked up his fork, eyes still on Daniel, he lifted a bite of pancake to his mouth and ate it.

"Was I not correct?"

The lad nodded.

"'Tis all right to speak, lad. You are among friends here." Maybe that word—friends—would someday mean as much to Alexander as it did to Daniel. There was power in that word. And soon, he'd be able to call himself a Friend in a whole new way.

Zachary would arrive shortly, and the two of them would meet with the elders about Daniel's membership. He wasn't anxious, exactly, but a little apprehensive.

Cora placed a stack of golden goodness in front of him and slid a pot of maple syrup closer. "I can make more if these are not enough."

"Fill your plate and join us. I have news to share."

When Cora was seated, Daniel stabbed a forkful of pancake and pointed it at Alexander, then at Cora. "As soon as you have this young man fit and ready to travel, Zachary will take him on north to another place where he will be safe."

"He will need at least another week, I should say." Cora studied the boy. "Indeed. At least."

Alexander shook his head. "I can go now, suh."

"Nay, I think Cora has the right of it. If you leave too soon, you will only weaken again. Let her feed you well. Grow stronger, and then you will have a better chance to make it all the way to Canada."

Daniel had wiped his plate clean with his last bite of pancake when a knock sounded on the back door. "Come in," he shouted, hardly pausing to wonder what Margaret would have said about that breach of etiquette.

Cora smiled her approval, and that pleased him. Maybe more than it should.

Zachary entered the kitchen. "Are thee ready?"

Daniel wiped his mouth on a napkin. "I believe I am."

"Are thee working on at the business today?" Cora asked.

"Not today." Daniel shrugged into his coat. "I will be home for supper."

He followed Zachary to the door.

"Thee sound like an old married couple in there," Zachary said.

Married? To Cora Johnson? What a preposterous idea. Wasn't it?

"I hope thee do not mind." Zachary's voice pulled his startling thought back to the mission at hand. "Some people wished to join us today."

"What? Who?" Daniel stepped outside, where Evie and Sapphira sat on the high seat of the wagon.

Bran sat on the tailgate, legs dangling, gap-toothed grin wide. "I figured it be about time I get myself settled here in Mount Pleasant proper like, but I can see them elders another time if you—thee—prefer."

"Of course not." There was safety in numbers, after all. Not that Daniel thought the elders would banish him, but they were likely to ask a lot of uncomfortable questions. Questions he might not have the right answers to. But we was ready to embrace the Quaker way of life.

Zachary had dropped Daniel at his house and Bran at the doctor's before turning the team toward home. "Hup, Justice. Hup, Jubal." He slapped the reins against their broad black rumps.

The wagon's wheels rumbled over the dry road, raising a veil of dust in their wake. The sun shone from its zenith, glinting off the early tinges of yellows and oranges in the trees. Ahead, a doe and her half-grown fawns bounded across the road and disappeared into the trees, white tails flagging. A breeze picked up and carried the scent of freshly cut hay as they passed a farmer working a scythe, swinging it in a broad arc to harvest a second cutting of hay.

It was the perfect setting for a wonderful day, one in which he'd witnessed four people pledge their belief in the Light of Christ working in their lives. A man he'd come to regard as his friend, a boy he'd been trying to disciple for years, the woman who'd given him life, and her years-long companion who was already like an aunt to him.

"I never thought." Sapphira broke the companionable silence around them. "I just never thought."

"Remember when we called Quakers saints?" Momma asked.

Sapphira nodded and dabbed her eyes with a handkerchief, not for the first time since leaving the elders.

"We is saints now too." Momma squeezed her friend's hand. "After all these years. Umm-hmm." Momma rocked gently back and forth.

Joy—the kind that came from outside of himself—filled Zachary. Not a fleeting kind of happiness or a giddy feeling of expectation. True joy. The kind that settled in a man's heart and lightened his burdens. The kind that let him know he wasn't walking this earth alone.

"Thee are Friends now, Momma." Zachary cleared his throat of the emotions that threatened to clog it. "Thee are free, and thee are home."

Epilogue

Mount Pleasant—1825

Z ACHARY RUBBED THE DAMP neck of the reddish-brown cow. "There now, Bossy. 'Twill not be long."

The animal stretched on the straw bedding and strained, ending with an all too human-sounding grunt. The tips of a pair of hooves appeared and then disappeared. She was making good progress.

Turning up the wick of the lantern he'd brought to the barn, Zachary hung it on a nail and settled on a barrel close by. He pulled an envelope from the pocket of his coat, fished spectacles from his pocket, settled them on his nose, and then smoothed out the paper against his lap.

Dear Zachary,

I hope this finds thee well and thy farm prospering. Our family is growing. Beth and I thought we were done at nine children, but God had other plans. She is expecting again in the spring, perhaps before this letter reaches thee.

A tenth child. What a full house they would have. At one time, Zachary might have been envious, but the years had passed, his hair was more gray than black, and he'd made peace with being childless. After all, he couldn't have done all he did if he'd had to worry about the safety of a wife and children. And he was never alone for long.

Bossy bawled a long, low protest, and then strained again. This time, a nose appeared, resting on top of the hooves. Then the straining stopped and everything slid back inside. The cow rose and walked around the roomy stall with the low ceiling before pawing the straw and lying down with a gusty sigh.

"Thee are getting closer." Zachary adjusted his spectacles and returned to the letter.

> My shop is busier than ever. It seems everyone needs a new bucket or barrel to start the new year. My oldest works beside me now and is becoming an accomplished cooper, and two of the younger boys are helpers, so I have enough hands to meet the demand.
>
> Beth keeps the girls busy, and the two oldest have hired out as housemaids this past year. Both have completed their schooling.
>
> The most important thing thee ever told me was to get an education. I dare to dream that one of the boys might go on to college someday. They are bright enough.

Bossy strained again, and the face appeared and then disappeared. He went to her and rubbed her neck, the motion taking him back to a ship a long time ago. The original Bossy—grandmother to this one—had been in the hold, sharing space with the white goat, Tiny. And huddled next to her was a frightened young girl, Gwen.

It'd been Gwen who'd saved him from the first slave catchers, at great risk to herself and her son. Little had he known back then that he would be the one risking everything to help others evade slave catchers.

Bossy moaned and strained, bringing the calf's head into the world for a moment before it slipped back inside. But this time the hooves and nose remained out.

"Almost there, girl. Just three or four more good strong shoves."

The cow heaved herself to her feet and walked around the stall. Zachary returned to his barrel. Nature was going to take its course and didn't need his interference. He picked up the letter.

> I cannot tell thee how many times I wish I could visit thee. Beth and I discussed it before she knew of the new babe on the way. I could not leave her now. And there are the same dangers, dangers thee still face every day.
>
> Just last Sunday I met an older woman named Lizzy who came to meeting. Beth introduced her. She was visiting family in our area. She mentioned thee, and we shared fond memories.

When he'd first read the letter, he'd had a hard time remembering Lizzy. She'd been one of the first Titus had brought to the farm, even before the secret room. So many years had gone by, so many people had passed through his farm.

Bossy strained while standing, the calf's head fully in view. Its nostrils twitched, and Zachary smiled. It would be healthy, hopefully a heifer. Bossy was getting up in years and had steadfastly refused him a heifer, giving bull calf after bull calf. He didn't want to break the line, but it was up to the Lord to provide the next Bossy—or not—as He willed.

The cow paced another circle, then dropped to her knees and settled on her side with a groan.

> Above all, I wish my children could meet thee. I, of all people, know thy work there is vital. I am living proof of it. But I will hold out hope that in the future, we will see

each other again.

Until then, I remain thy friend,
Darius Cooper

After all these years, it still pleased him that the boy had kept the name he'd given him. He folded the letter with careful fingers and slipped it back into the envelope before tucking it in his coat pocket. With luck, there would be another in six months or so. And tomorrow, Zachary would pen a response, as he always did.

Letters from Titus were few and farther between, but he wrote when he could. They'd lost Miriam of a fever a few months after reaching Canada, but Dinah and Tabitha were married with children, and although Titus never married, he was a doting uncle. He'd made several more trips south once the sisters were settled and had brought more fugitives north, stopping to see Zachary each time. He hadn't joined the Society of Friends, but had joined a Methodist church, and after a few years, had taken on the role of pastor. That had stopped his smuggling activities, but he'd felt the Lord calling him to his new occupation. And the Lord knew best.

A few others wrote to him from time to time. Some he remembered more clearly than others, but none were as dear to him as Titus and Darius. Titus, who had taught Zachary how to help the fugitives and set him on the path the Lord intended him to live. Darius, who had taken Zachary's father's name, became forever linked to him as if he were family.

Bossy stretched out her legs and pointed her nose in the air, releasing a bawl as her sides tightened.

The calf's front legs slipped out, followed by the shoulders, and finally, after several more contractions, the hips. The cow panted and rested on the straw. The calf shook its head, wet ears flapping against its head. As if that were the signal, Bossy rose, and the calf's long back legs slipped from her, landing with a plop onto the straw.

The miracle of birth—it never grew old. Soon, the calf was licked dry and standing on shaky legs beneath the circle of the lantern's light.

Zachary rose from the barrel, and Bossy snorted at him.

"Easy there, Bossy. 'Tis only me, and I have been here all along."

She pushed her nose toward him and sniffed, then returned to licking her calf.

Zachary ran his hand down the calf's back and between its back legs before patting the cow's rump.

"Good job, Bossy. Thee have finally given me a heifer. Thy grandmother's line will continue."

And so would the flow of milk that had nourished countless fugitives over the years.

Thank Thee, Lord, for confirmation that my work here is not yet done.

Author's Historical Notes

T HERE IS NO SINGLE place where the Underground Railroad began, but Mount Pleasant, Ohio, was one of its starting points. The term Underground Railroad would not be coined until the 1830s when actual railroads started to dot the landscape. The network grew organically from people—especially Quakers—who wanted the fugitive slaves to reach freedom. As one person learned of another trusted person, they began to help one another. But it was rife with danger. Even though Ohio, Indiana, and Illinois were brought in as free territories, there were plenty of people there who believed in the right to hold slaves. And they were backed up by the law, such as this clause in the Constitution, which was effectively nullified much later by the Thirteenth Amendment's abolition of slavery:

Article IV, Section 2, Clause 3:

No Person held to Service or Labour in one State, under the Laws thereof, escaping into another, shall, in Consequence of any Law or Regulation therein, be discharged from such Service or Labour, but shall be delivered up on Claim of the Party to whom such Service or

Labour may be due.

The Fugitive Slave Act of 1793 tightened the screws by spelling out exactly what could and couldn't be done as well as a fine of $500 *(roughly $15,860 in 2024 dollars)* and up to one year of imprisonment.

Those who helped the fugitives did so at great risk to themselves. But it didn't stop them. And as the networks grew and merged, more and more men, women, and children were released from bondage. It was a testament to the human spirit, ***starting with the people who found the courage to break for freedom*** as well as those who found the courage to help them.

The Quakers of this period referred to the "inner light of Christ" much like today's evangelical Christians refer to the Holy Spirit, that Person of the Trinity who indwells a believer.

Greenesville, North Carolina, is now written as Greenville, but was named after "the fighting Quaker," Revolutionary War hero Nathanial Greene.

Reviews are Golden

REVIEWS ARE THE LIFEBLOOD of authors. Leaving a review on **Amazon**, **Goodreads**, and/or **BookBub** means that more readers will find our books! Reviews can be long or short - your honest opinion of the book. Shout-outs on any social media platforms also help!

Pegg Thomas lives in Michigan's Upper Peninsula with Michael, her husband of *mumble* years. She creates American stories with real history and fictional characters inspired by her ancestors who immigrated here in the early 1600s.

Pegg won the 2019 FHL Readers' Choice Award for novellas, was a double-finalist for the 2019 ACFW Carol Award for novellas, and a finalist for the 2019 ACFW Editor of the Year. She was a finalist in the 2021 FHL Readers' Choice Award for novellas. Pegg won the 2022 Selah Award for historical romance and placed 2nd with her second entry. She was a finalist for the 2023 FHL Selah Award, placed 2nd in the 2024 Selah Award, and won the 2024 Will Rogers Silver AND Bronze Medallion Awards. Pegg spent 3 ½ years as the managing editor of Smitten Historical Romance.

When not writing or editing, Pegg can be found in her garden, her kitchen, or sitting at one of her spinning wheels creating yarn to turn into her signature wool shawls. https://PeggThomas.com

PeggThomas.com

Facebook

Goodreads

BookBub

Amazon

Newsletter signup